Cyberchicks

Book 1
Cyberchicks in Love:
A Satire for the Star-Struck

Book 2
Cyberchicks go Wild:
What Happens Next May Shock You!

Cyberchicks GO WILD

Title: Cyberchicks go wild:
what happens next may shock you! / Barb Dwyer
Series: Dwyer, Barb. Cyberchicks ; 2

ISBN: 9780645948783 (hardcover)
ISBN: 9780645948790 (paperback)
ISBN: 9781923212398 (ebook)

BISAC codes:
FIC028120 Science Fiction / Humorous
FIC02725 Romance / Romantic Comedy
FIC027130 Romance / Science Fiction
FIC016000 Humorous / General
FIC009080 Fantasy / Humorous
FIC027030 Romance / Fantasy
FIC052000 Satire

A catalogue record for this book is available from the
National Library of Australia

ABN 67 099 575 078
PO Box 345, Shoreham, 3916, Victoria, Australia
www.leavesofgoldpress.com

Cyberchicks

GO WILD

What Happens Next May Shock You!

Cyberchicks Book 2

Barb Dwyer
(*Virtual love-child of Douglas Adams, Nora Roberts,*
Terry Pratchett and Jane Austen, though unacknowledged due
to implausible genetic mutations.)

Critical Reviews

"This lavishly told masterpiece is stylish, sophisticated and thrilling, with moments of gut-wrenching realism and intense emotion. The language truly sings. Terrifically satisfying stuff!" ~ A. Lyer, *The Daily Undependable*.

"Let yourself be carried away by the read of a lifetime! Make no mistake, this is a monumental literary experience." ~ V. Gullible, *Sunday Telephone*.

"Reading this story was an indescribable experience." ~ Ophelia Payne, editor of *Tripe Odd's Alien Taxi Service Weakly*.

"They never had anything like this when I was in the Gnus and Loyals." ~ Major Blooper, ex British Army.

"This story is so instructive it ought to be standard military issue!" ~ Private Parts, US Marines.

"What can the publishers these days be thinking of?" ~ Evan Elpus, *Londinium Evening Standup.*

"Cyberchicks" is like a never-ending sailor's yarn. Bring more rum!" ~ Captain Albert Ross, SS Minnow.

"They use just the right number of vowels" ~ S. Johnson, Author of a Most Illustrious Dictionary, Who Does Not Wish To Be Associated With This Book.

"Some of the greatest works of modern fiction have been created by the most seriously deranged minds" ~ S. Freud.

"I have read this book and now I would like to get back into my grave." ~ A. Einstein.

"Name your price for the movie rights" ~ S. Spielberg. "~~No matter how cheap, I'm not interested.~~"

"The punctuation is unusual." ~ L. Tolstoy.

"It may have frayed my sleeve." ~ Moliere.

"Not as good as my books." ~ J. Austen.

"I am very attractive man. Place me in your story upon several alluring women of marriageable age." ~ Borat S.

"Tess is my kind of woman. Please give me her telephone number." ~ Ra Ra Rasputin.

"Could you please forward to me a copy of the TOATS Rule Book on Etiquette?" ~ Secretary-General of the Untied Nations.

"The penmanship in "Cyberchicks" is extraordinary. My husband and I hope ~~never~~ to see more literature of this quality throughout the Commonwealth. Keep calm ~~and please go away~~." ~ E. Windsor.

"I am biggest "Cyberchicks" fan in my country." ~ Terry Bull, editor, *Air Banana In-flight Magazine.*

"If you hate political correctness, this is for you. If you like political correctness, this is for you. If you don't care either way, this is for you. Also, if you don't know what political correctness is, this is for you. Have I missed anybody?" ~ Journal of Plausible Reviews.

"Geheim habe ich meinen fictional Abenteuern in dieser erstaunlichen Geschichte gefolgt. Ich schauen vorwärts zu jedem Kapitel."
~ Siegfried B. Hinkelheimer . . .
(. . . which AltaVista®'s Babelfish online translator rendered as "I followed to mean secret fictional adventures in this amazing history. I look forward to each chapter.")

EPISODES

RECAP OF BOOK 1

The story so far . . .
Have you read Cyberchicks Book 1 yet? Have you bothered?
Hmm?
Well if not, here's what happened.
In a nutshell. . .

Gorgeous movie star. Oozing charisma. Amazing actor.
Has a German accent. Is actually German.
Pack of incredibly hot fan-girl chicks.
They are all crazy for him.
Clueless.
They visit his fansite on the new-fangled "Internet".
It's 1998, so this is ancient history, when THINGS were
possible. Mysterious, arcane things.
Like a whole new Virtual World called "UnEarth" arising
in cyberspace, born purely from the passions of some star-
struck, obsessed, fashion-slave air-heads.
Avatars.
Mayhem ensues.
Everyone now exists in two places at once, or they pop
back and forth between them. Your guess is as good as mine.

Anyhoo, everyone now has an Original version and an UnEarthly version of themselves.

Madcap adventures unfold. A horde of beautiful young women, all unfeasibly pursuing the same guy through cyberspace.

So far, in their quest to elbow each other out of the way and be alone with their idol, the cyberchicks have travelled to Artificial Australia, Almost Africa, Implausible Ireland, Inauthentic Iceland etc.

Too many stereotypes to keep track of. Sure to offend somebody.

And their life-story has taken on an acronym— "TOATS".

Stands for "The Original and the Sexy", or "The Obsession and the Story," or The Old and the Senseless". Take your pick. Make up one of your own.

Who knows where they'll go next in their interminable quest? Or what they'll find, what they'll do, or who they'll meet?

Other characters include Nicolas Birdhouse, Daniel de Licious, Gabriel Yearn, Lance Boyle, Ray Fiends etc., who are completely fictional. I swear. No resemblance to anyone. Pure satire and parody. No lawyers please.

This is a work of literary genius mangled together with atrocious prose. Verbal trash-and-treasure.

When you get to a boring bit, just keep reading. Something better will be along soon.

Fanfic, chick lit, bodice-rippers, movies, pop culture, virtual reality and travel guides all rolled into one.

Or two.

(There are two books in the series, don't forget.)

So, if you didn't read Book 1, and you're just picking up this book for the first time, don't blame me if it doesn't make sense.

No, seriously.

It barely makes sense even if you have read Book 1.

(Which is a rollicking read, by the way. Treat yourself.)

You have a lot to look forward to.

New characters.

New scenes.

Completely extinct volcanoes.

Gorgeous Portuguese models (model aeroplanes, that is).

A visit to Bogus Brazil.

Stiletto heels.

Expensive, designer clothes and accessories.

A hastily-assembled Ratintosh computer.

The Rainforest Rondaybooze Bar.

And more.

Now you've learned something.

Enjoy.

~ Barb

UnEarthly Character Bios
(. . . so far, and in order of when they were written)

SIEGFRIED (our hero)

Tall . . .Amazing eyes, like chips of heaven. Lean, athletic frame. High, moulded cheekbones.

He is the perfect sea-captain; a strong, quiet, lonely man, somewhat remote, but always accessible, always humane, compassionate; a man to trust implicitly; to love; a captain whose crew would die for him.

But almost above all, he has that magnetic inner gleam—what is it?—a vast sense of humor?—profound knowledge of the world?—has he perhaps discovered the meaning of life?

BARB

Barb's origins are obscured by the mists of legend and romance. Some say that as an infant, she was discovered, washed up on a lonely island shore, by a lighthouse-keeper.

Raised by the lighthouse-keeper and his wife amongst their own family, Barb grew up to be a young woman of astonishing beauty—some said an exact replica of Cloudy Chiffon®. It was whispered that she had strange powers. Had it not been for the remoteness of the windswept isle and the treacherous seas incessantly pounding its rugged coastline, she surely would have been sought by hordes of young suitors.

The news of her stunning looks travelled across the ocean, borne by tall ships, their sails unfurling against the grey and stormy skies like the wings of wild swans. . . .

When one evening a tall stranger with long, dark hair arrived at the isle enquiring after the lighthouse-keeper's adopted daughter, Barb mysteriously fled the place of her childhood and ranged out into the world, where she now roams, writing or doing what I wot not what of.

These are the only heretofore known facts about the history of Barb, scribed by the oracle Myopia and subject to change without notice.

EMILY

Emily, a well-endowed lass with a fiery spirit, was born in the Forests of Southern Europe. Raised by a band of roving circus performers, she learned the art of juggling and knife throwing. Due to a slight miscalculation while blindfolded, she missed her target by inches and wounded an innocent spectator (who actually wasn't so innocent, but that's another story).

Deciding it was time to take her vivacious personality on the road, she left the troupe and headed for the high seas.

Emily became an expert with pistol and cutlass and was considered as dangerous as any male pirate. She was fearless in her exploits and the life of any boarding party.

Her last confirmed sighting was as a fire-eater in the Virgin Islands. Rumour has it she has since settled down, preferring to write novels about her exploits in a great, oak-panelled library with the scent of almond blossoms and frangipani wafting in from outside.

DONNA

Donna was kidnapped in childhood and raised by Tibetan Monks in the belief that she was the true Dalai Lama, until the arrival of puberty when her incomparable beauty and stunning femininity revealed the depth of their error.

Striking out across Asia alone on horseback, she conquered kingdoms and plundered hearts in search of her true destiny. Her youthful exploits are the subject of the biographical best-selling epic, "Magnificent" by J. Michener.

LOTTIE

An (almost) descendant of King Edward I, Lottie was born in a magnificent castle on the banks of the river Nore in Ireland.

Two days later her family were turned out of the castle, bankrupt and destitute. They stowed away in the hold of a three-masted barque, bound to Chile for nitrates. But the ship foundered in mountainous seas off Cape Horn with the loss of all hands. Lottie and her family swam across the Pacific Ocean to Australia, where she has lived ever since.

Stunningly beautiful and dazzlingly intelligent, Lottie almost gained three university degrees, and would have achieved international fame as an artist, if they had only printed her name on the catalog. She just missed out on being the first woman to sail solo around the world, and she gave back her Olympic Gold Medal for showjumping after she realized she'd accidentally ridden someone else's horse.

She went on to write what would have been a best-selling novel, but the only copy of the manuscript was stolen from the back seat of her car. She is presently at work on a film script which will star Siegfried B. Hinkelheimer in a truly heroic role. Needless to say she is sure to make millions and win numerous awards...

JULIANA

The Oracle representing Juliana says.

I think that picture[1] says it all.

No bio needed in this case.

What magnificent hair, what beastly horns! That IS Juliana, born of unborn souls, drenched at birth in herring skin and the tousled hair of elkhorn maidens!

She is lost in timewarps for eons at a time and is the most inconsistent in devotion to the Object of Desire, she might be off chasing the Man in the Moon tonight, never mind the aforementioned.

And oh yeah, she was born in Walhalla by some unborn souls.

Came to earth to get her little horns in a little twist.

Which happens now and again, well that is destiny for you!

---

1   The frontispiece.

Commercial passenger vehicle services on UnEarth

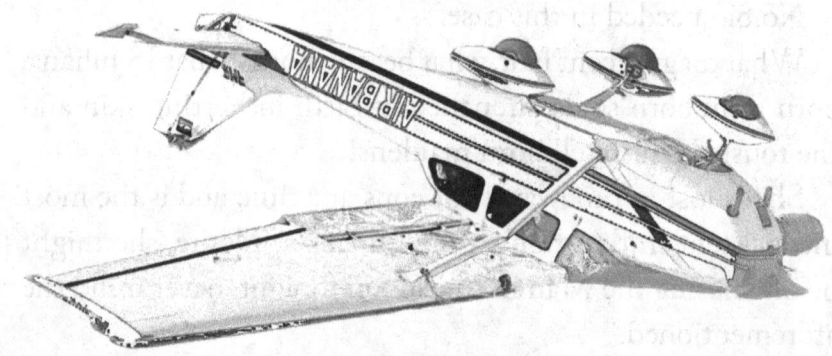

Air Banana

Tripe Odd's Alien Taxi Service

1

A BRIEF DETOUR

UNEARTHLY BARB
20 January 1999
Juliana, having managed to flag down a convenient (although typically unroadworthy) TOATS taxi, had zoomed off to the airport and flown back to Inauthentic Iceland. There she dwelled as queen for the next eleven-one episodes, surrounded by lusty latter-day Vikingers, trolls, a Norwegian Siegfried B. Hinkelheimer clone, a novelist whose name I can't remember, a crocodile which has miraculously been restored to life, some stereotyped fish-stinking villagers, a few giant spiders, Tammie, Tinfingers, Nicolas Birdhouse, Connie, Tess, seven hundred Vulgarian sailors and a few Australian blowflies.

They are all having such a great time they have become too boring to write about and so are best forgotten for the moment. This also makes it easier for prospective TOATS authors to untangle the grossly over-complicated plot.

UNEARTHLY LOTTIE
21 January 1999

Connie groaned and rolled over. "Wha . . . ?" she said, opening her eyes to see a bleak, black bay before her, dotted with little icebergs. She recognised it straight away. "Oh no! Ich hab's ja geahnt, dass etwas schiefgehen wurde!"

"What?" said Nic, climbing out of a mound of snow nearby.

"Sorry," Connie said, "it's this website. Sooner or later everyone starts speaking German. It's just . . . well, I thought things were going too smoothly. There we were, happily trotting back to Siegfried and His Idiots aboard the beautiful horse Brian and suddenly, here we are—back in bloody Inauthentic Iceland! But I know who's behind this. It's that bitch Barb—just because the love of her life is stuck on some mangy, flea-ridden planet and she can never return to him because she foolishly left her spaceship in outback Australia where, no doubt, it's been carted off and dissected at some top-secret stupid place . . . anyway, in her insane jealousy she used the force of her evil Splingian-air-powered mind to zap us back here! Grossly over-complicated plot, eh? I'll give her over-complicated plot! She thinks she's got a monopoly on revenge, but she ain't seen nuthin' yet!"

"How are you going to . . . ?" began Nic, but Connie interrupted, "Well, I'm not likely to get any help from you, am I?"

"Connie, you know I can't do anything, this is not my web-si . . ."

"I know, I know . . . Look, after I've finished dealing with Barb, how about we fly off to some bit of cyberspace devoted entirely to you, where you can be hero?"

"No, nothing happens there," he replied. "Anyway, I like it here. I get to travel in unexpected ways and see interesting places. Besides it's too crowded back there; you'd be lost amongst thousands of desperate females and I'd never see you again. Oh look! Here comes a TOATS taxi—that'll get us back to More-or-Less Morocco."

Connie flagged down the taxi. "Quick, take us to More-or-Less Morocco!" she said.

To her surprise, the driver was human. "I'm very sorry," he said with unexpected civility; "but I already have a passenger."

Connie noticed the taxi was bouncing up and down. She peered into the back seat. "Get out, Juliana," she snapped. "We need this taxi. You can do that anywhere."

The young Norwegian Siegfried clone looked up from his pleasant occupation and said politely, "I'm sorry, but we got here first."

Juliana looked up. "Push off," she said.

"Anyway," said the driver, "although some TOATS taxis fly, this one is totally land-bound. I'm very sorry." He wound up the window and drove on. Connie stamped her left foot in a fury and started to foam at the mouth.

"Well, how about this?" said Nic. "Here comes our transport!"

Connie turned to see the four-masted Vulgarian barque, every sail set, come bashing and bumping through a small fishing fleet and several icebergs, to grind straight up onto the beach.

UNEARTHLY LOTTIE
21 January 1999

Connie rushed down the beach flapping and screeching like a deranged albatross. Mishka the exceptionally good-looking Vulgarian sailor threw a rope ladder over, and she and Nic climbed up the ship's great black steel sides.

"What are you doing here?" Connie asked Mishka. "I thought you were in More-or-Less Morocco."

"Yes, wery strange for it seem a moment ago ve vent crashing in ze dock of Conjectural Casablanca," said Mishka, "but you see, ve haf not kapitan, ve still search for our perfect kapitan, but he is alvays torn from our grasp by a pack of foolish vomen. Until ve find him ve are destined to vander ze vorld forever, Siegfriedless, directionless and doomed! Ve must go vere ze vind take us, till our sails hang in tatters and our dead sailors cry from ze rigging vith ghostly woices, and gaze horribly from eyeless sockets in gaunt, dread faces! And efen vorse, ve vill be accompanied by corny old Wagnerian music verefer ve go, to strike horror and boredom into ze souls of all who hear it! I ask Herr Schumm, 'Vy can't ve haf Ze Red-Hot Jalapenos®?' but he say 'Wagner—it's in ze TOATS Rule Book.'"

"Well, I'm your kapitan for now!" shouted Connie, "so let's get this baby turned round and moving! Leg it!"

Tess was already aboard, of course. She appeared to be painstakingly assembling something on the quarterdeck. "Connie," she said proudly, "have a look at my jigsaw puzzle."

"Great," said Connie, kicking it all over the deck. "Now, clear some space here! We're gonna see some serious sailing! And give this woman some vodka! Chuck that cocoa and fruit-juice overboard!"

Connie's orders were carried out and soon the ship was pounding down through the North Atlantic.

Mishka approached Connie tentatively. "Um, Kapitan . . . a fax just arrive via Wonasat®[1], from TOATS headquarters. New rule—it state zat from now on Siegfried B. Hinkelheimer must be mentioned at least tree times ewery chapter."

Connie ripped the fax to shreds and threw it to the rising gale. "See if I care!"

"But you vill be expelled if . . ." began Mishka.

"Not before I've expelled That Woman!" cried Connie as the ship headed straight into the worst storm of the decade.

Container ships foundered in the mountainous waves and sank without trace, tankers crashed into rocks and broke asunder, spilling dread cargoes. Thousands of sailors perished and half the coasts of Ersatz Europe washed away.

"Ve must reduce sail!" bellowed Mishka in Connie's ear.

"Never!" she shrieked. The mighty ship smoked her way south, lying over till her yards dipped in the wind-shredded waves, her rails under, her decks awash, her old hull shuddering with the strain. The gale howled and shrieked through her rigging like an orchestra from hell and, one by one, her loftiest sails exploded with a noise like cannons firing and disappeared in tattered grey ribbons to eternity.

---

1   Worldwide Nautical Satellite Organization

Connie rode the bowsprit, shaking her fists at the elements. "Vengeance is mine!" Suddenly remembering the new TOATS ruling and quickly counting on her fingers, she cried, "Yes, that's what I'll do—one of the things I'll do anyway—I'll steal Siegfried from them—he won't be able to resist my charms! See how they like that—the whole pack of senseless idiots. And you Barb—I've got something special for you— don't know what it is yet—but you just wait!!"

Meanwhile, on the Siegfried B. Hinkelheimer Fan Site's Feedback Page, a familiar name had reappeared, and a new fan called Heather had joined in.

ORIGINAL NATHANIEL HINKELHEIMER
Marktberg, Austria — 21 January 1999

Hi guys, you haven't heard from me for ages, I know. Er . . . not my fault—for several months I was employed in a place with no access to the Internet. I have returned at last —yeah I know I said that long ago and then I went away, so apologies for that, please don't be angry :o)

Best wishes from Nathaniel, who does NOT know Siegfried B. Hinkelheimer!

ORIGINAL NATHANIEL HINKELHEIMER

Marktberg, Germany — Friday 22 January 1999

PS I have to teach you some more German. As before it is about the page that pops up after we post feedback to this site. It's only a small mistake. You must put umlauts over the 'u' in 'für'. I couldn't help pointing this out! :o) Hope you don't mind!

By the way, Siegfried is fantastic! :o)

ORIGINAL DONNA

22 January 1999

Hi Nathaniel, I am so glad to hear that technical problems kept you away. I thought we'd scared you!

ORIGINAL NATHANIEL HINKELHEIMER

Marktberg, Austria — Friday 22 January 1999

Hehe, nobody could scare me because I am a Hinkelheimer like Siegfried, which means I am strong and brave! :o)

By the way I'm wondering about that saga you guys are writing. I don't really get it.

ORIGINAL HEATHER

23 January 1999

Hi Nathaniel. The fan fiction thing is a multi-authored never-ending story "about" Siegfried B. Hinkelheimer and his fans. It started off being quasi-realistic and has degenerated into complete unfeasibility. Incidentally, your address seems to waver between Marktberg, Germany and Marktberg, Austria. Do you commute? :)

After that, Nathaniel Hinkelheimer was barely glimpsed again on the SBH fan-site.

On Original Earth—"Oh dear," Barb said to herself. "Lottie says that Siegfried B. Hinkelheimer must be mentioned at least three times in every chapter, eh?"

Nervously she chewed on an empty chocolate wrapper.

With a shrug she concluded, "Oh well, if it must be done, then so be it. There's gotta be some way. . ."

2

BACK TO THE "DESERT"

UNEARTHLY BARB
23 January 1999
As the convoy of cars carrying Siegfried B. Hinkelheimer (mention #1) and Emily made its way across the dehydrated and sunburnt desert landscape of More-or-less Morocco, a small crowd could be seen gathered around beneath a few dead palm trees, peering down at a hole in the ground.

The convoy squealed to a halt (there was a lot of sand in the brakes). A few Oylimans, along with Siegfried B. Hinkelheimer (mention #2) and Emily, were disgorged from their vehicles. Inquisitively, they joined this crowd.

"ان ه يرجي اذام" asked Siegfried B. Hinkelheimer (mention #3) in impeccable More-or-Less Moroccan. (Or should that be Arguably Arabic?)

"Someone has fallen down the old, dry well," explained a crabbed old man in impeccable English. "He has been down there for three days. Unfortunately nobody is brave enough to venture down there to save him. Besides, there is no rope."

Siegfried B. Hinkelheimer (Note: that's four mentions now. Can I save up my extra mentions in case I don't mention SBH in a subsequent chapter? In a chapter like this I could get quite a few credits . . .) Siegfried B. Hinkelheimer (mention #5) looked down into the darkness of this dismal orifice. In the gloom he saw the face of Herr Schumm looking up at him.

"That's the face of Herr Schumm looking up at me!" Siegfried B. Hinkelheimer (mention #6) exclaimed. Without further ado, he commandeered everyone's dressing-gown cords. And of course, most people were wearing dressing gown cords around their middles, to give some sort of shape to those robe thingys they wear in the desert. In fact there were so many dressing-gown cords (I think they call dressing-gowns 'bathrobes' in the USA) that when they were all tied together they were long enough to reach all the way to the bottom of the dry well.

Siegfried B. Hinkelheimer (mention #8) secured one end firmly to a withered and somewhat fragile-looking, rotting palm tree stem. Dashingly he vaulted over the crumbling stone lip of the well and rappelled down.

The dressing gown cords began to fray where they rubbed against the stone edge, and somewhere some violins were playing fast, suspenseful music as the life-line parted, strand by strand.

Would the cord hold for long enough for our hero to make it back to the top with his burden clasped in one arm?

Another strand snapped. Only one was left.

Just as it was about to give way, the handsome head of Siegfried B. Hinkelheimer (actually mention # 8, since I cheated on the last count) surged above the well's rim. He clutched the stone coping with one lean, tanned hand and heaved Herr Schumm over the top to safety, before scrambling out himself.

The crowd (not having lifted a finger to help) cheered. Emotionally, Herr Schumm thanked Siegfried B. Hinkelheimer (mention #9).

"Here," said the penguin-suited little man, wiping a grateful tear from his eye. "You deserve this, Siegfried B. Hinkelheimer." (mention #10) He produced a paper from inside his coat pocket, scribbled something on it and handed it to Siegfried B. Hinkelheimer (mention #11).

The sexy German proudly held it high for everyone to see—a genuine Hero Certificate, at last! With Siegfried B. Hinkelheimer's mention (#12) name on it, and signed by Herr Schumm!

The crowd cheered more wildly.

"How did you pass the time down that well for three days?" asked a reporter from 'Theoretically-Tangier TV', shoving a microphone under Herr Schumm's dripping nose.

"I was reading this script," explained Herr Schumm, just before the microphone shorted out. He turned to Siegfried B. Hinkelheimer (mention #12). "You must read this also, my friend," he said ardently. "It is a fantastic script. Written by a talented girl who signs herself merely 'Lottie'. I was never bored, down that well, while I had this to read."

Siegfried B. Hinkelheimer (mention # 13),took the script and speed-read it from beginning to end. "But zis is superb! He shouted enthusiastically. "Brilliant! How did you get hold of it?"

"A goddess passed this way some time back," explained Herr Schumm. "She had with her two handmaidens.'Get me out, get me out of here I beg of you!' I prayed to them, but only one of the handmaidens took any notice. She looked over the side of the well and said, 'Cheer up! Look on the bright side! You'll have plenty of time to read my script.' Then she added, 'SOMEONE'S got to read it.' With that, she dropped the script down the well and went off with her goddess."

"Himmel!" breathed Siegfried B. Hinkelheimer (mention # 14). "I haf got to get to the Citadel to see Lottie. Zis script is a potential goldmine! I would suit so much ze lead role!"

About two seconds later the entire convoy was packed up and roaring off once more towards the Great Citadel . . .

As a tiny black speck appeared on the uttermost dunes, the distant figure of an outrageously beautiful red-haired girl walking, walking inexorably . . .

UNEARTHLY BARB
23 January 1999

The stunningly attractive Barb had been striding across the desert sands for a day or two, dressed whimsically in a harem costume made out of otherworldly silk from the planet Splinge. At times she had happened upon an oasis, where she had paused for brief refreshment.

Travelling Bedlinen tribes, recognising (by the merciless fire in her eyes) that she was on a mission of revenge, felt a brotherly affection for her, and donated for her sustenance tasty morsels such as stewed camels' eyeballs and fried camels' other bits, when she stalked obsessively by. Having rid themselves of their rubbish, they headed for McDecoy's Family Restaurant.

Barb shaded her delicate, unwrinkled skin with a TOATS Rule Book on Etiquette, thus avoiding severe sunburn. By this means she arrived unblemished at the outskirts of Make-Believe Marrakesh, the place known to the Oylimans as "The Great Citadel". The wind fanned out her long red hair and rippled like water through the silk of her harem pants (outlining her superb physique) as she stood atop a vertiginous dune rising three hundred feet into the blind blue skies of More-or-Less Morocco.

Below, she saw the auburn city seething with crowds. Her eagle eyes, sharpened by the evil-producing airs of an alien world, spied Donna loaded down with jewellery, seated in an ornate palanquin on the back of an elephant, from which position she was supervising the construction of a new temple which may or may not have been part of a movie set.

Two girls flanked Donna. One was in purple silk, wearing a badge which read "Katie, Handmaiden to the Goddess".

She was sitting upon a golden lion, harnessed with silver. The other was Lottie on a donkey.

Barb's burning eyes scanned the scene. They came to rest upon Siegfried B. Hinkelheimer, (mention #1) his arm linked through Emily's.

"Aha!" Barb would have said, had she been in the habit of talking to herself, which she wasn't, "there is my quarry!" But before she could begin to descend the dune, a bird fluttered down and landed on her wrist. "What's this?" said Barb with a frown. "A carrier pigeon?" (Talking to the bird.) She detached the scrap of paper from the pigeon's leg. Unrolling it, she began to read.

At her first short, sharp bark of laughter, the pigeon took fright and rushed into the air with a clap of wings. Its flight was pursued across the landscape by the uncontrollable peals of hilarity issuing from Barb's lips. On finishing the missive, Barb crumpled it into a ball with her fist, dropped it on the sand and ignited it with a glance.

"Well," she said aloud to a passing ant which narrowly avoided getting fried as the paper flamed, "it was a joy to read Lottie's latest three chapters, so cunningly yet benignly sent to me from TOATS Headquarters. So she's got Connie pursuing me, has she?" She threw back her lovely head and laughed loud and long. Lightning flashed intermittently like illuminated nerve branches. Even the weather was nervous.

Barb abruptly fell silent. She rolled up her sleeves. "Bring them on," she snarled. "Bring them all to me. You think I can't handle these bleached blondes?" She mentioned Siegfried B. Hinkelheimer a second time for good measure, then with a bound, she was off down the slope.

Slyly, unnoted, she slipped into Make-Believe Marrakesh. Everyone was too busy kowtowing to the goddess and the famous movie star, Siegfried B. Hinkelheimer, (mention #3), to notice the advent of a tall, statuesque red-head with eyes like lasers.

Barb made her way to the industrial sector, where squatted a strange and forbidding factory. She entered illicitly. Presently, those who were paying attention might have seen her exit, driving a large, unmarked truck. Amber dust from the tires rose in clouds as the truck lumbered towards the temple/movie site. The dust hung in the air for a while, then gradually settled on a sign over the factory door—

"Sadis el-Fire & Co. Pty Ltd"

"Manufacturers of More-or-Less Morocco's Finest Beauticians' Equipment ...

... and Instruments of Torture."

UNEARTHLY BARB

24 January 1999

"Since I have ten Siegfried B. Hinkelheimer credits to my name from Chapter 126, I do not need to do this, but I will do it anyway, just in case. "Siegfried B. Hinkelheimer, Siegfried B. Hinkelheimer, Siegfried B. Hinkelheimer." That gets the new TOATS ruling out of the way right at the start."

Thus The Evil Barb advised the ant perched beside her on the faded vinyl seat of the unmarked truck she was driving—that self-same ant with whom she had held a one-sided conversation in the desert, earlier that day.

15

Barb honked the horn incessantly as the truck bumped through the noisy, colorful streets of Make-Believe Marrakesh. Street urchins and market crowds scattered. Finally she pulled in to a quieter part of town and parked the clumsy vehicle. Leaving the ant to devour a crumb, she climbed out of the cabin and into the back of the truck.

Presently, sounds of hammering, sawing and cursing emanated from the truck's insides. The vehicle trembled slightly, rocking on its faulty suspension. Its sides developed unexpected dents from within, almost as though someone was hurling large chunks of machinery at the walls.

Eventually Barb poked her head out of the back doors. She sported a spanner behind her ear, a screwdriver clenched between her teeth and a bandage on her left foot.

"These modifications are taking more time than I had allowed for," she growled, directing her comments to a scarab beetle crawling up a nearby wall of sunbaked clay bricks.

Throwing down the spanner and screwdriver, she leapt out of the truck carrying about a dozen cans of spray paint. With incredible speed, she decorated the truck's exterior with bright colors, finally adding, in large letters, "Madame Sangfroid's Mobile Beauty Clinic. Special Rates for Movie Star Hangers-on and Desperate Fan Fiction Writers."

Throwing away the empty paint cans she ducked inside the truck one last time and emerged clad in a disguise so perfect it was impossible to penetrate. By the amateurish use of rubber masks and someone's stolen washing, Barb had accidentally made herself look exactly like Attila the Hun in drag. Not exactly the feminine look she had been aiming for . . .

UNEARTHLY EMILY
24 January 1999

Emily, still arm in arm with Siegfried, was bored.

"Does it have to take all day to shoot three minutes of film?"

Siegfried nodded "I'm afraid it does. That's why we don't usually allow writers on the set. They get cranky."

Emily's eyes narrowed slightly. "Cranky?"

Siegfried, sensing he may have said the wrong thing, tried to recover. "I don't mean *you're* cranky I—"

Emily raised her hand to his lips to silence him. "Siegfried, I've baked enough in this desert heat and put up with this movie madness long enough. Besides, I didn't write this brilliant screenplay—Lottie did. So as far as I can see I don't need to be typecast as a Movie Star Hanger-on or a Desperate Fan Fiction Writer. I'm leaving."

Emily turned to leave and Siegfried grabbed her arm. "Vere are you going?"

Emily thinking fast but not fast enough said, "Verisimilitudinous Vegas."

After Siegfried had overcome the awe engendered by her perfect pronunciation, he frowned. "I thought you said you were sick of the desert?"

Trying to recover quickly Emily replied, "I am, but the Beaujeudi® is open and I've always wanted to see Dwayne Newt in Concert®."

Stunned, Siegfried allowed her to walk away. Emily went to her tent to pack her backpack. Being a natural beauty, she didn't need much to look spectacular and always packed light.

A knock on the tent-post interrupted her.

"Emily?" Nic pushed back the corner of the tent flap and stuck his head in.

"Hi Nic, come on in." Emily finished closing the tabs on the pack.

"Fatima told me you were headed to Verisimilitudinous Vegas. Is it true?"

"Yes, why?"

"I think I can safely say I know more about Vegas than most."

Emily put her pack on. "Really?"

"Yeah, I did 'Hangover in Vegas', 'Being Vague in Vegas', 'Pros and Cons Air', where I crashed a plane into the Hard Rock Cafe in Vegas . . . "

Emily laughed and sat on the edge of the cot. "Okay, okay, I get the point. I'd love for you to come along, but what about Connie?"

Nic looked a little sad as he related Connie's plan to seduce Siegfried and go after Barb.

Emily sympathetically replied, "There's not much money in the revenge business."

Nic offered Emily his hand as she got up. "Nope, but there's plenty of money in Vegas, and I've always wanted to see Dwayne Newt."

Emily smiled. "Me too!"

"Then what are we waiting for? I'll call a TOATS taxi." Nic reached for the cell phone.

"No!" Emily startled him.

"Why?"

"Don't you know by now? If you get in a TOATS taxi you'll end up goodness knows where. It'll be much safer to take a regulation Gingham Cab®."

"You have a point there. I'll call for one."

Moments later a Gingham Cab® pulled up in front of Emily's tent. Emily and Nic climbed in, not saying goodbye to anyone (knowing chances were they wouldn't be gone for long) and headed to the airport.

As the taxi sped off towards the horizon a strong wind started to blow. A corner of the Gingham Cab® sign began to peel away in the wind until it finally tore off and floated on a current back towards the citadel.

Emily and Nic, unaware that this had happened, did not think to look at the cab door to see if any damage was done. If they had, they would have been horrified to find out that instead of an innocent Gingham Cab® they actually were riding in a TOATS Taxi Gingham Express Cab—headed straight for the Planet Splinge!

Dum De Dum Dum Dummm . . .

UNEARTHLY BARB
25 January 1999

Having finished disguising herself as an ageing beautician and camouflaging her pilfered truck, Barb happened to glance skywards. She saw a TOATS taxi flying towards her at low altitude, trailing the last remnants of a peeled-off Gingham Cab® sign.

Springing into action she hurled a half-brick at it with deadly accuracy, knocking out the taxi's anti-gravity magneto-axle.

The vehicle plummeted towards the ground, at the last moment employing its safety device—a gigantic air cushion, on which it landed, battered but undamaged. As the air cushion slowly deflated with a long-drawn rather vulgar sound, one of the occupants stumbled forth, looking dazed.

What luck! thought Barb, *It's Emily!*

"Hello my dear," Barb-as-beautician squawked. "You look a little shaken. What you need, my dear, is a refreshing pick-me-up. Today we are offering free facials to natural beauties who fall out of the sky. Step this way!"

"Wha—?" said Emily according to TOATs custom. She was a little groggy. So much so that she forgot about Nic(k) and the taxi driver, leaving them both unconscious in the taxi, and allowed herself to be led into the truck by the cunningly disguised Barb.

Inside, Emily was startled to see a vast assortment of strange and inexplicable machinery.

"No need to worry," soothed Barb with an odd gleam in her eye (she actually had two eyes, both gleaming, but for the sake of literary convention I'm only mentioning one).

"But these machines look . . . terrifying!" stammered Emily. "Quite punishing!"

"Everyone always says that," clucked Barb. "After all, what could be more punishing than the LEG WAXING MACHINE?" (Emily shuddered) ". . .except maybe the BIKINI LINE WAXING MACHINE," continued Barb with relish, "or the machine which does ELECTROLYSIS of the NOSTRILS and EYEBROWS." (Emily went weak at the knees.)

"Er—what's this thing here?" asked Emily, almost wishing she hadn't spoken.

"Oh THAT!" gurgled Barb. "That's the CLOSE-FITTING HAIR TINTING & HIGHLIGHTING CAP."

"You mean—" Emily felt faint.

"Yes," her tormentress confirmed. "It is indeed that skull-hugging cap of plastic, sprinkled with tiny round holes, which the hairdresser fits tightly to one's tender dome before—" Barb paused for effect, smacking her lips—"before using a thin hook of shining steel to pull one's hair through each tiny hole, strand by agonising strand."

Emily winced. Her eyes watered at the thought. She was beginning to wish she had never stepped into this place. Suddenly recalling Nic in the taxi, she blurted "I must go!" and raced for the door.

UNEARTHLY BARB
25 January 1999

"Not so fast my pretty," reprimanded the "aging beautician", whose voice (Emily now perceived) bore a striking resemblance to Barb's. "We also have a special deal today on our CELLULITE MACHINE."

Emily stopped in her tracks.

"Yes, I said cellulite," purred Barb, "the scourge of womanhood. The dread of the female species. Armageddon. Ragnarok. The craters of hell, made manifest in fleshly form."

"I agree with your description," said Emily. "Who wouldn't? But I don't have any cellulite. See?" Emily swished the hem of her skirt and displays her long, lean thighs, sleek, smooth and undimpled.

21

"True," agreed the creature before her, who looked like George Clooney in drag, "but THIS machine will make sure you never, ever develop any."

"Oh really?" gasped Emily innocently, eagerly.

"NO!" shrieked Barb, pushing Emily into the Cellulite Machine and slamming the door, "I lied!"

Barb threw a switch and machinery whined into motion.

UNEARTHLY BARB
25 January 1999

Throwing off her disguise, Barb laughed like a drain. The needles on the dials of the "Cellulite Machine" swung around until they entered the red zone. At length they swung back into the green and the machine grated to a halt.

Emily emerged. "What have you done to me, Evil Barb?" she fiercely shouted.

"Ha ha, that once was a real Cellulite Machine," said Barb. "The prototype, the only one in existence. I made some modifications—it's been PUT INTO REVERSE! Now you are cursed with the scourge of femininity, the blight of beauty. You have cellulite! Awful, bubble-wrap-type cellulite all over your thighs!"

"Noooooo!" wailed Emily. "How can I face Nic? Or Siegfried? Or Gabriel? That's the worst possible thing you could have done to me!"

"I know," said Barb irritatingly.

But Emily, thinking quickly, said suddenly, "Oh, look out there through the crack between the doors. Isn't that Daniel de Licious walking past? I thought he was on the planet Splinge ..."

Instantly, Barb bounded out of the truck. While her antagonist was thus diverted, Emily picked up some tools which had been lying on the floor. Attacking the Cellulite Machine, she became a whirring mass of flailing spanners, welders, screwdrivers and hammers. Before Barb could return from her fruitless search, Emily had finished the job, jumped back into the machine and turned it on the from the new switch welded to the interior. By the time Barb reappeared, Emily was stepping out of the machine looking better than ever.

"Aaargh!" wailed Barb. "What have you done?"

"Reversed the reversal." said Emily smoothly. "And now, Evil Barb, I am going to find a way to cure you of this evilness and make you into the goody two-shoes you used to be, the kind who donates soup to deserving villagers."

"Nooooo!" screeched Barb in turn. Shocked, she fell backward out of the truck. At that precise instant, Nic (now fully recovered), turned up.

"Come on Emily," he said, stepping over Barb. "The taxi can't fly but it can still drive over land ..."

UNEARTHLY EMILY
25 January 1999

" . . . We can still make it to Dwayne's 10 o'clock show if we hurry." Nic said as he cranked up the engine.

Emily leaned in the window. "I can't go."

Nic looked at her with those baby blues. (Has anyone noticed that Siegfried, Gabriel and Nic all have blue eyes?) "What do you mean? It's your chance to get away from these luna— I mean lovely, lovely ladies, with the exception of the crazy one of course."

Emily pondered which one he considered crazy. "Sorry Nic, I can't. I must to the noble thing and save Barb from herself and show her the error of her ways."

"Do you want me to take you back to the set?"

"No, that's okay, I'll walk. I'm a little paranoid I didn't get all the cellulite off. Besides I could use the exercise."

Nic tossed her the cell phone. "Here, just in case."

"Thanks." Emily stood alone in the desert as Nic drove off. Realizing a TOATS Rule was about to be broken if she didn't mention Siegfried at least three times she threw her arms up in the air and yelled at the top of her classically trained lungs, "Siegfried B. Hinkelheimer! Siegfried B. Hinkelheimer! Siegfried B. Hinkelheimer!" Her voice seemed lost in the vast expanse of sand dunes. Lost except to one—Barb was regaining consciousness behind her.

Emily noticed her stirring. She deftly picked up what looked like a Viral Monsoon® Model AK-47 Hair Dryer and knocked Barb out cold.

"That hurt me more than it hurt you," Emily said as she tossed the hairdryer aside. She picked Barb up by the feet and dragged her into the truck's shadow. Not realizing Barb was REALLY going to be annoyed when she woke up with a "sand wedgie," Emily rummaged through the glove compartment of the truck looking for the travel size version of the TOATS Rule Book on Etiquette to see what it said about reversing evil.

"Eww an ant!" She got ready to squash it, but deciding that it would be really bad karma, changed her mind and left it alone.

ORIGINAL LOTTIE
26 January 1999
Barb, if you are still amazed that Connie is still a Nic fan after seeing "Knit Me a Bagel", you'd be totally astounded (knowing how passionate I am about a certain German actor) if you saw some of the films I've seen Siegfried in! They make *Knit Me a Bagel* look like a supreme masterpiece.

If we all went off our favorite actors because of a dud film or two (or three, or four . . .) Siegfried wouldn't have a single admirer, let alone the bunch of idiots that frequent this site!

Original Barb

UnEarthly Barb

3

EVIDENTLY-NOT ENGLAND

UNEARTHLY EMILY
26 January 1999

. . . Lottie felt the oddest sensation. Slowly everything turned milky white.

Clouds. It felt as if she were floating on clouds . . .

. . . When she returned to full consciousness, she looked out across a lonely black moor. A cold wind howled.

Trying to ignore the oppressive solitude of the night the bemused beauty, shivering in her harem outfit, began to yell as loudly as she could. "Connie! Tess! Hello? Anybody here?" The sound echoed emptily across the silent landscape.

"Looking for someone?"

Lottie jumped and turned around instinctively. In front of her was a crumpled old face, with two dark eyes staring straight at her.

The man's pale skin glinted eerily in the moon-light, the rest of his form shrouded in dark. "Have you not heard of Merlin?"

Alarmed, Lottie almost ran off there and then, but she realized she had nowhere to go . . .

The path looked somehow familiar, but the night seemed to be getting darker—darker than Connie and Tess had anticipated. Connie looked over to the west at the clouds boiling towards the town. She shivered. A wild storm was approaching. They had better find Lottie soon. Trust her sister to get separated from them on a night like this...

A crag of grey stones overhung the path, and Connie clambered up. "Just over these rocks, we should be able to get a clear view of the ridge above," she said. Just as she had finished helping Tess mount the stones, she lost her balance and fell onto the bracken in front of her. Crackling, it gave way beneath her weight, giving her just enough time to feel herself falling, along with Tess.

"What on earth are you doing down there?" said an exasperated female voice from overhead.

"I was trying to find my sister, and we fell," Connie said, experimentally wiggling her toes and fingers to check whether anything was broken.

"Yes, yes, now, are you hurt?" said the voice.

"No, I don't think so." Tess sounded annoyed. "Will you be able to get us out?"

The woman smiled at them, an expression almost invisible in the dark sky. "Yes, I can, but there's going to be a violent storm. I will get you out and then and we can shelter while the worst of the weather goes by."

Already, rain had started to fall and the wind was rising. The woman threw a rope over the lip of the cleft and with some difficulty the damsels climbed out. Once they were back on firm ground their rescuer said, "Didn't you bring a cloak?" Sardonic amusement and annoyance played across her face. Despite the rain lashing down around them, she seemed amused, a smile brightening her features.

Tess and Connie's eyes, however, were bleaker than the storm. The clouds overhead parted for a moment, though the rain continued to pour, and the brief flash of moonlight allowed them to make out something of their rescuer. She was dressed in English medieval garb, with wild hair and a fairy quality to her.

Tess said under her breath, "After that last adventure in Ireland I've had just about enough of fairies."

Connie looked around. They weren't quite at the top of the crag—there was still some distance to travel before that—but they still had a magnificent view of the bleak, silhouetted landscape.

Both of them were totally confused.

"What happened?" Connie asked the woman.

"Came through a time tunnel to an island off the coast of Evidently-Not-England, you did. So did your friends—they're out there in the night somewhere. Just think what its going to be like for them when they wake up and discover when they are. Its really quite amusing," said the crone, sounding jubilant. "Come along," she continued. "Don't want to wake the dragon, you know."

Numbed by the enormity of their bizarre situation, the gorgeous damsels walked on past silent houses, beautifully illuminated by candlelight.

Tess turned to Connie. "You know you're pretty calm. For a beginner you seem unaffected by all this. You sure you haven't done this before?"

"Well, I've always enjoyed excitement," Connie replied, beaming.

"Oh ho, is that so?" The old woman's eyes twinkled.

Presently, unnoticed among the shadows, she faded and disappeared. Perhaps she had been an illusion all along...

ORIGINAL LOTTIE

OZ — Tuesday 26 January 1999

Emily, what have you done? You've completely lost me . . . I feel baffled, bewildered and bamboozled . . . (who accused ME of over-complicating the story?) I hadn't finished with Morocco, and I don't want to be in smelly sixth-century England (Arthur/Merlin's time) where there are no flushing toilets (come to think of it, there aren't many in Morocco either) and what punishment is due to you Emily . . . you have broken the new TOATS rule that Siegfried must be mentioned three times in each episode . . .

I suggest that we must all be back in the Sultan's Citadel sucking on LSD!! How else could we have all so dramatically changed our locations . . .

Lottie Having a Bitch Session

ORIGINAL EMILY

Tuesday 26 January 1999

Good heavens! What have I done? Well if Barb doesn't like what I've written I guess Donna the goddess of the webpage can delete them and go back to the desert with Nic and mention Siegfried B. Hinkelheimer, Siegfried B. Hinkelheimer, Siegfried B. Hinkelheimer three times in each episode.

ORIGINAL BARB

Wednesday 27 January 1999

Hey, Emily, I never said I didn't like what you'd written—that was Lottie having a bitch session! Check recent postings— 'm not to blame! :) I indiscriminately like everything everyone writes. The reason is, I am just glad someone else is writing besides me. Usually I fall out of my chair laughing at each episode.

ORIGINAL EMILY

Wednesday 27 January 1999

Hi Barb! I meant that since you write as much as I do if you didn't like it I knew you would whip up a couple of chapters that would work!

Anyway since I'm off for San Diego for a couple of days I won't have access to the computer. We'll probably be in Tibet by the time I get back!

ORIGINAL CONNIE

OZ — Wednesday 27 January 1999

Emily, Lottie and I were discussing your chapters and neither of us disliked what you'd written, but the continuity thing was a bit of a mental block . . . we're discussing ways we can go on from there, but with an explanation of how everyone comes to be in such a radically different place than Morocco! I love everyone's stories; they are all so funny and witty and entertaining. I wish I had the time and the mental ability to write with such profusion!

ORIGINAL EMILY

Friday 29 January 1999

Hi guys! I had an idea for a chapter so I wrote one to tie England in with the desert.

UNEARTHLY EMILY

29 January 1999

(Flashback to More-or-less Morocco.) While everyone was busy running around the Citadel, Katie (handmaiden to the Goddess Donna) was bored, as she had nothing to do. She was hungry too, and sick of dates and tabouli.

The director, busy setting up a scene, was shouting at everyone. "Can't anyone here speak English? I need props! Props! Vases, candles, rugs, lamps, P - R - O - P - S!"

Katie, seeing her big chance to maybe get a bigger part, leapt up from her satin cushions to start looking for props. She went to Sultan Siliman's tent to see what she could find.

In the corner stood a well-travelled wooden trunk, and

she went over to investigate. It was locked. Since all TOATS women are clever, she used a hairpin to pick the large padlock. A few quick turns and the lock sprang apart. She opened the lid slowly. It smelled really musty. Inside there were treasures from all over—silks, jewellery, scarves, gold candlesticks.

Those would go good in my dining room!

Out of the corner of her eye as she was trying on a tiara, the lovely young handmaiden spied an old dented tarnished oil-lamp. She thought to herself, I wonder. . . then picked it up and polished it. The lamp began to tremble and purple smoke started pouring out of the spout.

A booming voice was heard. "Who dares wake the Genie of the TOATS Lamp?"

Shaking, Katie answered. "I do, Mr. Genie sir."

The genie materialized, looking remarkably like Daniel de Licious as Sparrowfoot, long hair and all. "Then I am at your service. Three wishes I will grant you—with one exception. No wishing for more wishes."

Excited, Katie scrunched her face in concentration. "Okay, three wishes." Her stomach started to rumble. Again she checked her portable sundial. It was four pm. "Gosh, I'm hungry. I wish we were all in Evidently Not England— at least I could get decent tea and scones."

The earth began to shake and an eerie fog descended upon the Great Citadel. The genie voice boomed for all to hear. "AS YOU WISH!". . . .

UnEarthly Lottie

UNEARTHLY LOTTIE
29 January 1999
(Back to Evidently-Not-England...)

Under angry skies and through endless rain driven horizontal by the rising gale Tess stumbled down a narrow path behind Connie's retreating back. Still clutching an empty vodka bottle, she slipped and slid on the loose shale and occasionally muttered and whimpered to herself.

Connie rounded on her. "Good Heavens, girl, can't you get a bit excited? Here we are, fallen through a time-warp into God knows which dark, dank, dismal, soggy century, where everyone lives in a swamp and they probably haven't even invented the potato, and you're still snivelling on about that rotten jigsaw!! I said I was sorry!"

"It's not just that," mumbled Tess, balancing on one foot to empty a shoe, "it's ... well, we seem to have been squelching along in this for hours ... and I don't understand why. I thought we were going to More-or-Less Morocco so you could wreak vengeance on Barb, then all of a sudden we're back home looking for Lottie ... Well, Lottie can fall into a black bog for all I care; I was dying to see Siegfried again—I haven't seen him since Inauthentic Iceland and I think my brain's shrivelling up through lack ... "

"That might have something to do with this," interrupted Connie, tearing the empty bottle out of Tess's hand and tossing it over the precipice beside the path. Moments later they heard it crash and ... was that a little howl of pain? No ... just the wind.

"Do you think we'll ever see him again . . . darling Siegfried?" Tess sighed dreamily as rain-water poured off the end of her nose.

"Look, I'd be willing to bet," said Connie, "that we're still in TOATS. (Though why you're still here is anyone's guess—I thought you got written out ages ago.) Because, after all, this is typical of the silly things that happen in TOATS. And if I'm right Siegfried's sure to be around somewhere. By the way, where's that old hag got to? She was supposed to be leading us to shelter, but she seems to have vanished. Oh well, good riddance—she ponged. I vote we go and knock at the door of the nearest castle!"

"Can't we go back to those stereotypical thatched cottages we passed a while ago?" moaned Tess as she set off after Connie, "They looked warm and dry." Suddenly the wet shale under her feet started to slide. Flailing her arms she cannoned into Connie's back and they both catapulted over the edge of the cliff to fall, screaming, through the dark, rain-swept air.

Connie landed with a thump and a squishy noise, her fall strangely cushioned. A second later Tess thudded down on top of her, driving her further into the bony, but softish thing she'd landed on.

The softish thing moaned, "Aaahoow—get off me."

"Oh, thank goodness, Lottie; it's only you," said Tess. "As I was falling, I had this terrible feeling that I was going to land on Siegfried and squash him and I'd really hate to injure HIM."

"Tess, would you kindly get off me?" said Connie.

"And will both of you get off me?" gasped Lottie. "You've hammered me into this smelly black bog and I'm going to drown in a minute."

After some splashing and floundering, Connie and Tess stood on solid ground watching Lottie through the gloom and driving rain as she sank, struggling, into the black ooze.

"So you fell through the time-warp too, did you?" asked Connie. "Exciting, isn't it! Wonder where on earth, or should that be when on earth, we are. Looks like . . ."

"We're in the time of King Arthur," interrupted Lottie. "I met some old geezer who turned out to be Merlin. Now will you help me out please?"

"Merlin?" said Connie, "How did you know it was Merlin?"

"Because it looked like him," said Lottie, "and he could read my mind. He got a bit bored with me though—he said: 'Zounds damsel, thou hast a one-track mind . . . who be this Siegfried fellow anyway?' Before I could enlighten him a bottle came mysteriously hurtling out of the sky and knocked the poor old blighter out. He's back there somewhere in the mud. Do you think Siegfried might be here too? What a lovely knight of the Round Table he'd make! Can someone help me out of this mud . . . please?"

"Anyone got a TOATS Rule Book?" asked Connie, ignoring Lottie's pleas.

"Yeah," said Tess, extracting the invaluable volume from her pocket.

"Arthur . . . King Arthur," mumbled Connie, flipping the pages. " . . . blah, blah, blah . . . ah, here we are . . . 'If you meet The Real Arthur you are in the 5th century. You will find yourself swamped by wave after wave of brutal Saxon savages (as well as a few Angles and Jutes); pillaging, burning and slaughtering. Behind your back some hairy Picts and Scots will be doing more of the same. If you are a serf you will live in either; a) the mud; or, b) a hovel in the mud. If you are a well-heeled Briton you will live like a starving animal in the sacked ruins of your house. If you are Arthur you will live in a castle (i.e. wretched timber & thatch hut atop muddy earthworks surrounded by dank, waterlogged ditch)."

"Do you think we're still in TOATS?" spluttered Lottie (the mud had reached her mouth). "Only that means Siegfried will be here somewhere. He'll come and rescue me and carry me off to Camelot and we'll get ma . . . oh no! I've just realized . . . ! People around here haven't invented movie-cameras yet . . . just when Siegfried's finally read my script! What am I going to do?"

"Hurry up and sink," said Tess. "Keep reading, Connie."

"If you meet the Mythical Arthur (of, for example, Sir Thomas Malory or Lord Tennyson) you are approximately in the 15th century. If you are a knight you get to wear shining armour . . ." ("Ooh", bubbled Lottie, "I can visualize Siegfried in shining armour!") " . . . and gallop around the countryside knocking other knights off their horses and bashing them with your sword. If you are a damsel you get to wear a pointy hat and languish in a tower.

"'All damsels (unless they are evil sorceresses) must languish helplessly until rescued by Sir Lancelot or some other hero . . .'"

"Yes . . . a hero; must be my Siegfried," burbled Lottie breathlessly.

"Look, you foolish twit," said Connie, "if we're in the time of the Real Arthur (God forbid!), who's to say your Siegfried won't choose to join the savage Saxons (they are, after all, a Germanic tribe), and go round pillaging?!"

Lottie's mouth dropped open and she swallowed a gallon of swamp-water.

Connie took pity on her. "Anyhow, I reckon your Siegfried is out there," she said, flinging her arm in the general direction of a distant fortress dimly illuminated by the stars. "That abandoned castle. I have this really strong fee—"

"Castle? Where?!" With superhuman strength Lottie surged from the mud like some monster from the black lagoon. Shouting: "Siegfried! Siegfried! Please don't go pillaging! I'm here . . . your bride!!" she rushed off into the storm, leaving a trail of black ooze behind her.

UNEARTHLY EMILY
13 February 1999
The sun did not shine, It was too wet to write.
They trudged through the mud all through that cold, cold night.
So they sat in a castle and waited with fear.
Who would write next? (Connie said, "How I wish Nic were here.")
Too wet to go out and too cold to stay in,
Tess said to Lottie "Go to the Blue Bottle, get us some beer—no—make that some gin!"
But Lottie was asleep, so all Tess could do was Sit! Sit! And Sit!
She did not like it, not one little bit.

And then, the door went BUMP! Lottie woke with a jump!

They looked! His foot stepped onto that ancient stone floor!

They were thrilled when they saw him! It was Siegfried! Who could ask for more?

Followed by Barb, Donna and Katie.

Siegfried said "I know it is wet and the sun is not sunny,

So let's get out of England 'cause it just isn't funny!!"

And we can't stand it, not one more day.

But Katie stepped in and said "No, No! I can't go away!

I haven't had crumpets and buttered scones yet today!

"We have to stay here!" She said with a shout.

"You're out of your mind! We all just want out!"

"How about Iceland?" said Connie. "It would be fun."

Lottie looked at her. "That won't work, it's already been done."

Just then Emily walked in and said, "What's going on?"

"We're leaving England and soon will be gone!"

Emily responded, "I'll write the next episode that's what I'll do!"

"Can you really?" Lottie asked, while Tess sipped some gin .

"Give me paper and pencils—and I will begin!"

Just then some travelling performers came inside.

Barb asked them "You're both here too?"

"Of course we need to know where to go!

"As they say in the business 'On With the Show!'"
Emily broke into a sweat. She wrote with clenched fists as if in a rage.
Cuss words were heard as she crumpled a page.
"Almost finished!" said Emily, her head in a whir.
"It's almost as good as the classic BEN HUR!"
"Don't cast it yet. It's time to get drunk!"
Tess replied. Emily yelled "No I have to write more, I'm out of my funk!"
"But that is not all, not all I say. Now I will tell you where we will stay…
"A quick rub of Katie's lamp is all that needed,
"For her Genie to send us to were we will play.
"Say goodbye to England girls, we're going away!"
"Where?" said everyone at the same time.
"Ahhh," said Emily, "it's all in the rhyme."
They all gathered closer as Emily spoke:
"When it comes to Siegfried, he's always the star!
"And where we are going is very far,
"I promise you adventure! Excitement? A must—
"Hang on to your hats, it's Nairobi or BUST!"

THE END???

4

ALMOST AFRICA

UNEARTHLY EMILY

13 February 1999

It was a quiet evening at the safari campsite. Barb was relaxing in the portable swimming pool, playing with the cute rubber duckies, sipping Diet Kemi-Kola® and watching Siegfried silhouetted against the fiery African sky. Nearby, Connie and Katie were sitting on the couch eating pizza and watching the final moments of *Knit me a Bagel*, beamed down by the mini satellite-dish. Tess was asleep in a hammock, and Lottie, all thoughts of revenge against Barb forgotten, was sitting beneath a cowabunga tree adding a few paragraphs to her never-ending screenplay.

Suddenly, Emily and Donna ran up and hurled themselves in the pool with a huge splash. Instead of hitting Barb they ended up squashing twenty rubber duckies. Siegfried and Lottie, hearing the commotion, joined the group.

Barb watched in horror as the duckies gracefully spiralled to the bottom of the pool. "Oh my gosh! You killed my innocent rubber duckies!" she yelled.

Just when another TOATS fight was about to take on titanic proportions, a banged-up jeep pulled to a halt in front of the camp. The man in the passenger seat had a gun on his lap. Noticing it, the driver saw it and grabbed it from him, hiding it under the seat. "We want him delayed, not dead, you idiot!" he whispered.

Siegfried walked over to the jeep...

UNEARTHLY EMILY
13 February 1999

... Siegfried approached the jeep. "Hello," he said.

"Uh ... hello," said the driver. "We were wondering if you have seen two women in safari clothes nearby."

Siegfried turned around and noticed at least five ravishing women. "I have seen several."

"Oh, um ... so you have," said the driver, whose eyes must previously have been clogged with dust. "Well, we wanted to warn you that there is a large elephant herd nearby that's been very aggressive, and to tell the ladies that it isn't safe to be out alone. Would suggest you stay put for a day or two till the elephants move on."

Siegfried thanked the visitors for their concern and assured them he would take care of the ladies. After they drove off he walked over to the pool where Barb was trying to rescue rubber duckies and Emily and Donna were hiding underwater breathing through straws.

"Would vun of you like to tell me what is going on?" he asked sternly. "Why don't you vant those two strangers to see you?"

The submerged ones burst up through the water, scattering droplets. Donna was the first to speak.

"Emily and I were looking for a very early start this morning and we were a bit disappointed to find that no one had been dragged off by a lion during the night, but those are the breaks I guess. Anyway we wandered over to the next camp—the one on the other side of that rocky outcrop—because Donna thought she saw Lance and . . ."

Emily chimed in " . . . and we started talking to this skinny Englishman—"

Donna interrupted, "And he asked us if we ever heard of the Suliman Mountains up to the northwest of the Mashukulumbwe country. I told him I never had. And then he said, 'Well, that was where Solomon really had his mines—his diamond mines, I mean.' So I asked 'How do you know that?' 'Know it?' he cried, 'why, what is "Suliman" but a corruption of Solomon? and, besides, an old Isanusi (witch doctor) up in the Manica country told me all about it!'"

At that point, Lottie, Katie and Connie gathered around to listen to Donna's story.

"Did somebody say diamonds?" one of them blurted. Everyone was hanging on Donna's words except Barb, who was on the other side of the pool trying to punch a rubber duckie back into shape.

Donna continued, "And then the Englishman got a weird look on his face. 'There it is,' he cried stretching out his long, thin arm, 'but I shall never reach it, never. No one will ever reach it!' Suddenly he paused and seemed to take a long time to continue. 'Aye,' he said, 'I shall rest soon; I have time to rest—all eternity. Listen, I am dying! You girls are young and beautiful. Diamonds would pale in your presence, so here, I will give you this paper.'" Pausing, Donna pulled an old and tattered piece of paper out of her pocket. "He said, 'Perhaps you will get there if you can survive a trek through the desert.'"

Siegfried asked, "Is that a map to King Solomon's Mines?"

"Exactly!" Emily replied excitedly. "But those two strangers saw the Englishman give it to us, and we suspect that they are on the trail of the diamonds!"

Lottie burst out laughing. "Thank goodness you didn't buy the map—then I'd really think you were crazy!"

Connie interjected, "What if it is real?"

"We're supposed to be on safari," said Lottie, "and I haven't seen any elephants yet. You're not dragging me to Masha—Mashuum—whatever that place is!"

Donna, whose miniature elephant collection was displayed in the National Museum added, "There are lots of elephants if we go beyond Bamangwato…"

"Donna," said Connie, "can I ask you a question?"

"Sure."

"How come you can pronounce all these names with a perfect African accent?"

"Donna smiled like the Cheshire Cat. "The TOATS Rule Book—I forget what chapter—said 'if you can spell it you can say it'."

"Interesting!"

"Well, anyone up for a treasure hunt?"

"Of course we're in," said Connie. "Diamonds are a girl's best friend! Next to you Siegfried darling" she added with an ingratiating smile at their hero.

ORIGINAL BARB
Wednesday 24 February 1999

Whoever writes the next chapter — we have a guest star appearing. Her name is Alice. She is stunningly attractive (duh!) and is wearing a seductive outfit. Maybe she wanders in out of the desert or else wakes up in the back of a TOATS taxi in Africa when her original destination had been London, or Bakewell, or something . . . whatever.

The Original Alice is actually the only one of us crazed fans who has actually bumped into Siegfried in the flesh, so maybe she deserves honor and glory in TOATS for a while.

ORIGINAL ALICE
Wednesday 24 February 1999

Seen from afar, rather than "bumped into".

UNEARTHLY EMILY
24 February 1999

Siegfried got behind the driver's wheel of the lead Alpine Ambler® as Barb, Katie, Lottie, Emily and Donna pushed and shoved each other for the front seat.

"I'll go first—I have the map!" exclaimed Donna, squeezing past the rest. The others relented and piled into the other vehicles.

Barb, stunning as ever, was riding sidecar with her Splingian anti-elephant gun resting across one knee. "What's the map for?" she wanted to know. "Where are we going?"

Everyone was too busy to pay her any attention.

As our band of merry TOATS travellers headed off for the Suliman Mountains, Siegfried and Donna pored over the map. "Vere do we start Donna?" Siegfried asked, with his usual stereotyped German accent.

"Well, this squiggly line ~~~~~ is heading towards those mountains ^^^^^^^ but those [][][] are in between."

"Those [][][] are huts. It's ze village of Jambo." Siegfried got a far away look on his face Returning to the present he said, "Ve'll stop zere first for supplies."

A short time later, the convoy entered the village of Jambo. Dusty and thirsty the travellers disembarked to find the nearest watering hole. Amidst all the natives coming to greet the weary travellers was Alice, looking stunningly attractive in the traditional dress of Jambo, which hugged every curve.

"Who is that!" Liz exclaimed.

"I dunno." Connie replied.

Siegfried wandered over to the newcomer. He took her hand and kissed the back of it tenderly. "Jambo, Alice."

She smiled seductively. "Jambo. It's been too long since the last time I saw you. What brings you here?"

"We're on our way to find Solomon's Mines."

Alice laughed. "Must be a new map floating around."

"Why do you say that?" Siegfried asked.

The entrancing young woman took him by the arm as they walked towards the Pink Elephant Bar. "It's just that two men were here yesterday. They claimed to have the part of the map to King Solomon's Mines."

On overhearing this, Donna quickly pulled out her map. Sure enough, just past the ^^^^^^, part of the document was missing! "Approximately half the map has been torn off!" she exclaimed. "Those two nefarious men must have the other piece!"

UNEARTHLY BARB
5 February 2009

Just then Barb pointed out a cloud of dust fast approaching. "Oh look! It's a TOATS taxi."

She was correct. The loud yellow automobile slewed to a halt in front of everyone and out stepped Juliana!

As evening stars emerged in the voluptuous African skies, nine stunning babes congregated in The Pink Elephant with Siegfried and the other happy campers. They spent the next day clustered around their inflatable swimming pool squishing rubber duckies and planning their diamond-seeking adventure.

Even the best-laid plans, however, can go awry…

UNEARTHLY BARB
14 March 1999

Nine horsemen were thundering across the plain towards the village of Jambo. The cloud of dust kicked up by their steeds' hooves glowed orange in the light of the dying sun. They looked like the horseman of the Apocalypse. Except that there were too many of them.

This spectacle is what the bartender beheld from the window of The Pink Elephant, and he was not sure whether he liked it . . .

In order to explain what the bartender had just seen, we must slightly regress in time. A few moments earlier, nine incredible babes could be seen at the edge of the village, clustered under a thatched roof with no walls (just one of the unexplained architectural monuments typical of Jambo).

Barb stood pondering beside a potted flowering plant. Donna, Emily, Connie, Lottie, Tess, Katie, Alice and Juliana had just finished an argument over a map. Or to be quite accurate, half a map.

The argument petered out.

After a while, Lottie looked about wildly. "Where's Siegfried?" she demanded.

"Who knows?" said Connie with a shrug. Lottie started walking in circles calling Siegfried's name.

"How pathetic!" snorted Barb, eying Lottie.

"What's your problem? asked Donna, walking over to her. "Are you in a bad mood or something?"

"No," said Barb politely, "I'm just trying to work out whether I am evil, in this chapter, or good." She began to pluck petals, one by one, from a flower. "I'm good, I'm bad, I'm good, I'm bad," she repeated, with every petal she plucked.

"Hey, wait a minute!" shouted Tess, "that's the Zamzoozoo Flower! There's only one in the world and it only blooms once every thousand years! Last night it was stolen from the Jambo Botanical Gardens!"

"Well, that decides it then," said Barb, tossing the Zamzoozoo Flower over her shoulder. "I must be evil." Without warning she snatched something out of Katie's pocket and held it triumphantly aloft. It glimmered in the flamingo radiance of the sunset. (Out on the plains, lions roared and somewhere in the village someone very hip was playing a cool reed pipe.) "Aha!" said Barb, "I guessed you still had the magic lamp, Katie. Now, I am going to use the last wish to completely short-circuit TOATS and destroy everything!"

"My gosh she's really turned wicked this time!" breathed Alice. Juliana lunged at Barb, but before she could reach her, Barb had rubbed the magic lamp and made a wish . . .

UNEARTHLY EMILY
17 March 1999

One by one the riders revealed themselves. Wide-eyed with disbelief, the crowd stared at the throng of men that suddenly appeared.

"It's . . . it's impossible!" Siegfried managed to utter. "They all look like..."

"Like you!" Alice exclaimed, clinging to Siegfried.

Lottie and Katie fainted dead away from the shock. Emily's jaw dropped in amazement. She said to herself, *I assumed it would have been Gabriel and Daniel and Nic and Lance... but this! How can this be?!*

Tess, being perfectly pickled from her sojourns in The Pink Elephant blurted out, "I thought they all melted, when we were back in Reykjavik . . . hic . . ."

Original Lottie

UnEarthly Lottie

5

THEY'RE ALL DIFFERENT CHARACTERS FROM YOUR MOVIES, SEEGUMS!

UNEARTHLY LOTTIE
20 March 1999

"Wait, ladies ... look again; these are not exactly clones," said Siegfried, a look of horror crossing his face. "Barb, you wicked woman .... what have you done?"

"Oh Seegums, dearest," crooned Barb, "I am naughty aren't I, but I just can't help myself when these evil moods come over me, and this is going to be such fun!" She was trying so hard not to fall into her usual clichés that her face was beginning to twitch.

"Oh my gosh!" gasped Donna, "you're right—these are not ordinary clones . . . they're all different characters from your movies, Seegums! Where's . . . !" She frantically scanned the line of dismounting horsemen, then suddenly spied *him*, in uniform and looking absolutely heavenly—in fact, just like he does at the beginning of That Film!

"Oh Captain!" she cried, with desperate emotion tearing at her voice, "I've dreamed . . . I've yearned for this moment sixteen long years! Now, at last, you are mine!" With a strangled sob, she rushed headlong towards him, her arms outstretched.

"No! He's mine!" screeched Emily. "I saw him first!"

"No you didn't . . . I did!" screamed Katie, suddenly recovered from her fainting fit.

The dust rose from stampeding feet as the mob charged, sweeping even Connie up and dragging her backwards into the fray. The poor, bewildered Siegfried-as-Captain-lookalike was engulfed by a tidal wave of desperate and maddened women. Claws, fists and elbows flew. Shreds of svelte, glamorous and highly impractical safari outfits floated through the African dusk. An elegant lace-up walking boot hit Tess (too drunk to join the scrimmage) in the head. Vultures, scenting blood, circled above in the vast, darkening sky.

Lottie crawled from under the seething mob with half her gorgeous curls missing, a black eye, bloodied nose and slinky leopard-skin-print outfit hanging in tatters.

UNEARTHLY BARB
20 March 1999

"Lottie, are you crazy?" screeched Tess, rubbing the expanding lump on her head. "You can't just import characters invented by other people into TOATS! They're copyright! Do you want to get us sued?"

"But I—" Lottie began.

"Relax!" interrupted Barb, assuming her most annoyingly patronising air. "Those gorgeous-looking hunks aren't really anyone else's characters. They are just fakes that resemble Siegfried dressed up as those characters."

"Oh yeah?" Tess snorted derisively, suddenly rendered sober(ish) at the prospect of litigation. "Tell that to the prosecution!"

"No, really," Barb assured her. "Those Siegfried clones winked into existence because Lottie is lazy and we're all shallow. Lottie can't be bothered with writing down their all physical descriptions, so she's just said they look like Siegfried's movie characters. It's called reference material. If anyone really wants to know how Siegfried looks when he's acting the role of one of these characters, all they have to do is go and watch his movies. That saves Lottie all the trouble of describing."

"Yeah, yeah," agreed Lottie hastily. "That's what I meant." She was catching on quickly. Her eyes darted nervously back and forth as she scanned a local clump of baobabs for possible signs of lawyers waiting to pounce. "It's not the *characters themselves* who've landed here in Almost Africa, it's clones that look like Siegfried dressed up for the roles. There's a huge difference, you know!"

"Okay, that explains how Lottie is lazy," said Tess, turning to Barb, "But how does that make the rest of us shallow?"

"Because as long as these figments of Lottie's imagination look like Siegfried, we don't much care which character they're dressed as, or what their personalities are like, or whether they even have any personality."

Tess pondered, nodding thoughtfully. "True," she said, reflexively searching the nearby sand for signs of lawyer-spoor.

Lottie murmured to Tess behind her hand, "Barb is even more paranoid about litigation than we are. That's why she carries around pocketfuls of those '®' symbols and sprinkles them everywhere she goes, even in unnecessary places—have you noticed?"

Tess nodded. She swigged heartily from a bottle of vodka and said, "Okay, then let's—"

UNEARTHLY LOTTIE
20 March 1999

"Oh Tess . . . look!" Lottie croaked. Tess blearily followed her pointing finger to see a simulacrum of Siegfried as the skipper from *Thrill Schmooze* standing bemusedly beside his horse. "If I can't have the other, he'll have to suffice," said Lottie.

Tess and Lottie approached in their most alluring style— Tess on her hands and knees in the dust, hiccupping, and Lottie squinting through a swollen eye, limping and wiping her dripping nose on the back of her hand.

"Will you take us to Barbados please Skippy?" said Lottie, tilting back her head to stop the bleeding. "We can sing your favorite song really well—we've been practising ever so hard—and Tess here is a dab hand with a harpoon."

"Scheisse!" said the skipper lookalike; "I need a drink!"

"Best idea I've heard in ages," hiccupped Tess happily. "Let's . . ."

She was interrupted by one of the nine horsemen, who suddenly came galloping up, yanked Barb violently off her feet and threw her across the saddle before him. The captive struggled wildly but he forced her into submission.

"I've been looking everywhere for you, sweetheart," the rider said in harsh tones, "and it's put me in a foul mood. It's high time I taught you some manners, my sweet!"

Yes! It was a replica of Siegfried as the dreaded Charlie Dude from the movie Sugarcane Smith! As his horse thundered off across the darkening African plain, something strange was happening. One second Barb was swinging like a sack of potatoes across the saddle in front of him, the next she was behind him, the next she was up in front again! The lack of continuity associated with this character was giving the poor girl a very bumpy ride. As they disappeared into the night, from every direction a bizarre tapping noise could be heard. It was the busy racket of a typewriter . . .

Have the women killed the Captain? Have they killed each other? What other Siegfried character lookalikes have arrived? What is the real Siegfried doing? What's with the typewriter? Who will rescue Barb? The answers to these and other equally unimportant questions will be revealed soon.

On Original Earth, Barb scratched her head, trying to recall the names of those nine characters Siegfried had played, (and whose copyright was owned by their respective creators). More importantly, she was trying to remember their idiosyncrasies, just in case any of these clones were still trying to portray the character they were dressed as.

Siegfried usually took the role of villain, so it might prove vital to everyone's survival to know what made those villains tick; some of them were pretty nasty.

In *Das Rat*—Siegfried had portrayed The Captain; courageous, loyal, competent and resourceful.

In *Sugarcane Smith*—he'd played Charlie Dude®; murderer, torturer and all-round bad guy. Apparently, Lottie had just had Barb's avatar abducted by Siegfried-as-Charlie. Some friend Lottie turned out to be!

In the movie *In the Nostrils of Idiocy*—Siegfried was Justin Sain®. Endowed with special powers, this character was a writer of horror fiction. All the nightmarish events he wrote about came true.

The British Are So Impatient—Siegfried's Major Mullet® was a sadistic officer who oversaw the severing of a man's toes.

Thrill Schmooze—Siegfried took the role of The Cap'n®; a sailor past his prime but still pretty darned good-looking.

In *Sandhill*—Siegfried played Duke Lego® A'Freebies®; aristocrat and military commander on the planet Arachnid®.

And in *Der Polizist und Die Junge Dame*—Siegfried was a tough cop with a good heart.

That made seven characters, so far. For the moment, Barb could not recall the other three.

UNEARTHLY DONNA
26 March 1999

There was a general sense of disbelief among the troupe that anyone could possibly overpower Barb—as several "in-character Siegfrieds" and one apparently "real" one gazed doubtfully after the disappearing dust cloud around Dude®-Siegfried's horse.

[Clack-clack!]

"This is NOT planet Arachnid®!" bellowed a familiar voice over the [clickCLACKclick] noise of Tess and Lottie [taptaptatapTAP] trying to perform a clever dance number for their Cap'n®. [DING!]

"You won't type so [handily] without those thumbs" growled illusory Mullet®-Siegfried at the clickety-clack of delusory Justin Sain®-Siegfried's ancient Myth-Verona®.

UNEARTHLY BARB
26 March 1999

"Waydaminute! waydaminute!" Tess held up her hand in the universal gesture for "stop". "Donna, are you crazy?????" (This question was so urgent, it was worth more than one single interrogation point, query, or eroteme.) "You can't give Siegfried-as-Justin-Sain's typewriter the same supernatural abilities that the screenplay writers gave to the typewriter of character Justin Sain in *In the Nostrils of Idiocy!* The lawyers might—ouch!" She broke off, leaped sideways to dodge a passing aardvark and fell over awkwardly.

"Well, what do you expect me to do about it?" said Donna exasperatedly.

"Oh. . . I dunno. . ." said Barb lamely. "Ouch!"

Donna sighed and shrugged.

UNEARTHLY DONNA
26 March 1999

"TaptapTAPTAPtap!" came the sullen reply, and the landscape shifted and began to melt. The group shied farther away. Katie, suddenly ejected from the seething mass centred on so-called Captain-Siegfried, stumbled into another Siegfried persona who was emitting a bright glowing radiance from his midsection. He smiled paternally at her and headed off alone into the distance.

"Waiiiiiit!" She [ding!ClackCLACKcluckclick] tried to follow, but a harsh wind was rising that filled the air with stinging red sand. "Ouch!" [tippety-tap] she cried as the tiny missiles shredded her diaphanous wraps.

Suddenly she was attracting the attentions of a CROWD of Siegfried clones. "MmphH!" uttered the Captain lookalike from under a thrashing pile of female perfection. "I vas safer at ze bottom of ze ocean! I vish I vas zere again!" [clickclackclick] and he disappeared!

Donna, Emily, Connie and Alice thudded crankily to the ground in a cloud of dust, hair, and blood.

The wind howled around them until it drowned out everything but the [clickety-clickety-clack] of Justin Sain's magical typewriter . . .

"How peculiar", said Original Barb aloud, as she finished reading Donna's latest chapter. "Here's the real me writing stories that come true in cyberspace, and out there in cyberspace a fictitious character is writing stories that come true there, which for him is the real world!

"Well, if that "Justin Sain" can control events by writing, I'm sure Cyberchick Me can do it too. After all, Connie wrote herself out of a bad situation on the back of a napkin. Here goes!"

UNEARTHLY BARB
16 April 1999

Barb's complaints were abruptly cut off as her chin jarringly banged against the horse's flank. Her teeth rattled rhythmically to the beat of the gallop, her eyeballs rolled around in her head as she bounced up and down.

Gosh, this is uncomfortable, she thought stoically, her liver flapping about inside her like a freshly-caught fish. She shot a sidelong look into Siegfried-as-Charlie Dude's® saddle-bag, in case he had a keyboard she could use to get herself out of this situation. No keyboard was evident, although the saddle-bags were bulging with paraphernalia, including leather thongs, a whip, a bar of dark chocolate and a complete scuba-diving outfit, including flippers.

"Oh well," Barb said resignedly to herself, her skull vibrating to the clicketty-clack of her teeth (which sounded like a type-writer), "I might as well just go with the flow and use this moment of extreme discomfort to take stock of the current situation."

She began to make a list, ticking items off on her fingers as she enumerated them.

One: I am being abducted for nefarious purposes by a clone supposedly called Charlie Dude®.

Two: He looks exactly like a character who was played by Siegfried B. Hinkelheimer.

Three: This means he has amazing eyes.

Four: And a hot body.

Five: He can do anything he wants with me, until I get access to a keyboard.

Six: Being raced off by someone extremely masculine on horseback is one of my favorite fantasies.

Seven: I'll bet I lost five kilos sweating with fear when those slimy monsters came at me, which means I can eat this chocolate with a clear conscience.

Eight: All those other stunning-looking Siegfried fans are back there, still hanging about at The Pink Elephant, which drastically reduces the competition.

Nine: This situation is beginning to look better than I first thought.

Ten: I wonder what I'll do when I run out of fingers to count on ...

"Hey Charlie®!" Barb yelled erratically, her head gyrating dizzyingly as the horse's hooves pound the desert sands. "Let me sit up again, will you? I've run out of fingers and I'll have to enumerate on my toes."

"You'll have to WHAT?" her abductor reined in the horse.

"Enumerate," repeated Barb. "You're an educated man— you ought to know!"

"That's enough of your impudence," velvetly said the Siegfried-clone, "You seem to forget that out here in the African wilderness I am virtually omnipotent."

"Oh really?" simpered Barb, wiping chocolate stains off her face with her sleeve, "In that case I do not have to fear being deflowered, after all."

"I said OMNIPOTENT!" roared Charlie®.

Barb's heart pounded against her lacy bodice, which was already ripped. (By her, in anticipation.) "You look gorgeous when you're acting angry," she breathed. "This role really suits you, Siegfried—I mean, Charlie®."

Taking her in his strong arms he threw her to the ground, then jumped gracefully from the saddle. "You are too bold, woman. I shall have to teach you a lesson!" he said huskily.

"Hang on a minute—" (Barb hastily gobbled the last few squares of chocolate)— "Right. Now, where were we?" She clung to him, her aching lips searching for his. They kissed—hungrily, passionately under satanic African stars. Fleetingly, between moments of ecstasy, Barb thought, *I bet Lottie thought I'd write my way out of this . . .*

The next episode contains many pseudonyms for Latin-named parts of the body. It is X-rated and has to be censored. Sorry readers, you'll have to imagine it for yourselves.

UNEARTHLY LOTTIE
16 April 1999

Carried on balmy night breezes across the vast African plain, the raucous laughter of hyenas drifted in through the open windows of The Pink Elephant and woke the "real" Siegfried where he had nodded off at the bar.

"Ach du liebe Himmel . . . what a horrible dream," he muttered.

He rubbed his eyes and looked around with a grimace. Tess and Lottie, attired in little (very little) sequined dresses, were still attempting a pathetic song and dance routine for the stupefied replica Skipper from *Thrill Schmooze*. It appeared that a karaoke night was in full swing. The light from the bar spilling out through the windows illuminated half a dozen battered women engaged in digging a deep hole in the dirt in a desperate search for their vanished captain from *Das Rat*.

"Scheisser," moaned Siegfried. "I wake up to find reality's even worse!" At the other end of the bar the harassed skipper-from-*Thrill Schmooze*-lookalike downed another vodka.

"All I have is you, so why not come and take me . . . I cannot bear, you're leaving me . . . you're leaving meeeeeee!" yodelled Lottie, while Tess, waving her harpoon, hiccupped tunefully and fell over.

On hearing the word "leaving", it dawned on Siegfried that all his senseless admirers had deserted him to go off chasing his film characters. He pushed away his empty glass, put some money on the bar and got to his feet with a smile. "Es war recht nett, ladies, aber . . . I'm going home. Auf wiedersehen," he said quietly as he pushed open the door and walked out.

Earlier, on their arrival at The Pink Elephant, he'd conveniently noticed a sign at the crossroads outside: "To the Airport". He followed the sign and, oblivious of the ominous rustle of dangerously restless elephants, the bloodcurdling growl of hungry lions and the heart-stopping choke and splutter of an Air Banana plane flying perilously low overhead, he walked heroically off down the dark, pot-holed road into the horrors of an African night.

Like a gorgeous moth to a candle flame Barb, leading her horse, wandered towards the very distant light of The Pink Elephant twinkling on the horizon. Somewhere far behind her, the Siegfried-as-Charlie Dude®-lookalike was lying on a carpet of indigenous Sweet Hottentot Fig plants. He was unconscious from exhaustion.

Curses, Barb thought, old "Charlie" and me . . . we could have made an evil team! If it wasn't for his boringly limited vocabulary . . . hah! . . . kept telling me I was 'bait for the sharks'! Hasn't the stupid man realized by now that that particular fate is reserved for him?

Barb was so deep in thought that she failed to notice the clicking of a typewriter.

"Barb, how nice to see you," said a voice close by.

A being who looked exactly like Siegfried-as-Justin Sain® sat at his desk under a baobab tree, typing furiously in the darkness. He wrote:

<Barb recoiled in shock then looked down to find herself poised, wobbling, at the rim of a bottomless pit. She stared into the illimitable gulf of the unknown; the stygian world yawning blackly beyond.

Her eyes refused to close. She did not shriek, but the hideous, unholy abominations shrieked for her, as in the same second she saw them spill and tumble upward out of an enormous carrion black pit choked with the gleaming white bones of countless unhallowed centuries. She began to back away from the rim as the army of unspeakable figures, twilit by the glow from the bottomless pit, came pouring at her towards our world!>

Justin Sain stopped typing. The unspeakable figures advanced towards Barb, their claws and fins gleaming, a low growl in their throats and their dripping fangs bared.

"I wrote about you . . . that's why you're here," said the typist, immune to the predators produced by his writings, "but I wasn't expecting such . . . you're unimaginably beautiful you know . . . exquisite . . . "

"You wrote about me?" snapped Barb, kicking and hitting out at the bunch of slimy abominations crawling up her long, shapely legs. "You've got it all wrong, you fool—I wrote you into TOATS—that's why you're here!"

Justin Sain laughed softly. "You poor deluded woman. I'm a god now, you understand. I don't go anywhere at another's beck and call. You only exist—all of you," he waved an elegant hand towards the heap of women grovelling in the dust; "because I wrote about you. But you needn't worry; one look at you and I've gone right off horror. Hop it you guys," he said to the unholy abominations, whereupon the stygian pit sucked them back in and closed with a thud, squashing some of those nasty slimy things. "I'm now going to write bodice-ripping romances and you, Barb are my first heroine!"

Sain typed rapidly:

<Barb whimpered as Justin Sain picked her up and flung her across the pommel before him. Her luxuriant tresses of Icelandic red hair floated down across the rippling black hide of the great stallion as it pranced and curvetted. With one strong arm Justin held Barb to him and her wild struggles subsided. She clung to him, her aching lips searching for his (after all, he did look like Siegfried). They kissed—hungrily, passionately, until with an easy mastery he set his heels to the horse's sides and it leapt forward, its mane and tail streaming like ragged banners across the blazing red sunset.>

"Hey, you can't do that!" yelled Barb, being bounced around once again on horseback. "We've just had a sunset!"

"I can do whatever I want," smiled the replica of Siegfried as the bad-guy movie character whose copyright belongs to the actual writer (just covering all legal bases, here.)

"Where's my computer?" wailed Barb, pulling an old shopping list out of her pocket. She scribbled on the back of it as fast as she could:

<Barb twisted in the arms of that wicked man and drew her dagger! With its point poised before his heart, she lunged . . . >

"Sorry, Barb," laughed her intended victim, "but I can out-type you any day."

As he carried her, slung like a bag of potatoes across his horse's wither, off into the day's second glorious sunset, her voice could be heard wailing; "Why didn't I listen to Mum? She said I'd need those shorthand lessons some day!"

UNEARTHLY BARB
16 April 1999

Lawks-a-mussy-me! mentally exclaimed Barb, as soon as she had figured out what a horse's wither was. *It's quite incredible how this guy can hold a struggling woman across his steed with one hand, grasp the reins of the galloping steed with the other, balance a typewriter on his lap with the other, and still manage to "out-type" me with whatever hands he has left over. Lottie seems to think Justin Sain is some kind of genetically engineered man crossed with an octopus.*

UNEARTHLY EMILY
17 April 1999

The smouldering remains of another Air Banana flight illuminated the moonless African night. Wearily, Siegfried, still several kilometres from the airport, decided it was safer to climb a nearby tree to get some rest than to remain below it with all those hungry, growling carnivores prowling about.[2]

As he gazed toward the wreckage and thought of home he noticed a tiny intermittent glow in the distance. A firefly perhaps? It drew nearer and nearer still. Siegfried remained motionless as a figure began to take shape, then another.

"I told you we should've taken the Fjordstream airliner®," said a voice, "but no! This will be quicker you said!"

---

2   (Hopefully the lawyers had not scared away the ravening hyenas, which were, by comparison, benign.)

"Will you stop complaining for one second," said another, "and shut off that flashlight before we're lion-burgers."

One figure halted. "Did you hear something? I thought I heard something."

Siegfried couldn't quite place the voices; one of them sounded very familiar. Suddenly he realized who was approaching.

"It's your overactive imagination, Alice." Emily's tones were quite distinctive. "I didn't hear anything. Come on."

"It is you!" Siegfried blurted out, scaring the two women half to death as he jumped out of the tree.

Alice nearly fainted from fright as a screaming Emily instinctively did a perfect aerial roundhouse, knocking our hero completely unconscious.

"You idiot! You killed him!" Alice threw herself across Siegfried's body to shield him from further harm.

Emily, stunned by her own lightning quick reflexes, rationalized the situation. "He's not dead, he only dies if he's shot in the back, remember!"

Alice felt a wave of relief. "Oh yeah, but what do we do with him until he regains consciousness?"

UNEARTHLY EMILY
17 April 1999

Meanwhile, back at The Pink Elephant's karaoke night—

"At first I was afraid, I was petrified, just thinking I could never live without you by my side[3]. Come on! Sing it with me!" Tess belted out.

---

3   "I Will Survive", ©Gloria Gaynor® Lyrics by Freddie Perren and Dino Fekaris.

A group of Vulgarian sailors, lured by Tess's singing, like sailors to the Siren, joined in. "Then I spent so many nights, thinkin' how you did me wrong. And I grew strong, and I learned how to get along. So now you're back, from outer space I just walked in to find—Katie!"

Lottie looked up over her Rum Tum Tugger[4]® punch. "Hey Tess, that's not how it goes."

Tess rubbed her eyes in disbelief hoping it was just the cigarette smoke playing tricks on her. But no, it was Katie looking fabulous in her new ensemble, huddled in a corner not with SBH or a SBH character, but with a very handsome Irishman.

Lottie spun around on her barstool to see what Tess was looking at. "Oh my gosh! I don't believe it! Is that in the TOATS Rule Book? Can she do that?"

Tess put down the microphone as a loud burst of feedback caused everyone to cover their ears. She stumbled towards Lottie. "I think so." Feverishly she searched her bag for the TOATS Rule book. "Except that if— (her conversation was drowned out by a Vulgarian sailor who had started singing 'Back in the Useless Mess Bar®) …" —so I wouldn't want to be Katie when she finds out Katie's with her man!"

"Right you are," agreed Lottie, getting a sudden hit of inspiration. "We could sell tickets. We could bill it as the best fight since Krystle and Alexis Carrington on 'Dynasty'[5]®! Hey there's an idea!"

---

4   © T.S. Eliot

5   © Richard and Esther Shapiro

She started looking around the room for the other TOATS crew. "Funny I don't see everybody. I wonder where the others are."

UNEARTHLY EMILY
18 April 1999

When Siegfried regained consciousness, out by the smouldering wreckage of the Air Banana flight, he didn't say anything. He merely gazed into Emily's eyes.

"It's not fair!" said Alice. "He likes you better than me!" And before Emily had time to explain that the glazed look in Siegfried's eyes was not love but confusion, she had sulkily rushed off towards The Pink Elephant.

Awakening to clarity Siegfried stood up, nodded politely and walked away in the direction of his lodgings.

Emily was scared. Her "real life" self had written Siegfried back into the story just when he had been about to fly out and escape— he couldn't possibly be pleased about that! Furthermore, her cyber-self had kicked him in the head— knocked him out cold, for goodness' sake! He must at least be badly bruised.

Spontaneously leafing through the medical glossary of her TOATS Rule Book on Etiquette, she realized to her horror that he might even have Concussion, Contusions, Fractures and Hematomas, although he certainly looked okay.

Maybe her friends were right when they called her "paranoid", but the fact that when he awoke he hadn't mentioned any of the night's earlier events warned her that he could be plotting revenge. His silence seemed ominous.

Vengeance could happen at any moment, and knowing Siegfried's usual roles, it could take any form. The more time that passed, the more time he had to think of something and the worse it would be. Emily sighed and headed for her own bungalow down the path. This was going to be a long night.

Little did she know how right she was…

UNEARTHLY DONNA
18 April 1999
Alice burst into The Pink Elephant in tears.

"Emily's run off with Siegfried!" she moaned. Donna yawned, took a slow look around a room chock-full of Siegfried clones and character lookalikes and answered, "Relax. Have a replica. No calories." She turned back to the poker game. "How did I get ten cards in my hand?"

"That's it, you're cut off!" answered Lottie, reaching over and plucking Donna's magic wand out of her overalls. "No spell casting in YOUR condition."

Suddenly the tall and briefly forgotten Irishman stood up and yelled at the top of his lungs "I demand to know where in hell I am and how the hell I got here!"

The outburst even momentarily subdued the singing Vulgarians.

Lottie looked flustered and began rifling through the TOATS Rule Book. "You're … well it's … ."

Donna tried to stand up but couldn't tell whether she was already. "This is the TOATS Universe, Gabe baby, we can conjure up anyone, anywhere, anytime," she slurred, focusing on one of several Gabriel Yearn® clones in her field of view.

"All any one of these vashtly talented and ravishing women," she gestured around the table at the semicircle of beauties, "hash to do is just type shomebody's name, and the next thing you know . . . here they are."

As if on cue, a complete set of "Marx brothers®" flashed into the room.

"Am I having some kind of nightmare?!" cried "Gabriel".

"Ha! And what's more, you're all STUCK here, all of you, shtuck here until we lose interest, that is. For as long any TOATSH author wantsh you around, you'll shtay right here, right here in our own private Dishneyland®."

The "Marxes" winked out of existence.

Donna reached instinctively for her wand but couldn't remember where she left it. "I need a shobriety shpell," she mumbled as she pitched face forward into the bean dip.

"What's she going on about?" mused Connie, as the sailors and Tess started another round of "Ninety-Nine Bottles of Wodka in the Foc'sle."

"Does anyone know what happened to Barb?"

UNEARTHLY EMILY
18 April 1999

Siegfried entered his bungalow. He had to get revenge for what Emily had done. He'd never thought of her as devious before. But to write him back to Jambo just when he had been about to escape—how could she? And how did he end up unconscious for so long? Was it her doing?

Which was why he wanted to bang his head against the wall.

His revenge would have to be perfect and he couldn't think of a darned thing. Except for kissing her. But that wouldn't be revenge. That would be fun.

Siegfried sighed. What had he gotten himself into? Had TOATS finally torn away that last bit of reality from his mind? Was he past suspension of disbelief and stuck in this madness forever?

When Emily returned to her bungalow, she found a notice taped to her door. She took it inside and read it.

"Great. Just great," she muttered. The note stated that her bungalow had termites, and that this was her third notice that bug bombs would be set that evening and continue through the next morning. "What happened to notices one and two?" she demanded aloud. She had less than an hour.

After going into her bedroom to pack, she dialled the phone. If she didn't know it was impossible, she'd think Siegfried had arranged this termite scenario.

He answered on the first ring. "Hallo."

"Siegfried. It seems my bungalow is being fumigated."

"And?" She could tell from the question that she was required to beg.

"Can—can I please stay with you?" Silence. She hated asking, knowing she was setting herself up. But she'd rather worry about revenge than spend the night in a TOATS taxi… "Please?"

"OK," he said at last, "but there's one condition. We play by my rules."

"Of course; it's your room. I'll be over in a little bit." Emily hung up before she could change her mind.

This was Siegfried's big chance. He had to think of something, fast.

UNEARTHLY EMILY
18 April 1999

In Siegfried's bungalow, Emily eyed the plastic mat on the floor. "Tell me again how you talked me into this?"

"This is as good a way as any to decide who gets to use the bed," Siegfried explained.

"We could flip a coin or we could share it if you were nice," Emily suggested. She recognized the dark look in his eyes and felt the electricity in her stomach.

"I don't feel very nice right now, Emily," he said. Emily nudged the spinner with her toe so she wouldn't have to meet his eyes. When she looked up, he was smiling. "One more thing. Whoever loses has to do one thing the winner tells her to."

"You're assuming you'll win?" Emily scoffed.

"Scared?" he asked teasingly.

"Of course not."

Their eyes locked. Emily's heart started beating faster. Siegfried was looking at her like he was the Big Bad Wolf. No, she told herself, he only looks like that because he's waiting to get even with me.

"Let's play." she said.

"You first," he said and spun the spinner. "Right foot to red." Emily put her foot on the Pretzel® mat and he handed her the spinner. That worked fine until they both had two hands on the mat.

"I don't think you can play this with two people," Emily said.

"Sure," Siegfried said. "It's more interesting that way. You just say a color and I'll move what I can."

"OK," Emily said, not thinking it would work. It was true, they were at opposite ends of the mat. Not twisted at all.

Siegfried smiled slowly, knowing that would change. "Just wait," he promised.

Emily and Siegfried were facing each other balancing precariously. She was pretending to be fascinated by their socked feet on the spotted plastic.

"Blue," he said.

She contemplated what she should move. None of the choices looked good since the only blue spot open was right between Siegfried's feet. She moved her right foot. Slowly. Careful not to touch him. She eased out a breath when she was balanced.

"Green," she told him. His eyes met hers and held as he slowly, deliberately, dragged his arm across her leg, and finally touched the green spot. He was now leaning over her.

"Red," he whispered. She had to close her eyes. This was like a slow dance on the horizontal plane. (You know; sex) Her eyes opened again. She couldn't see where the damned spots were. She knew she couldn't move either hand, because they were bearing most of her weight. She stretched her bent leg, edging toward the red spot on the far side of the blue one—trying hard to ignore the fact that it placed her body more squarely beneath Siegfried's.

"This is physically impossible," she muttered.

"Do you give up?" her playmate inquired.

"Never . . . oof." In her effort to reach the dot, Emily's foot slid and her delicate balance collapsed. She fell the rest of the way to the floor. Siegfried didn't move, hovering over her, and she didn't have room to get up.

"I think you just lost," he told her, his eyes amused, his body still not moving.

"Two out of three?" Emily asked. Here she was, lying on the floor under him only he wasn't touching her. So it was to be torture then. She couldn't breathe. She couldn't think straight. For a split second he didn't want revenge any more. He wanted her. But he realized her defences were down and a moment after that a smile flashed across his face before he backed away and headed to the kitchen. Without saying anything.

Emily walked to the window and opened it, breathing the cool night air. It cleared her head. She closed her eyes and imagined herself in his arms.

"Do you like gelato?" Siegfried's s voice came from the kitchen. Her eyes flew open. That wasn't what she had expected to hear.

"What?" Emily's voice was too high. Siegfried appeared holding a pint container in his hand. "Gelato, it's Italian ice cream . . . " He saw the crimson blush on her face. "What did you think I said?" he asked, chuckling.

"Nothing," she said.

He was smiling. "Would you like some?"

"What?" she replied a little too quickly.

"Gelato. Ice cream." He was laughing at her.

"No thanks. On second thoughts I think I'll take a walk instead." Totally confused, Emily hurriedly left the room.

A TOATS taxi was parked outside.

"You know, if it wasn't for you," said Emily, "I would be having a healthy relationship with Siegfried!" She angrily kicked one of the tires and, turning her back on the taxi, headed off into the night.

UNEARTHLY EMILY
18 April 1999

Soon she re-entered the village of Jambo and made her way through the winding streets. After rounding a corner she passed The Pink Elephant. The pounding of music could be heard for miles. Emily glanced at the front door wondering if she should go inside.

"Hey Emily," the slurred speech came from behind her. Emily turned slowly to reveal a very inebriated Tess.

"Tess," she replied. "Hello."

"So," Tess began. "Do you think Katie's having fun with your boyfriend?"

Emily stared at her with a blank look. "What do you mean?"

"Well, you see Katie still had her third wish for some inexplicable reason, and . . . hic . . . since she saw that movie *The Predictable Lineup* she thought she'd wish . . . hic . . . for Gabriel, and we thought that since we need one last night of excitement . . . hic . . . before we leave tomorrow, a good fight would be nice."

Emily, showing no emotion, entered the bar. She walked up behind Katie, who was buying a drink.

"Aren't you going to say hello?" Emily said evenly.

Katie stopped dead and whirled around. *Oohhhhh drats,* she thought. "Emily, hi!" she nervously chuckled. "I was looking for you."

'Really?" Emily replied sarcastically, looking around for Gabriel.

"Yes, I was wondering where we were off to next . . . and . . . um . . . thought you might know."

Emily raised a finger and pointed northwest. "Detroit's that way," she snapped. "Now, what have you done with him?"

The jealous cyberchick turned around and began searching for Gabriel, but temporarily lost her footing when Katie pushed her from behind. Emily wheeled around, feeling anger wash over her. "You'll regret that!" she yelled.

A crowd begin to gather as Connie ran around yelling, "Cat fight! Cat fight!"

"You're not woman enough to handle Siegfried and Gabriel," Katie countered.

Emily's forehead wrinkled with rage. "I don't see either one of them here with you. Did they BOTH turn you down?" she asked acidly. A chorus of "Oooo"s came from the surrounding throng of people. Katie growled, her temper taking over. Leaping for Emily, she yelled as she miscalculated the distance between them. Emily grabbed hold of her shoulders and tackled her to the floor.

The crowd cheered, some placing bets. "Five on the American!"

"They're both American."

"Okay then, ten on the blonde!"

Suddenly, Katie lashed out and hit Emily, who spun into her former lover's arms.

77

"Emily!" Gabriel asked. "Are you okay?"

Emily opened her eyes and looked up at him. "M—Mom? Is that you?"

"No," Gabriel replied. "It's me. Gabriel. The original lookalike."

"Gabriel . . . " The feisty beauty frowned. It was if she couldn't remember him at all. "Oh!" she exclaimed. "Gabriel. Okay, yeah. Hey, how's it going?"

"Not too good," he replied. "You're losing to Katie."

"I'm WHAT!?" Emily stood up and faced Gabriel, leaning in close to him. "Did . . . did you j-just say that I'm losing to . . . " She cringed. "… to Katie?" Gabriel nodded. Emily straightened up and threw her shoulders back. "Well then," she said.

"Uh, Emily," Gabriel tried to divert his fan's attention as she turned to her opponent with a look in her eyes he had never seen before. "Doesn't the Bible say, 'Thou shalt not kill?'"

"I'm not going to kill anyone," Emily answered, stalking towards Katie....

 **UNEARTHLY EMILY**

18 April 1999

Emily turned to the crowd and inquired, "What odds am I at?"

Gabriel checked a notebook. "Uh . . . Forty."

"Is that all?" The ex-pirate wench shrugged. "I'm just going to have to work a little harder I guess."

Suddenly someone yelled. "Emily! Behind you!" Emily turned a split second too late. Katie immediately nailed her in the left side of the jaw and she fell backwards into Gabriel's arms for the second time.

Gazing up at him with blood dribbling down her chin she said, "Hey, you look familiar. Don't I know you?"

"Yeah," he replied with a smile.

Realization set in for Emily. "Gabriel," she murmured. "I'm so sorry Katie dragged you back into this." After pausing for a moment to think, she went on, "I'll tell you what, Gabe darling. If the bets go into three digits, I'll give you that stupid magic lamp—which I nicked from Barb's carryon bag after she nicked it from Katie—and send you back home . . . okay?"

Instantly Gabriel helped her back into the "ring". "A hundred bucks on Emily!" he cried.

Emily looked back at him, her eyebrow raised. Gabriel smiled at her. As a new adrenaline rush surged through her body, Emily stood tall. She laced her fingers and pushed her palms out. Katie covered her ears to drown out the sound of the cracking knuckles.

Afraid for her life, Katie kicked out, hoping to connect with Emily. Instead, she found her leg being held by her opponent. Emily smiled disdainfully at her before tossing Katie's leg in the air, sending the rest of her body backwards. The crowd cheered. A moment later it was all over, and Gabriel declared that the victory had gone to Emily.

"I believe you owe me a trip home," he said giving the conqueror an enthusiastic kiss.

She turned and wiped the blood from her nose. "As you wish," she said softly, pulling out the magic lamp from a pocket of her jacket and handing it to him. A second or two later Gabriel vanished as quickly as he had appeared.

Emily picked up her jacket and left the bar as Lottie and Tess divided their winnings. Turned back down the main street of Jambo, Emily left the frenzied crowd behind in search of peace and quiet.

Later, she spotted a shadowy form standing on a street corner. "Emily?" that familiar voice asked. "What are you doing out here?" Siegfried stepped closer to her. "What happened?" He touched her cheek where a dark bruise was forming.

"What do you mean?" she asked innocently.

"What do I mean?" he repeated. "I mean where did you get all these cuts?"

"Oh, those," she said. "I got into a fight."

"A fight? Mein Gott, Emily!"

"Siegfried really, I'm okay."

He took her arm and they started down the street, all thoughts of revenge now completely forgotten. Suddenly, a supple, silhouetted figure stepped out into their path. Siegfried and Emily stopped, unsure of what to make of this.

"Well, well, well," a small voice said. "If it isn't Emily."

"What's going on?" Siegfried look nonplussed.

"Siegfried," Katie said, "would you mind stepping aside?"

"What?" he asked.

Emily began backing up slowly. The face in front of her was slightly mangled; hideous at best. Emily drew in a deep breath. She cleared her throat. "Katie."

Siegfried looked from woman to woman. His eyes suddenly widened. "This is who you got into a fight with?"

Emily was fed up with this whole situation. First Katie conjures up Gabriel, then Lottie and Tess stage this fight, and now she was this close to having some quality time with Siegfried . . .

That was the clincher. She balled her hands into fists and regarded Katie with a stony glare. "All right," she said finally. "You want me." After handing her jacket to Siegfried she rolled up her sleeves. "Well come on then," she taunted.

"Emily . . ." Siegfried made as if to stop her.

The lovely ex-pirate wench held out her hand in a gesture of admonition. "Siegfried, please. Not now."

Calmly, Katie walked up to her adversary and looked her in the eye. Emily stared back. Suddenly, Katie's hand came across her face and slapped her.

Emily laughed. "That was it?" she sneered. "What the hell was that? *Barb* hits better than that!" Next moment, Katie's fist came flying at her, knocking her back a few steps.

Fingering her jaw with the air of someone reaching an important conclusion, the ex-pirate wench turned to Siegfried. "Remember when you asked me how you became unconscious?" she said. "Well pay attention."

In one deft movement, using all that was left of her strength, Emily leapt into the air and spin-kicked Katie square in the jaw. Katie flew several feet into the air before sprawling unceremoniously on the ground.

"Wow!" Emily exclaimed as she landed. "I've never got air time out of anyone before!"

Siegfried stood motionless, his mouth hanging open. Never had he seen Emily fight like this before—it was strangely exciting.

"This has been one heck of a night. I'm going to bed," Emily managed to say as she grabbed her jacket from Siegfried and, totally exhausted, walked back to the bungalow. Siegfried stood staring after her as the first rays of daylight touched the sky.

There was a new visitor to the SBH fansite. Her name was Ingrid and she seemed interested—yes, interested!—in TOATS.

"Write her in!" cried Original Barb.

UNEARTHLY BARB
21 April 1999
As the sun rose cautiously over Africa, somewhere in the middle of a desert this scene was taking place: Barb and Justin Sain, a man who strikingly resembled Siegfried B. Hinkelheimer portraying Justin Sain®, a probably-copyrighted character out of one of Siegfried's movies, were sitting cross-legged in the shade of a horse, playing chess.

At least, there was a chess-board between them but nothing was moving. It might be supposed that both players had fallen asleep sitting up. In fact, Barb was not asleep—she was reminiscing about the events of the preceding night. She recalled the way she clung to him, her aching lips searching for his. They kissed, hungrily, passionately under satanic African stars.

Eventually she became aware of a scratching sound behind her left ear. "What are you doing?" she mumbled thickly, twisting her head around to take a look.

"What do you think?" replied Justin Sain, continuing to scribble with pencil in his notebook, "Everything I write comes true, remember? I am writing what's going to happen to you next, darling," he continued with a suggestive leer.

Barb noticed he was up to the last page . . .

"Ooh, ow, ah!" cried Justin Sain.

"What's the matter now?" Barb shouted.

"I have writer's cramp," he moaned. "It's killing me." Doubling over, he cradling his clenched hand.

"Oh dear," said Barb, picking up the discarded notebook. She read it over while Justin Sain writhed in agony on the sand. "Too bad," said Barb, tossing the notebook into a nearby mine-shaft. "It might have been interesting."

Searching through the saddlebags, she found no more pencils, no paper, no type-writers, and no computer keyboards or modems of the plug-in-to-palm-tree type.

"Nothing to write with," she announced to the tormented Kutter, who wasn't listening. "What happens now?" she said conversationally, turning to the horse, who seemed more attentive.

"Baa," said the horse.

Barb's brow furrowed. "Egad, with nobody writing this thing it's getting out of control. Starting to get weird, even. It's time for me to take the reins again, so to speak."

With a "ding!" a light-bulb appeared, flashing, just above her head. "An idea," shouted Barb joyfully above Justin Sain's moans.

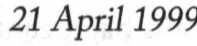

UNEARTHLY BARB
21 April 1999
(Barb's reminiscences of the preceding night—continued.)

Barb picked up a dead twig and began writing in the sand.

She glanced across at the clone, who was now unconscious. In her hand the dead twig raced across the sand, writing, writing, as follows…

<The drunken beauties pour from the Pink Elephant Bar,> Barb inscribed in the free-flowing mineral grains, generally yellowish-brown in color, generated by the erosion of siliceous and other rocks[6]. <All with gigantic hangovers, they squeeze themselves into the line of TOATS taxis that forever wait sinisterly outside the pub, like hyenas vigilant for the leftovers of a lion-kill.

<The cyberpeeps are all present (except Emily). (And, of course, Siegfried.)

<There is Katie, wrapped up in so many bandages she looks like an Egyptian mummy.

<Carrying Katie's stretcher are Tess (with one shoe missing and a bottle of vodka sticking out of her pocket) and Lottie, her hair all messed up, gazing mournfully at the tattered photo of Siegfried B. Hinkelheimer she always carries around with her.

---

6   Authors are told not to use the same word too close together, and I've already mentioned "sand" twice on the preceding page.

<Donna is still dazedly looking for her magic goddess-wand. Tammie is wondering how she got back into TOATS when all she ever wanted to do was be an innocent bystander (it was due to Katie's magic lamp). Newcomer Ingrid, who looks sensational in Verbose®, is wearing a gown entirely made from the naturally-moulted plumes of an albino peacock (she hasn't been in TOATS long enough to appear weather-beaten).

<Connie is dressed in yet another see-through harem outfit, and is in danger of being viewed as a shameless hussy; Alice looks exotically alluring—absolutely fabulous considering what she's been through and is probably about to go through. Between a pair of lusty sailors, with her arms linked through theirs, is Juliana wearing a houppelande with a matching hauberk over the top.>

UNEARTHLY BARB
21 April 1999

Having written the preceding scenario, Barb pulled a chess set out of the saddle-bags, propped up Justin against a tree and proceeded to play chess.

"Might as well while away the time until the TOATS taxis arrive," she smiled, still inscribing the future in the sand with one hand while the other moved her Queen's Bishop's Knight and the other hand broke open another packet of chocolate and the other hand was playing the piano. She had decided that if Justin was allowed to have more than his fair share of arm-extremities in this universe, she was too.

"Mmph," groaned Justin Sain. (He was not being permitted to say much, as you may have noticed).

"By the way," said Barb, one ear cocked for the roar of TOATS taxis in the distance, "Why did you bring a full scuba outfit compete with flippers?"

Justin Sain suddenly revived.

"Because after I had finished with YOU," he said, "I was going to climb down that mineshaft over there. The bottom of the mine-shaft is filled with water. BUT to those who know—and to those who have the MAP, the water is not all that is down there. Those are King Solomon's Mines, and if one scuba-dives beneath the water, one will come upon a hoard of diamonds the like of which has to be seen to be—"

"Yes, yes, I know," interrupted Barb, "believed." Her eyes narrowed. "How'd you get the map?" she snapped.

"Lottie gave it to me."

"Lottie?"

"Aye, Lottie." Justin Sain's eyes glistened as if moist remembrances filled them. "Ah, Lottie. She would never have treated me so cruel. I should have abducted her, not you. Regrets, I have a few . . ."

"Shut up! barked Barb, savagely knocking over all the chess pieces, She leaned closer to him. "I need a friend," she hissed. "I need a best friend. I need lots of them."

Leaping up she paced back and forth, whirling abruptly. "DIAMONDS are a girl's best friend!" she appended, tossing back her incredible mane of red Icelandic hair. "Had I known of this treasure earlier, I would not have written what I did."

She paused as the revving thunder of TOATS engines approached and a haze of dust, billowing on the horizon, came pelting towards them. Through the dimness could be discerned a ravening pack of yellow automobiles, their rooves topped with giant radars and other complicated apparatus.

"No time now to re-write. The taxis will be here in a nano-second." Barb gritted her teeth. "I'll have to get to the diamonds before they do. Else there'll be some sort of cat-fight and someone else will end up with the sparklers . . ."

UNEARTHLY BARB
21 April 1999

In the last taxi, Alice was seated. She was wearing a dress of palest primrose silk, trimmed with ostrich feathers. Tiny, jewelled fireflies were laced through her hair. As the taxi hurtled through the desert she sat back comfortably, filing her nails.

"Where are we going?" she asked presently.

The driver looked back at her, over his shoulder. His eyes were all white—there were no pupils. His forehead was ridged and scaly. His eyebrows bristled like two greenish hedgehogs. Alice did not bat an eyelid. This was a typical TOATS taxi driver—an alien from outer space.

The driver grinned, displaying six rows of stained teeth filed to extremely sharp points. "WE'RE ON THE ROAD TO NO-WHERE!" he uttered with a terrible laugh.

"Oh, so you've got us lost already, have you?" said Alice. With one lithe movement she vaulted over into the front seat. Reaching across the burly bulk of the driver she opened his door and pushed him out.

The door slammed and she took up the recently-vacated position at the wheel. Stepping on the gas she hummed a tune as she turned the taxi around and headed for King Solomon's Mines.

UNEARTHLY EMILY

21st April 1999

A previously untold chapter of the TOATS Rule Book—The TOATS Ten Commandments.

1) Thou Shalt insert a disclaimer in thy images all of thy days.

2) Siegfried Shalt not covet a TOATS woman for more than three chapters.

3) Thy Stories Shalt always include lots of adjectives and prepositional phrases.

4) Thou Shalt wear designer clothes at all times unless in a natural state.

5) Thou Shalt always be fair to other authors before using their characters, lest need stock in flame retardant underwear.

6) Thou Shalt not kill off main characters, lest they be clones, replicas or aliens.

7) Thou Shalt keep true that no such things as spelling mistakes exist, only new words.

8) Let not thy postings be bogged down with befuddling storylines, lest we spend two weeks explaining what they be to others.

9) Keep Thou thy stories neatly divided into chunks, preferably, so that all, yea verily I say all, may enjoy thy creative endeavour without pain.

10) Thou Shalt obey all the above commandments and keep thyself in humor at all times.

UNEARTHLY EMILY
22 April 1999

The ceremony was beautiful. The champagne was now flowing among their guests as a string quartet quietly played and candles cast their romantic glow across the room. His new wife, Emily, was breathtaking, and he was the luckiest man alive.

NO, wait!

Wrong fantasy.

Where was I? Oh yes.

Emily shivered. It felt strangely cold all of a sudden. She reached for the blanket, only to find that it had mysteriously disappeared. Raising herself on one elbow she looked over to where Siegfried was sleeping. He was lying sideways warmly wrapped within the blanket.

With a tug, Emily pulled the blanket to her side of the bed, taking more than necessary. A few seconds later, Siegfried switched his position slightly and yawned, pulling it back to his side.

Emily's eyes flicked open as she felt the blanket being drawn back in the other direction.

"Siegfried!" She sat up, crawled over to Siegfried's side of the bed and dragged the entire blanket back to her side. Wrapping it around herself tightly like a sleeping bag she snuggled back into a deep sleep.

A few hours later, Siegfried shivered. With half closed eyes he looked around and groped to find the blanket. Shifting to the right side of the bed he gave it a tug. Emily rolled out of the blanket and fell on the floor with a thump.

"Oh great, I've pulled too far." Siegfried muttered. He rolled over to her side and couldn't help but laugh, his fair companion looked so ridiculous. One long leg, and one arm was still clinging to the bed. She didn't even seem to notice that she had been pushed off. Siegfried reached a hand down and shook her cautiously, remembering what had happened to him last time he startled her. "Emily? Emily, wake up!"

"Hmmmmhh?" Emily opened one eye tentatively. She realized where she was and tried to get up, hitting her head against the bed side table. Siegfried laughed as he watched her try to stand up. "Would you mind giving me a hand instead of laughing at me like that?" she said frostily.

Siegfried leaned down, and offered his hand to lift her up. After several minutes with Emily thumping against the wall, they finally reached the bed once more. "I want to get some sleep Siegfried," said the ex-pirate wench, "so if you stay on your side and I stay on my side, I won't have to hurt you."

Just then the door to the bungalow burst open. "Quality time is over darling!!! shrilled a loud voice from the vicinity of the door. Emily winced involuntarily. It was all over—her luck had just ended. She turned toward the voice with trepidation. And there she stood—Juliana.

Siegfried gaped in wonderment at the astonishing sight of a strapless leopard print, floor-length sheath, a wild mane of hair the color of the most powerful Coast Guard flares, a pair of terrifyingly bright sequined stilettos modestly peeking out from beneath a thigh-high slit, which showed enough fishnet to make one of Tess's hardiest sailors blush. Riot Red® Lipstick and matching nails were complemented by a three-inch wide diamond bracelet. (The houppelande with a matching hauberk over the top had proved to be a tad warm for this time of year.)

"Up! Up! Up!" cried Juliana. "I need a necklace and earrings to match this, and the meter's running on the taxi!"

UNEARTHLY EMILY
23 April 1999

Later . . . the TOATS taxi screeched to a halt in front of an enormous crowd. Juliana hopped out followed by Siegfried and Emily.

Emily stared in amazement at the horde of people gathered around a deep well. "What the hell happened here?" she asked in astonishment.

"Oh, nothing. Donna kept writing characters in and here we all are!" Juliana nonchalantly replied.

"This will never do!" cried Emily. "Too many characters to keep track of. My God there's . . . one . . . two . . . at least five Siegfried characters here! Hold on—" she looked overwhelmed. "I need to sort this out. Okay, "Justin" has diving gear, Barb was writing in that frightful notebook and what happened next?"

"Don't forget there are at least a hundred Vulgarian sailors and possibly a few more Gabriel Yearn clones back at The Pink Elephant too," Alice added.

"No, no, no—this will never do," Emily repeated, shaking her head.

"I have an idea!" Lottie ran to a taxi and talked briefly to the driver. Calmly, Lottie walked around to the trunk. With a POP it opened followed by a great WHOOSHing sound. Suddenly the whoosh turned into a gale force wind, swirling mercilessly upon all the superfluous characters and pulling them towards the trunk of the taxi.

"LOTTIE! WHAT HAVE YOU DONE!" Donna yelled over the roar of the wind. The extra characters bumped and banged their way into the trunk and with a tremendous sucking noise the trunk lid slammed shut.

"Take her away!" Lottie said to the driver with a smile, whereupon the cab became airborne and disappeared.

As the last grain of sand settled, Lottie looked around at the now manageable group of TOATS enthusiasts all together in the same chapter frame. "Now where did I put my spelunking gear?" she said as she went to find her backpack . . .

Who actually survived the TOATS clean-up?

Will Lottie find her backpack?

Has anyone ever been spelunking before?

Will Barb dump Justin once the chocolate is all gone?

Will Katie try to exact revenge on Emily, or is all forgiven?

After last night, does Emily want 'quality time' or just her own blanket?

Will Juliana find those matching earrings and necklace?

These are just a few of the questions waiting to be answered in the UnEarth universe... stay tuned.

6

OOMPHALALA LAND

OR

DIAMONDS ARE A CRAZED FAN'S BEST FRIEND

UNEARTHLY EMILY

23 April 1999

We had drawn straws to see who would go first into the foreboding well; Juliana, Barb, Lottie, Connie, Alice, Tess and myself. Anyone I've forgotten to mention either arrived late, was looking for an easier way in, or previously got sucked into an interplanetary taxi.

I was the last one to go over the side of the entrance to the mine. There I found out that I should have invested in better vertical gear as I plummeted three hundred feet. (Will someone please dig a staircase from the parking lot to the bottom of the well?)

Juliana, who had been there before, got started right away setting up a safety line and rigging. Connie and I headed towards the helectite room, where we generously sharpened the pencils that accompanied the guest register. (Obviously a frequently-toured mine.)

We picked up some sandwiches and a few "Official Maps to King Solomon's Mines" from the kiosk and then it was down, down, down once more. I for one was lucky—my Schmee Press-On Nails® held like glue, while Barb stopped the entire expedition to fix her French manicure.

Ultimately, we found ourselves at the bottom of the great pit. Looking around, we saw several tunnels once again branching off in all directions and angles. We all had a bite to eat before setting off on the next phase of the quest.

On Original Earth:

"Hi Barb, it's me," said Original Lottie, on the other end of the line.

"Hi. Nice chapters," said Barb.

"You too. But have you noticed what some of the other Siegfried fans have been saying about TOATS on the website?"

"What do you mean?"

"A couple of people called Sheila and RevInc, who don't contribute to it or even read it. They think it's crap."

"Well it is crap, basically. Anyway, they're entitled to their opinions."

"Yeah, but so are we. And I suggest it's about time these nay-sayers got written in. Do you think that's too cruel?"

Barb chuckled and rubbed her hands together. "Not at all. It's brilliant! Sweet poetic justice! Let's tell Emily."

UNEARTHLY BARB

8 May 1999

Sheila woke up with an aching head. She stared confusedly through the magnolia-colored cellophane surrounding her.

"Why is this magnolia-colored cellophane surrounding me?" she asked peevishly.

"There's no cellophane," replied Katie with a merry laugh which threatened to split Sheila's skull. "That's how your eyes look, viewed from your side. You ought to see them from this angle. They're much worse. Like road maps."

"What happened?" groaned Sheila, rubbing her forehead and her left foot. "Why have I got a hangover? I don't even remember drinking. Much. After we left The Pink Elephant, I mean."

"You fell down the mineshaft," explained Katie. "You've been out cold for twenty minutes. Luckily you missed the treacherous and fathomless waters at the mine's foot and fell instead on something soft—a pile of TOATS Archives, the Really Mouldy Ones." Katie brandished a flapping handful of papers.

"Keep them away from me," said Sheila, recoiling. "I can't stand TOATS. I find it a bore."

"Oh, so you've read TOATS have you?" smiled Katie.

"No!" Sheila quickly responded.

Katie looked puzzled. "Then how do you know it's boring?"

Fortunately, they were interrupted at this politically sensitive juncture by RevInc, who tottered past on a pair of spangled stilettos.

"Hey, where'd you get the shoes?" asked Katie admiringly.

"Souvenir shop," RevInc shot back. "Gosh Sheila, what happened to you?" she went on.

"Fell down the mineshaft," said Sheila. She sat up straight, as though she had suddenly remembered something. "I've suddenly remembered something," she squeaked. "I had the strangest dream while I was unconscious. There were millions of people, and we were all there, and we were all acting out of character . . ."

Katie and RevInc glanced at each other over the top of Sheila's head. They nodded knowingly. "Delirious," they whispered.

"Come on," said Katie brightly, helping Sheila to her feet. "There's no time to lose. We have to catch up with the others."

"Others?" repeated Sheila dazedly.

RevInc grabbed Sheila's elbow. "Yes. Just follow this rough-hewn, handrail-free stone track with the sheer vertical drop on the left side and the sheer cliff rising three hundred feet on the right. The path leads through the souvenir shop to the point of disembarkation, where the boats are moored. Everyone else has gone off along the underground stream, in a flotilla of inflatable rubber dinghies—even Donna, who came late via the tree-trunk elevator that no-one else knew about. Here's your map." She thrust a gooey bit of paper into Sheila's hand. "Sorry, there's melted chocolate all over it."

UNEARTHLY BARB

8 May 1999

"Oh good, now I can buy a pair of those spangled stilettos," said Katie happily as they sidled along the four-inch-wide path towards the souvenir shop. "They'll be just perfect for spelunking while looking great."

"Too late—Emily bought the last pair," said RevInc.

Five hours later, on reaching the mooring point while loaded down with souvenirs, the three gorgeous women squinted ahead into the torchlit gloom. The underwater river flowed like a black glass road beneath cavernous arches of living rock. The waters gurgled. Indescribable things splashed and cavorted in the shadows. There was no sign of the rest of the cyberchick group, all of whom had so carelessly gone on ahead in their typical thoughtless fashion.

A dark figure stepped forward. "Your vessel, *mesdames,*" he crooned in a soft, low voice which sounded at once somehow sexy and sinister. Overawed, Sheila, Katie and RevInc stepped into the dinghy. The tall, hooded figure cast off the mooring rope. As they drifted into the main current and were swept away, the three sensational beauties thought they heard a low, evil laugh drifting across the water.

"Er—are you sure this thing is safe?" muttered RevInc. "And who the heck was THAT?"

They swept around a corner. A barely-legible sign stuck on the rock wall with chewing-gum read,

> 'That woz The Ferryman. He iz an ex-TOATS taxie driver. Beware wot lies ahed. Turn back now, if you can.'

A sign further on read,

> 'But of coarse you can't, can you? You hav no ors.'

UNEARTHLY BARB
8 May 1999

The waters of the subterranean river gurgled like a leaky cistern, like soft maniacal laughter, like someone trying to ingest a Swiggee® without being sick. Or like someone actually being sick.

The rubber dinghy scudded along at a cracking pace, sliding beneath the vaults of living rock in the manner of a beetle being sucked down the plughole with the bathwater.

"So far so good," muttered Sheila optimistically. But RevInc wasn't so sure. With misgivings, she eyed the deformed and malignant shapes gliding along just beneath the surface of the dark waters. Eyes seemed to stare up at her. She fancied she saw gaunt claws reaching out . . .

It's not fair, she thought to herself, I don't even read TOATS. I've been hoping if I ignore it, it will go away. Why should I be trapped in it?

UNEARTHLY BARB
8 May 1999
"Get a load of THAT," said Katie, nudging RevInc out of her Gothic reverie. Katie was pointing to another sign chewing-gummed to the tunnel wall.

It announced, 'You are now passing beneath the border into Oomphalala Land. Please observe the customs of this police state or face the consequences. In Oomphalala Land polygyny is not only permitted, it is mandatory."

"Ooh good!" squealed Katie. "We can all have lots of husbands! As soon as I get above-ground I'm going to go and propose to the Yahoozi Tribe."

"Huh?" Sheila and RevInc stared at her, round-eyed.

"Haven't you seen them?" Katie cried. "Tall, ebony-skinned, smiles like flashes of white lightning, and they move like gazelles—"

"You can't marry the Yahoozi Tribe!" interrupted Sheila irritably. "The sign said POLYGYNY, not POLYANDRY. Difference is, people can have lots of wives, not lots of husbands."

"Damn, that's sexist," said Katie glumly.

"What's that over there? RevInc shouted excitedly.

The dinghy rocked violently as she jumped to her feet.

"Sit down!" Katie yelped, "before you capsize this thing."

"But look," shouted RevInc. "Someone's in the water over there! Man overboard!"

Peering into the eerily shimmering shadows which clung stickily to the rock walls like the webs of a giant spider, the three cute babes in the tub noticed something like the thrashing wheel of a hotted-up paddle steamer going full pelt. After a while they realized it was a female form splashing around.

"It's Barb!" trumpeted Sheila. "And she's wearing a Siegfried B. Hinkelheimer souvenir T-shirt. Hey Barb, what happened?"

"Glurp," replied Barb. Eventually she managed to get her head above water again. "My nail file punched a hole in our boat and we bounced and bumped along the tunnel like helpless creatures holding onto a deflating balloon," she gasped. "This is all that's left."

Holding aloft a limp piece of plastic like the hood of a chewed raincoat, she sank once more. The river closed over her head.

"Hey, great idea!" enthused Katie turning to RevInc and Sheila. "That's a good way to make ourselves go faster. Maybe we can catch up to the others!"

Grabbing one of RevInc's gold-spangled stilettos she punched a hole in the back of the raft with the ice-pick heel. Instantly the vessel shot forward with a sound of escaping steam and jet engines.

UNEARTHLY BARB
8 May 1999

Now they were really flying along. They zoomed past a few other struggling forms and through a cavern hung with the long pale green swords of stalactites. Soon an intact dinghy hove into view. They waved cheerily. As they approached, it became apparent that the occupants were Donna, Ingrid and Emily.

Katie and her companions could scarcely believe their eyes when they saw Ingrid. "What happened to YOU?" shouted Katie as they zoomed rapidly by.

"Barb took me into the Re-Describing Department of the King Solomon's Mines Souvenir Shop," Ingrid shouted back, her hands cupped around her mouth. "After I said I hated albino peacock feathers, she re-described my entire outfit."

"Oh, er, it looks—" Katie dissolved into a sudden fit of coughing.

"Never mind," Sheila yelled over the water, her voice echoing through the hollow halls and secret caverns. "Skin-tight snakeskin catsuits look good on some people. So do fake leopard-skin Smugg® boots." But her comforting words were lost to Ingrid as the half-deflated dinghy blasted away down the river.

"You've really got to get in first and describe yourself," said RevInc wisely. "Barb comes up with some really kitschy outfits. I mean, look at me in an electric blue mini with orange fishnet stockings. And a short, knitted jumper (sweater) of green mohair. I ASK you."

UNEARTHLY BARB
8 May 1999

"What happens when the raft runs out of air?" conversationally wondered Sheila, clinging to the jelly-like substance which was all that remained of the inflatable vessel's sides. At that precise moment, they careered around a bend and skidded up onto the shores of a large cavern-floor. The dinghy gave a last gasp and shrivelled to the size of a DirtyGreat Burger®.

"What luck! gleefully said Katie, stepping out. "And look, what a lovely place this is!"

The cavern was indeed spectacular. Lit by subtly-placed chandeliers, it was filled with natural limestone sculptures in the forms of angels' wings, organ pipes, great billowing curtains and turreted castles of stone.

As the three delicious damsels wandered through this glory, they heard several other dinghies pull up on the shore behind them. The babble of incoherent voices announced the arrival of the other TOATS protagonists. On rounding a row of fluted columns, they saw, spread out before them in the cavern's centre, a wide lake as black as liquorice. Moored at the edge of this lake was a five-masted schooner. Her hundred-and-fifty-foot-high masts scraped the cavern's ceiling.

"Welcome aboard!" cried a familiar voice, and there on the poop deck stood none other than—yes, you guessed it—Siegfried B. Hinkelheimer!

With yelps of joy the entire TOATS crew flung themselves across the gangplank; Donna, Emily, Lottie, Tess, Katie, Ingrid, Juliana, Sheila, RevInc, Connie, Tammie, a newcomer called Marilyn who had accidentally become separated from a party of cave-tourists and joined the cyberchicks in the naïve hope that they could lead her out of this subterranean labyrinth, a deranged woman who proved to be (Insert Your Name Here), and last of all Barb, exhaustedly dragging herself out of the river with a subaqueous-dwelling THING still hanging on to her half-chewed ankle.

Everyone surged towards Siegfried.

"Stay back, ladies," he said in a commanding voice. "You are on board my ship. I am the Captain and you must do as I say."

"Oh yes, anything you say, Siegfried," gabbled his fans, who hadn't set eyes on him for untold numbers of episodes. (Not since Emily whisked him away for some Quality Time.)

UNEARTHLY BARB
8 May 1999
The ship's crew cast off the moorings. Long oars extruded themselves from port-holes in the vessel's sides and she began to move out upon the crystalline surface of the lake, heading towards a distant glow which might have been the sunlight of the outside world.

As the passengers gazed upon their captain and hero with adoring eyes, he said, "I would like to introduce my crew to you. Look up!"

The beautiful wenches craned their necks. Down from the rigging swung several lithe, masculine figures. When they landed on the deck and bowed, the watchers gasped. Before them stood exact replicas of Gabriel Yearn, Lance Boyle, Nicolas Birdhouse and Daniel de Licious. And Ray Fiends.

And Andrew Huggins and Jeremy Northbound. And a guy called Gunter something. And any similar hunks I've forgotten.

"As the ship's captain," said Siegfried, "I have the power to marry people. I have decided to marry off a lot of you."

Squeals of delight greeted this announcement. Eventually they turned to cries of consternation as the quicker-witted babes started to wonder exactly WHO was going to be espoused to WHOM.

"But Seegums," they wailed, "who is going to marry YOU?"

UNEARTHLY BARB
8 May 1999
Siegfried sighed.

"Look," he said, "be reasonable. Even one of you crazed fans might be more than I could handle, let alone an entire harem. For a start, I DON'T want that bedraggled red-haired one there with the flesh-eating mud-crab attached to her ankle. Dar can have her. Any of you others can marry who you choose. I shall marry . . ."

He paused thoughtfully.

Everyone held their breath.

Who would Siegfried choose as his Bride?

UNEARTHLY BARB
8 May 1999
"Lottie!" Siegfried announced at last. "Lottie is to be the new Frau B. Hinkelheimer. After all, I was engaged to her once."

Predictably, Lottie fainted.

"But we all want to marry you!" sobbed Donna, Emily, Lottie, Tess, Katie, Ingrid, Juliana, Sheila, RevInc, Connie, Tammie, Marilyn, and the deranged woman who had proved to be (Insert Your Name Here).

Wearily, Siegfried consoled them. "We find ourselves now within the borders of Oomphalala Land," he said, "where polygyny is obligatory. I can probably marry a few more of you. The leftovers will have to marry lookalikes of Gabriel Yearn, Lance Boyle, Nicolas Birdhouse and Ray Fiends. And Andrew Huggins and Jeremy Northbound. And my friend Gunter."

The sobbing paragons of beauty blew their noses, looked at one another and nodded.

"Sounds like a good idea," they chorused.

Wedding bells began to ring out atop the mizzen mast. As the mighty schooner approached the massive arched exit from the cave into the outer world of Oomphalala Land, the crew unfurled the sails, ready to catch the wind. At the foot of the mainmast a hunch-backed figure was playing soothing church-type organ music.

Siegfried pulled a book out of his pocket and tossed it overboard. It was his spare TOATS Rule Book of Etiquette. He then produced a second book entitled "On-Board Marriage Ceremonies", opened it and prepared himself to read.

At that EXACT moment, (Insert Your Name Here) screamed "Wait!"

The gathering froze.

Upon her they turned gazes of frosty disapproval. Siegfried lifted his left eye-brow in a quizzical manner.

"Well?" he asked.

"It's one of the PRIMARY RULES in the TOATS Rule Book of Etiquette!" howled (Insert Your Name Here). "No married person can be a character in TOATS! If you all get married, TOATS finishes! At the end of the millennium, a Legendary Internet Saga shall fold, at great loss to the general public!"

"True!" agreed a multitude of voices. They all shrugged and turned away. "But who cares?"

 **UNEARTHLY BARB**
8 May 1999
Will Lottie regain consciousness before her honeymoon?

Will Emily's feet ever recover from those tight shoes?

Will Katie find another magic lamp?

Is Sheila reading this part yet?

Will RevInc ever read TOATS—or is it too late now?

Where are Tammie and Connie?

Will Tess be eaten by sharks before she gets to marry Siegfried?

Will Donna use her goddess powers?

Why is Juliana standing so close to Siegfried?

Is Ingrid really comfortable in that outfit?

Will everyone get married and thus bring about the doom of TOATS?

And does it really matter?

7

THE ORACLE AND THE TROLLOP

It's about time I wrote my sister Dahlia into this saga, Original Barb mused as she sat in front of her chocolate-covered keyboard. *Then I might be able to persuade her to actually read it...*

UNEARTHLY BARB
20 May 1999
The five-masted schooner was borne out of the caves into the sunlight upon the strong, long muscles of the river. As the sails bellied in the wind she began to cut her way towards the nearby river-mouth, seeming to sense the salt tang of the ocean as a dog senses ... yes, well, back to the story.

(Insert Your Name Here) threw herself down on the deck. She beat on the planks with her fists, kicking and screaming. "Shiver me timbers!" she cried, getting into the nautical mode.

"Got a problem?" casually asked Donna.

"It's all crazy!" wailed (Insert Your Name Here) lifting a tear-streaked face. "I've lost the TOATS plot. Here we are on a schooner, with Siegfried in his most beautiful role as Captain, but it looks as though we're all going to get married and become mundane housewives, thus spelling disaster for TOATS. I mean, after we're all married, the most exciting thing to write about will be how we dashed outside and grabbed all the washing off the line, rescuing it from a sudden downpour. Or how we found a gold earring when we crawled under the sofa looking for the other half of an odd pair of socks."

"We did?" gasped Barb. "I mean, you did? A gold earring? Gosh, I've been looking for one of mine for years, ever since —"

"Shut up!" screamed (Insert Your Name Here), jamming her hands over her ears. "Blast me barnacles, it's started already, and none of us are even married yet!"

"You forget, I was married many chapters ago," smirked Barb. "As Lottie just reminded me. I am now Mrs. Michoacan. I mean Moccasin. I mean Day—"

"Well clear off then," retorted (Insert Your Name Here). Barb bent her gaze on the woman sprawled tearfully on the deck. It hardened into an evil glare. A fight was evidently brewing, when unexpectedly a voice from the shadows said calmly,

"It's all quite clear, really. There is a way to rescue the plot."

UNEARTHLY BARB
20 May 1999
All around the schooner (by this time rolling and rocking on the waves of the ocean), heads popped up. TOATS beauties began gravitating towards the Voice like—um—things that gravitate towards things. Surprisingly, the sun was beginning to set (sunsets always make a good backdrop).

There in the glimmering shadow of the mizzen-mast stood a feminine form, lean and hard as a whip. She was clad in a black leather body-suit, rather like Travesty® in *The Prefix®*. Her fingernails were at least an inch long, and she was polishing a thin, elongated slice of moonlight—a rapier with a silver hilt.

Tossing back her mane of chestnut curls, she said in those same calm tones, "There is a way, if you will but listen."

As she explained, the TOATS belles drew closer, clustering cross-legged at the stranger's feet, spellbound, like acolytes before the Head Monk. While they listened, they passed around cups of cappuccino, (blissfully unaware that it was terribly unfashionable to drink it any more because these days cafe latte and chai tea are all the rage.)

UNEARTHLY BARB
20 May 1999

"There will be no weddings. We must sail due west," intoned the enigmatic stranger, "until we come in sight of several strange fingerposts sticking up out of the sea. Each post is topped with a runic marker. At the Seventh Sign we turn west-sou-west and Keep along that heading, battling through a rather large Hurricane called Smith, until we reach the darkening Mouths of Madness. These are terrible caves which lie on The Last Borders of Dangerous Ground. Aye, I would rather Lie Down With Lions or subject myself to The Tenderness of Wolves than enter into those subterranean orifices."

She shuddered, and at that the audience drew breath in wonder, for obviously this slender woman was not one to be trifled with. Over-awed, they did not think to ask her how she spoke with capital letters, or whether it should in fact be "The Tenderness of Beef".

Pausing reflectively, the storyteller held the rapier up to the starry sky. She eyed it measuringly, pulled a hair from her head, tossed it high and sliced it in two with one flick of her wrist. A sparkle ran along the blade's edge and vanished with a "ping!" at the point.

The stranger placed one hand on her hip and slashed a quick "Z" shape in the air. Instantly the sky fell apart in folds. The watchers fancied they saw, behind the star-dotted darkness, several pairs of huge eyes peering in.

"You see," said the swordswoman, "this rapier can pierce the very fabric of this virtual universe. Your alter egos are revealed." With a practised movement she made three reverse slashes and sewed up the sky somewhat raggedly.

"But I see into the future of this vessel," continued the stranger, in that same calm and certain voice. "For if she passes unscathed through these perils, then she will draw opposite the Forbidden Dune, near a couple of cube-shaped monoliths known to mariners as Surface Paradise—I mean, Devil's Paradise. Then, our look-out in the crow's nest will spy an Interceptor. It will be a privateer, which will fire upon this schooner with great cannons. Despite our Passion and Valor, despite our Water-pistols of Etiqu—I mean, Guns of Honor, we will lose the battle—but before our craft is sunk they will board her, taking all the passengers and crew into captivity on their piratical windjammer.

"The leader of this pirate crew will be a villain called Judge Mental—sorry, Judge Dredd—a trigger-fast psychopath who enjoys Killing Cars, and indulges in Murder by Reason of Insanity. You will know him: his flag carries the emblem of The Heliotrope Parrot..."

"But this is awful!" wailed Tess. "I don't want to be captured by pirates!"

"Never fear," the stranger reassured, "for also imprisoned on board the windjammer will be Princess Alisea. She will find a way to drug the pirates and when we have thrown them all overboard, we shall sail away.

"To California, Philadelphia[7] or somewhere like that," she added, rather lamely. "And if anyone is opposed to this plan, I suggest we kick 'em in das backside with das boot."

When this story was finished, the cyberchicks looked at one another in amazement. Everything then proceeded to happen exactly the way the stranger had foretold. After their adventures, they found themselves pulling into San Francisco[8] harbour, all still single, with Siegfried now captaining the windjammer.

No sooner had they berthed, than the black-clad stranger leapt lightly across the gangplank and strode away, vanishing amongst the thronging crowds of Australian tourists.

"Who WAS that woman?" breathed the TOATS heroines, staring after her wide-eyed.

"Once, near the Mouths of Madness," said Emily, "I asked her name. She replied, 'Some that know me call me Dahlia.' I asked her, 'Why is that?' and she answered, 'Because it is my name.'

"Dahlia!" everyone gasped. "Not—not the Oracle Dahlia of the Gilded Ford?"

Emily shook her head. "I do not know. Maybe we shall never know ...["9]

---

7   Counterfeit California or Pretend Philadelphia
8   Synthetic San Francisco
9   They never did know.

8

A VISITOR FROM BOGUS BRAZIL

In Original Brazil, a certain Siegfried fan had been "lurking" on the site for several months. Ideas had been forming in her mind. At this point she decided it was time to take the plunge —to jump off the edge of Reality into cyberspace…

UNEARTHLY MAYRA
25 May 1999
"Thank God I've found you!" It was Mayra's voice. She disentangled herself from the parachute knots, ropes, strings and other things she couldn't name and, ignoring everybody, headed straight for Siegfried. "I've been looking for you all over the world. You must help us. We have nobody else to turn to," she added, very Damsel-in-Distress-like.

Original Mayra

UnEarthly Mayra

"Who are you?" he asked. "What happened?" He actually said "vat happent" but Mayra, being a non-native English speaker and having a very bad accent herself, failed to notice it.

"The name is Mayra," she said with the self-control one can only find out one has in times of extreme gravity. "You are the only person who can prevent a major ecological disaster. You see, right now myriads of babelfish are swimming their gills out from the most distant seas towards the source of the Amazon River to spawn. The problem is that this year, for some unknown reason, there has been very little rain in the area (only seven hours a day) and the level of the Amazon and its tributaries is dangerously low. When the babelfish ascend the river to breed, they will fatally run aground somewhere between the Bogus Brazilian coast and Barely-Believable Bolivia. If they die before spawning, the species will go extinct!" she cried dramatically.

Siegfried was bewildered. Of all his crazed fans, this was a serious candidate for the prime position. All she wanted him to do was perform the simple task of changing the planet's delicate ecosystem in order to increase the annual precipitation over the Amazon basin.

"Look, lady," he replied, "I'm deeply moved, but that's a pretty tall order. I'm really sorry, but there's nothing I can do."

There was a long silence, then a THUD. It was Mayra's heart hitting the bottom of her guts. She just stood there with a trembling lower lip, dark clouds of disenchantment filling her wetted half-Indian eyes.

Oh, what the hell! he thought. If there is one thing a real hero can't stand that is to let down a helpless, distressed damsel. And one thing an actor shouldn't do is to disappoint his fans. Being part of both categories, he just didn't have a choice. So he sighed. "OK. Let's go save the babelfish."

Mayra, now conveniently unable to control her joy, leaped into his arms and kissed him passionately. "You won't regret it, I promise," she said with her most grateful smile.

"Everybody, back to the windjammer," ordered the Captain. "We're off to Bogus Brazil. Gabriel, set course to two, five, zero. Lance, hoist the sails. Ray, weigh anchor. Nicolas . . ."

"Wait!" cried Mayra. "We can't take this crowd with us. This boat . . ."

"Like hell you can't!" Barb cut her short, backed by a chorus of "yeah! . . . right! . . . no way! . . . who's this trollop?" uttered by the other TOATS belles. Seriously outnumbered, Mayra decided to take a more cautious course of action.

"I'm sorry, I think I didn't make myself clear. I meant it will be too crowded on this boat. Why don't we take a plane instead?"

As she spoke, an Air Banana sort of craft, coincidentally parked nearby, produced a bizarre figure in an even more bizarre airline uniform who asked, also very coincidentally, "Anybody know way for Bogus Brazil? I are very lost."

"We're in luck!" Mayra exclaimed. "I wouldn't take that plane to save my life if it were a National airliner. But since National Airlines merged with Banana Air, the quality, service and safety are state-of-the-art."

116

So they horded onto the airthing, but unfortunately there wasn't enough room for everybody, so all the male replicas had to be invited out, leaving some cyberchick feminine hands bidding a disconsolate farewell from the cracked window panes as they were airborne and fast approaching the end of the chapter.

UnEarthly Mayra

UNEARTHLY MAYRA
25 May 1999

"What if this Air Banana flying thingy predictably crashes in the Amazon jungle," wondered Lottie, "leaving our hero and we, his followers, in a very dicey situation? No food, no supplies, no mosquito repellent, no make-up kit, and worst of all, no paraphernalia to get rid of unwanted hair?"

That was no problem for Siegfried, of course. Gorgeous men look even manlier in filthy places.

Original Emily

UnEarthly Emily

9

CYBERCHICK COUNTDOWN

UNEARTHLY EMILY

14 July 1999

The engines roared deafeningly. The airthing smelled like stale motor oil, old pastrami and fear. Why, wondered Donna, had they happened to board this particular Air Banana airthing—one of the rare flights that forced you to parachute to your destination?

She leaned back, trying to make herself comfortable in spite of the bulk of the parachute weighing her down. Emily was in the back, engaging in animated hand-sign conversation with Juliana, but Donna didn't really want to talk to either of them right now.

Lottie finished checking her 'chute and crab-walked her way up to Donna. The headphones in Donna's jump-helmet sprang to life and Lottie smiled, her lips coordinating with the words through the earphones. "Are you ready to jump?!"

Donna gave her questioner a slightly queasy smile and tried to ignore the idea of intentionally jumping out of an airplane. The newcomer Marilyn, on the other hand, was visibly thrilled. This was much more exciting than the cave tour she'd signed up for. Little did she know that after she jumped, she would vanish inexplicably from TOATS cyberspace.

Donna's nerves got much, much worse when Emily yanked open the sliding door in the side of the fuselage. She could see land a long, long way down, without the proper, rational presence of a window between her and it. Tess was practically hopping up and down in her eagerness to do the stupidest thing she knew of outside naked bungie-jumping with two hundred Vulgarian sailors.

Connie bounced over. "This is gonna be great!" she yelled.

Oh gods. Donna realised Juliana was gesturing, trying to get her to climb over to the open door. Emily had unclipped from the safety rope. Donna watched her launch herself headlong out into the nothingness. . . and felt her stomach drop.

"C'mon Donna! You'll love it!" Lottie grinned as she disappeared next, but Donna wished she were off riding Brian, or fighting off the unwanted advances of the locals back at the Frosty Halibut or anything but this, anything at ALL. Taking a deep breath, she prepared to jump.

UnEarthly Mayra

UNEARTHLY MAYRA
15 July 1999

Yes, (Insert Your Name Here) was right. This was a setup. It had always been. Mayra was actually the villain who was missing in this episode. The villain, as everyone knows, is that character whose only reason to be there is to give the others something to do. Preferably dangerous.

Her original plan had been to drag Siegfried to Bogus Brazil and have a great time alone with him, but she had been outsmarted by the cyberchicks. She had planned to make the plane crash in the jungle, hoping to get rid of at least half of them in the process, but that failed, too. She was so infuriated that she decided if she couldn't get Siegfried for herself, nobody else could. (Very villain-like).

It was clear what she had to do now: systematically dispose of the competition to clear some room for Siegfried and herself. As the owner, Chairman and CEO of Banana Air, she had had the opportunity to sabotage the parachutes by attaching a mini rocket to each one that would automatically launch itself and the parachutist into a preset destination.

And that is how it happened. After jumping off the plane, the surprised heroines found themselves scattered around the world, totally unaware of the diabolic scheme Mayra had concocted to get rid of them.

Mayra proceeded to post an episode in which Connie, landed in Las Vegas and was hit with a ball of lethal green slime, hurled by Nic's jealous girlfriend.

ORIGINAL DONNA
16th July 1999
geeeez . . . what did you get hit with, Connie? Yuck . . . ! Mayra has us all at bay . . . wait . . . unless we write ourselves out of our particular predicaments I guess! I respond to Barb's cry in kind . . . SiegfriedSiegfriedSiegfried!

ORIGINAL MAYRA
To understand Connie's farewell chapter you must be familiar with *The Mineral Matter of Variable Composition*®. If you haven't seen it you won't know what that green ball is. (Ask Emily — she has seen it.) That goes for every chapter; they are all based on movies. All of the references in Connie's episode were Nic Birdhouse movies.

In Mayra's next episode, Tess's rocket plunged her into the North Atlantic's icy waters where she would have frozen to death if an Alpha-Class attack submarine crewed by her Vulgarian pals, hadn't rescued her.

Tess and the inebriated crew ran out of vodka and drank every other liquid on board, including the fuel and oil needed for the engines and defence systems.

So that when they got torpedoed, as in *The Hunt for Purple Friday*, they didn't stand a chance. . .

Meanwhile, in her secret lab, Mayra was crossing Tess's name off her list.

"Two down, twelve to go . . ."

UnEarthly Mayra **UNEARTHLY MAYRA**
17 July 1999
Juliana parachuted into Inauthentic Iceland, naturally. Who else could handle a place with absurd names such as Hofdakaupstadhur, Vestmannaeyjar, Skjálfandafljót and Hvannadalshnúkur?

She made a bee-line for that geothermal lagoon where she had spent unforgettably good moments with a young Siegfried clone innumerable chapters ago. Immersed in its cosy waters she was enjoying a nostalgic flashback, when she heard a sinister rumble.

That lagoon was actually a geyser, which erupted once a year. Juliana was ejected on a column of water, two hundred feet into the air. Coincidentally she landed on the deck of a nineteenth-century zeppelin headed for *The Archipelago in the Clouds®*, a heavenly place inhabited by gorgeous Vikings with golden hair and the physique of Valhalla gods.

There, the Icelandic wench found herself stuck in a well-behaved, insipid paradise with two splendiferous warriors, in a long-lasting, plato-moronic relationship. If three minutes in it don't kill her, I don't know what will.

Meanwhile, in her secret lab, Mayra was crossing Juliana's name off her list. "Three down, eleven to go ..."

ORIGINAL INGRID
18 July 1999
I am begging you to bump me off, Mayra! It's hilarious how you use such individual methods to murder people!

UnEarthly Mayra

UNEARTHLY MAYRA
18 July 1999

Ingrid found herself in Based-on Borneo trying to ask the bartender at The Rainforest Rondaybooze where the ladies' room was. Communications were proving kinda knotty, because Ingrid didn't speak Malay and the bartender only spoke Pig Latin.

At length the short-tempered fellow became so frustrated with the misunderstandings that he flung her out the door.

Unfortunately the bar was perched on the edge of a gorge and Ingrid would have plunged into the void if a feeble hand hadn't caught hers.

A drunken patron from the bar (who mistakenly prided himself on his heroism) held her by the tip of her little finger, while finishing his beer with the other hand. He was losing his grip, of course.

She looked up, wondering which movie this scene was from as she watched her last shred of hope vanishing. Meanwhile, in the secret lab, a voice declared, "Four down, ten to go . . ."

Original Mayra

ORIGINAL MAYRA
18 July 1999

I tried to pick well-known movies but it wasn't always possible, so I explained what Juliana's movie was about because I suppose only I have seen it (it's on LMAO® Brazil this month). Ingrid, I was saving your chapter for when you returned. There you go. Hope you like it. (By the way, after my character "disposes" of the protagonists, she has plans for Siegfried too. This time it will be ten thousand times worse than your worst nightmares — but it is going to be well behaved, I promise.)

ORIGINAL BARB
18 July 1999

Bravo Mayra, Bravo! Matching the impending dooms with the characters so impeccably! Juliana tormented by her continual proximity to a duo of gorgeous masculine hunks forever unattainable, like Tantalus in the legend. Tess faced with the twin, equally horrific fates of being torpedoed and running out of booze. Connie . . . well, I don't really get that one yet . . ,

Looking forward to the next eleven episodes of TOATS!

UNEARTHLY BARB
18 July 1999

Within the steely confines of her visor, (Insert Your Name Here) nervously chewed her lower lip. At this point in her pseudo-life, she was very rich and more than slightly deranged. Or to be more precise, she had recently been very rich and was currently on the verge of a nervous breakdown. Her erstwhile fortune had poured into her bank account last month, when she sold the amazing story of her Amazonian adventures in Bogus Brazil to "Wot?"® magazine. Despite the fact that the editor had heavily censored it, (or because anything known to have been censored was always more popular) the story had sold millions of copies, translating into millions of U.S. dollars for (Inse). But last week she had blown the lot.

(Inse) spoke into the tiny microphone balanced at the edge of her lip. Her voice echoed inside the metal helmet. "Red Five, give me the latest security report," she barked.

Her henchman, circling in a helicopter about five hundred feet above her head, replied, "All clear."

(Inse) relaxed imperceptibly. "Good," she said, shutting off the comsystem with a snap that rattled her ear-drums.

She tapped her gauntleted fingers on her iron-clad knee. Gad, it was boring, sitting there wearing a suit of armour, locked in a gigantic safe along with a thousand-years' thirty foot worth of oxygen, a closed-circuit self-purifying water supply and uncountable tons of food. She wished she had installed a video, but it was too risky—Mayra might have tampered with the circuitry before the goods arrived on the island.

(Inse) moaned. To think of all those Siegfried B. Hinkelheimer movies she might have been watching, year after year, while sitting there in the armour, locked in the safe.

The armoured cyberchick held her breath and listened, but no sound came to her from outside the thirty-foot-thick, lead-lined walls of the safe (whose keys had all been melted in a volcano). No sound came to her from the savage, android hounds which guarded the island fortress in which the safe was situated. She flicked on the intercom. "Green Seven, report to base," she snapped.

"All clear," returned the submarine commander.

"Roger. Over and out," said (Inse), adding the "Roger" bit to vary the tedium. She hoped the dozen helicopters, the fleet of subs and the flotilla of warships, combined with the high-tech alarm system, the booby-traps, the hell-hounds and the fail-safe hair-trigger laser-gun set-up, would be enough.

Enough to keep the fiendish Mayra at bay . . .

I forgot to mention—(Insert Your Name Here) was already crazed due to an episode involving a crocodile many chapters ago.

UnEarthly Mayra **UNEARTHLY MAYRA**
19th July 1999
(Insert Your Name Here) was getting really bored inside that safe. She looked around. Tons of supplies, life-support apparatus, medicine and medical equipment for any imaginable and unimaginable emergency, every possible detail to keep her alive, but that was that. She was stuck here for eternity. Alive and bored.

It was too depressing.

(Inse) was so down in the mouth she was seriously considering control-alt-deleting herself.

She placed her trembling fingers on the CTRL, ALT and DEL keys. For a long time she kept them there, as if she had been hypnotized.

"Green Seven to Base! Do you copy?" squeaked the intercom. (Insert Your Name Here) was brutally jerked out of her trance and with the scare she inadvertently punched the keys, accidentally triggering a computer malfunction that set off a chain-reaction hack.

As it passed across the entire Internet at the speed of electricity, the hack snowballed, triggering numerous other "sleeping" crack codes all over the world that were waiting to be activated. It sliced deeper and further than any hack had ever gone.

The screen went berserk, flashing graphs, maps, credit card

numbers, Pentagon passwords, blueprints of secret weapons, the real story of who killed JFK, the truth about the Roswell Case, Siegfried B. Hinkelheimer's address, a copy of his diary, a juicy picture of him—without his shirt and about to kiss a foxy redhead in a voluptuous black dress . . .

All this secret data flashed before (Inse)'s spellbound eyes.

Far away in Praetorian HQ, a state-of-the-art installation buried deep beneath a secret island, alarms shrilled and sirens screamed.

Boy, the last place you wanna be is stuck between the thirty-foot-thick, lead-lined walls of a safe whose keys have all been melted in a volcano when the Praetorians know that you know what they know, and you know that they know it. In clearer words, that evil cyber-terrorist group couldn't let (Inse) live now that she knew about the biggest conspiracy ever—and they knew where she was.

If you have seen the movie *An Open Fabric of String or Rope or Wire Woven Together at Regular Intervals*, you know that their power was unlimited. It would be just a matter of time. Short time.

Meanwhile, in her secret lab in the catacombs, Mayra muttered manically, "Five down, nine to go."

UNEARTHLY BARB
20 July 1999
While Mayra was occupied by her obsessive pursuit of deadly cliffhangers, Lottie had taken the opportunity to become engaged to Siegfried. At the very moment Mayra was crossing (Inse) off her list, Lottie was

walking down the aisle of an enchanting English chapel at the rural village of Great-Snoring-on-Nether-Wallop, to meet her beau.

Dressed in a magnificent tuxedo, he smiled affectionately at his bride-to-be as she approached. A brilliant shaft of sunlight struck through the erubescent glaze of the stained-glass windows, illuminating him, and only him. Bathed in radiance he looked even more gorgeous than ever. Lottie stumbled and almost fainted at the sight.

Almost.

Soon, she would be "Frau Hinkelheimer".

UNEARTHLY MAYRA
20 July 1999

Siegfried's cellular phone rang.

"Don't!" cried Lottie in despair as her husband-to-be flapped it open.

Too late.

"Hallo. Ja … ja … natürlich … ja … ich verstehe … Mary Oh Really?'s B & B? Das ist aber eine Überraschung! Um wievel Uhr? Ja, ich komme. Auf Wiedersehen, Herr Schumm."

Siegfried gave Lottie that you-know-what-it-is-like-to-be-almost-married-to-an-actor look.

"Listen, liebling," he said, "this will never work if you make me feel guilty for leaving you at the altar to catch a plane to Implausible Ireland in order to sign a contract. Herr Schumm and Mr. Isambard Moneybags are offering me a part in a new movie. It's my job. Implausible Ireland is pretty close. Stay right here. I'll be back in a minute, and then … "

He smiled warmly as he rushed out of that enchanting

English place of worship.

It took Lottie a couple of hours to recover from the shock. Then—

Stay right here, my ass! she thought, as she bolted out of Great-Snoring-on-Nether-Wallop Chapel with her lacy veil and train flying, hijacked the wedding limo (which had nine ancient boots tied to the rear bumper) and drove like a maniac towards the airport, the footwear furiously bumping up and down behind.

UNEARTHLY BARB
February 2009

Later, tired, bedraggled and extremely nervous after her Air Banana plane trip, Lottie trudged up the path to the threshold of Mary O'Really?'s Bed-and-Breakfast. As she raised her hand to knock on the door, she noticed that her knuckles were still white and her fingernails still bent from hanging on to the airplane's wings after the floor had dropped out of the fuselage (having been held on with gaffer-tape). What a miraculous landing it had been…

Mayra's next post had Lottie entering Mrs. Oh Really?'s B & B in Implausible Ireland, only to fall into the clutches of the evil Mr Hyde of "Dr Jekyll and Mr Hyde" fame.

He forced her to drink some kind of weird shape-changing potion, whereupon Mayra exultantly thought it was "Six down, eight to go," but …

UnEarthly Lottie

UNEARTHLY LOTTIE
23 July 1999

Lottie seemed to be surrounded by a sea of smiling faces. Amongst them she could see some replica characters who looked suspiciously like Jacqueline Basset-Hound, Patsy Transit, Daniel de Licious and ... the Prime Minister of Australia?—who the hell invited him?

Strange (she thought)—the TOATS women were noticeably absent... (but of course; they'd all be off somewhere seething in jealous rage.) Voices murmured Lottie's praises as she floated down the aisle through drifts of traceried sunlight and air laden with the scent of flowers. At last, after all this time, it was the day of her long-awaited, oft-postponed wedding!

She saw Siegfried ahead. He glanced around at her with that familiar half-smile. So dangerously desirable did he look that her knees start to wobble. One shoe fell off and then she found herself nose down on the cold flagstones, crawling on desperate hands and knees, tangled hopelessly in acres of veil. With a loud wrench of ripping seams, she lurched to her feet just as a gust of wind blasted its rude way into the little church and lifted her dress up around her ears.

Omigosh! she thought, *and I'm wearing those awful old faded knickers with the frayed elastic!!!* She struggled to push her dress down, only to find herself on a deserted platform of Flinders Street Railway Station. Hungry seagulls squabbled over a few squashed potato chips and hundreds of sheets of paper flew past her, scurrying helter-skelter before a savage wind. She realized in dismay that it was the only copy of her precious script and threw herself after it, desperate to salvage a few disintegrating fragments.

Her bridegroom peered round at her, grinning, from behind a cast-iron pillar, but it was not Siegfried; it was that creepy kid from High School—the surfer with hair like a pot-scourer.

"How come I'm marrying him when I can't even remember his name? I hate him anyway . . . hate him!!" Lottie started to scream and sob, just as a monstrous locomotive roared out of nowhere, huge, black and rust-streaked, belching smoke, hissing clouds of steam and scattering seagulls and shredded scraps of script.

This thing seems a little out of place—oh, of course, what a relief—I must be dreaming! thought Lottie, just as she woke up.

But she quickly discovered that reality was much worse, for that kid from High School, complete with quantities of facial hair in unlikely places, was leaning leeringly over her.

"Aaahhh", he sighed in a cloud of foetid breath, "you've come round at last! My own, my perfect Friday night date behind the school gym!"

"Clear off, jerk!!" bellowed Lottie in a voice like a super-tanker's foghorn. "Anyway, it's Mrs Hinkelheimer to you!"

She lumbered to her feet, picked up Pot-scourer Hair in one remarkably hairy hand and flung him across the room. "That Brazilian trollop!!" she trumpeted. "She'll rue the day she did this to me!"

As Lottie tramped from the laboratory the walls shook and the ceiling fell on top of Mr Creepy, squashing him like a cockroach. Lottie glanced at herself admiringly in the hall mirror as she left the B & B. Her Its MySaki® frock was bursting at the seams. From it issued arms and legs that resembled moss-covered tree-trunks. She sported a splendid set of yellowed fangs and copious amounts of attractive facial growth. And she had fine social skills and a personality to match! Yes; the old, wilting, fainting Lottie was gone!

"Cringe, Mayra!" growled the new, improved Lottie, pointing a taloned finger at the beautiful sight in the mirror. "Tremble and cower! Because I'll find you; no matter where that mangy little secret hideaway of yours is! Panic and quake, tart! Shiver and shake! And as for Siegfried . . . !"

At that moment a foolish, bespectacled little man burst in at the door. Yes! It was the Australian Prime Minister.

"You!" rumbled Lottie, "I dreamt you were at my wedding, you horrib . . ."

"No, no; I can't have this!" bleated the annoying little fellow. "I can't have you going around giving Australians a bad name. Next thing you know President Clinton will be putting trade restrictions on everything and I'll never get to have my photo taken with him again!"

"Ah, go choke on greenhouse gases, you twerp," rasped Lottie. Her karate chop dropped the babbling politician like a discarded toy monkey.

"Ooh, this is fun," said Lottie as she stomped from the building. "I should have tried this evil stuff ages ago. Who next? Ratchet? Blackbeard? . . . no, not him—he's a keen TOATS reader.

Mayra? Yes, Mayra! And then I'll get married—Siegfried won't dare abandon me at the altar this time! And won't he love my new look!!" Giggling in girlish anticipation Lottie loped ground-shakingly off down the hill and away across the fields into the night-enfolded streets of the slumbering city.

ORIGINAL INGRID
23 July 1999

Congratulations to Lottie for escaping that dilemma with her new chapter! It's exciting to see the first victim eluding her doom. I wonder if anyone else will try it. Keep writing, guys!

UnEarthly Mayra

UNEARTHLY MAYRA
26 July 1999

Emily fell through the very same time tunnel she had written into TOATS many chapters ago. Picking herself up from the muddy pool in which she had landed, she thought, *This won't be too bad if whoever is writing this has sent me to Camelot...*

Unfortunately for her, she had ended up not in Camelot but in a medieval Danish kingdom, just outside a castle owned by Hamlet.

Emily was unrecognisable beneath the crust of dried mud. Hamlet mistook her for a guy named Rosencrantz and insisted that she accompany him on a voyage to England. Since she was in one of Shakespeare's tragedies, certain doom awaited her ...

Meanwhile... "Seven down, seven to go," recited Mayra, who didn't yet know Lottie had not only escaped but was now plotting her revenge and immensely enjoying the pleasure of being evil.

UNEARTHLY EMILY
27 July 1999

"It was a dark and stormy night and the ship was sinking. The captain turned to me and said, "Let me tell you a story, my son. It was a dark and stormy night..."

Listening to the voice, Emily shook her head. She never should have shown Hamlet how to mix vodka with those oranges. He could be heard throughout the bar, still reciting the Dark and Stormy Night cycle, despite the fact that everyone else had grown bored with it after a nano-second.

The ex-pirate wench sighed deeply. Who would have guessed that those few misguided chapters about the time tunnel would end up haunting her now? Worse still—to be mistaken for Rosencrantz! Mud or no mud, maybe it was time to consider plastic surgery...

Her heart bled inconsolably. She got up from her seat in the bar and headed out onto the deck of the medieval galleon with its wildly anachronistic fittings and layout. Curling up on a lounge chair she covered herself with a nice tartan throw. (She was getting sick of all this misty, damp weather.)

Emily picked up her book "Rouge", its title printed in "Herotique"® font, with Flambio® on the cover. From the direction of the bar came the sound of Hamlet breaking into a loud rendition of "It's a Long Way to Tipperary".

Suddenly, Emily heard a ruckus on the Lido deck. Curious to get a closer look, she went over to the railing. Down there beside the swimming pool a man in black was stage-fighting with a young sailor. The watcher's heart skipped a beat.

Omigosh its… him! I recognize that technique from the Old Thespian Theatre®!

Of course, Emily wasn't sure whether anyone but Donna knew who she was referring to. "Ogosh" looked marvellous in black. Her inconsolable heart was suddenly consoled. All thoughts of older men vanished from her memory. Not only was this one gorgeous, he was in her age group!

Feverishly she glanced about, looking for anything that resembled a wardrobe. Next to the mast stood a large, iron-bound ark with an arched lid—clearly either a pirates' treasure chest or a clothes' storage box. On lifting the lid she found, to her delight, that it was the latter. In fact, the camphorwood chest was piled high with sexy female-pirate outfits.

Good old "Original Emily"! she thought. *She's written this in exactly the right place at the right time!* (Little did she know that it was actually pedantic Original Barb who had sneaked it there while Original Emily was busy drafting the next few paragraphs…)

After performing a quick costume change behind a handy sextant, Emily grabbed a nearby rope (which was unfortunately attached to a sail and sent the ship veering off course) and swung down onto the Lido deck in perfect pirate fashion.

"Well, well, well, if it isn't the Nubian Chieftain!" she declared.

Surprised, the man in black left off his swordplay and turned to gaze upon the loveliest pirate he had ever seen. "Emily!" Turning back, he quickly dispatched his opponent.

Emily smiled seductively. "Are you planning on keeping that sword unsheathed?"

It was a challenge, and he knew it. He grinned.

Thus commenced one of the two greatest sword fights on UnEarth (the other one happens later on).

The Ogosh-lookalike and Emily aren't close to each other—none of that swords-crossing "en garde" garbage. No, what we have here is a tango, too far apart to damage each other, but each time one makes even the tiniest feint, the other counters; then there is silence. They start to circle—feinting here, feinting there and—finished teasing, they begin to duel in earnest. Their swords cross, then again, again, and the sound comes so fast it's almost continual. "Ogosh" presses on, Emily retreating backwards up the steps to the Lanai Deck.

"You're using Confetti's defense against me, eh?" "Ogosh" inquires, thrilled at the challenge.

"I thought it fitting, considering the stairs," she replies.

He smiles. "Naturally, you must expect me to attack with dei Liberi," he says, shifting styles.

Emily tries to cope as best she can. "Naturally, but I find Marozzo cancels out dei Liberi, don't you?"

The lovely wench is now perched at the edge of the deck. With nowhere to go, she jumps to the deck below.

With a wicked smile on his face, "Ogosh" stares down at her. "Unless the enemy has studied his Palladini." With the grace of an Olympian, the young man flies off the stairs, somersaults clean over Emily's head, and lands facing her. Quickly disarming her, "Ogosh" grabs her in a passionate embrace. "Which I have . . ."

The mists roll in, blocking our view. (Good thing, or Donna would have to put an NC-17 rating on this one).

UNEARTHLY MAYRA
UnEarthly Mayra
27 July 1999
Donna, proprietor of the Siegfried B. Hinkelheimer fan-site, thought, *I would stop the slaughtering of the TOATS protagonists if only I could find my magic wand, which was whisked away by Lottie at The Pink Elephant. I would turn myself into an insect and teleport myself via the telephone cables into Mayra's computer, bugging her motherboard so badly that she would never be able to access the SBH feedback page again.*

A dream worth shrinking for.

That was going to be tricky though, without a magic wand, a magic lamp, Barb's Splingian kit or the Fairy Queen.

Then Donna remembered Mayra's grandfather, that fossilized medicine man countless centuries old. She deduced, *If those natives can shrink heads they might be able to shrink the whole body as well!*

Having heard that the ancient sage lived somewhere in the jungles of Bogus Brazil—no doubt in a small and leaky thatched hut infested by armadillos, short-horned grasshoppers and stick insects—she went in search of him.

At night, with her instincts sharpened by a sense of revenge, Donna crept with cat-like stealth up the old man's triplex Indian tent to the penthouse, where she found a skylight through which she swung herself in.

Now that she was inside she could search the place for the instruction book on the art of shrinking. She shone her flashlight into the gloom.

Suddenly the lights went on, illuminating the venerable patriarch sitting in a bergère, smoking a pipe and wearing a gold FauxLex® on his wrist. To cut a long story short, he shrank Donna to the size of a bug, picked her with his thumb and forefinger and flicked her out of the window.

Donna, *The Unbelievable Dwindling Human*® (don't ask me where I've dug up this classic movie), went flying aimlessly in the wilderness until she accidentally landed on a spider's web. More precisely, it was the web of a bird-eating giant hairy Brazilian pink tarantula. Nearby, she saw bits of a poor little ant, which apparently had been carrying a cookie crumb.

Sensing the wriggling of more prey, the merciless arachnid, a real monstrosity from Donna's point of view, stirred out of its sleep and slowly started closing in, eyeing the web prisoner's minuscule body and choosing which part of it should receive the first bite.

"Thanks, Grandpa," said Mayra through the intercom from the catacombs. She crossed Donna's name off her list.

"Eight down, six to go."

UNEARTHLY DONNA
27 July 1999
A giant spider?
Donna found herself alternately spitting, screaming, and vomiting forcefully (not necessarily in that order) in the "face" of the advancing monstrosity until she recalled having been properly (and fortuitously) informed of the great spiritual powers bestowed by her still-smarting snappish turtle-spirit tattoo. At the last possible moment

she withdrew hissing under its shell, confusing the (hideous) arachnid into temporary paralysis.

Thus spared for the immediate future, Donna found herself nonetheless reduced to gibbering hysterics at the prospect of being trapped in this chapter, denied access to her website and unable therefore to upload her latest updates and code enhancements, without which her cleverly crafted self-preservation stub will kick in . . . causing her SBH feedback program to AUTOMATICALLY stop accepting input from Mayra's IP !!

If only her laptop and cell phone had shrunk with her, and were lying nearby in her spidery grave . . .

Heehee maybe Emily's going to dump SBH for her new love?? Fickle! Fickle!

Siegfried! Siegfried!

UNEARTHLY MAYRA
28 July 1999

"So?" Mayra's eyes sliced the stifling Amazonian air like razor blades as she turned to her master hacker.

"We're working on it, Senhorita," the hacker muttered unintelligibly for fear his employer might understand and get into another one of her lousy moods. "We haven't found out what 'IP' means but apparently that's the source of the problem."

Fortunately Mayra wasn't listening. She was rambling incoherently. "Aramy . . . iramya . . . miara . . . airyma . . . aryam. . . ARYAM! Yes, if I could get Donna's computer to think I'm somebody else, somebody called 'Aryam', I might just have a chance to penetrate her system by using a decoy name and deactivate the self-preservation stub—whatever that is."

It worked! Mayra was back in business and more virulent than ever! "Nice try, Donna!" she growled with a rancorous grimace.

In her hubris she had, however, lost the ability to do math. "Nine down, five to go. . ."

Original Juliana

UnEarthly Juliana

10

ANOTHER BRIEF DETOUR AND SOME PARACHUTING

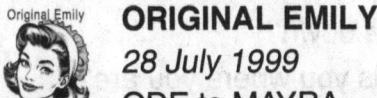

ORIGINAL EMILY
28 July 1999
ODE to MAYRA
(sung to the tune of "Mayra" from *The Sound of Music*®©[10])

How do you solve a problem like our Mayra?
How do you catch a fan and pin her down?
How do you find a word that means our Mayra?
A flibbertigibbet! A will-o'-the wisp! A-RYAM!

Many a thing Siegfried would like to tell her.
Many a time he's wanted out of the fray.
But why would he want to stay?
If we're all sent away?
How will we keep Siegfried from certain doom?
Oh, how do you solve a problem like our Mayra?
How do you keep an author's demise at bay?
We're the prey? We're confused!
Out of focus and bemused.
And we never know exactly where we are.
Unpredictable as weather TOATS's as flighty as a feather
We are darlings! We are vixens! We're on Mars?!
Mayra can out-pester any pest, Drive a hornet from its nest,
She's offing us one by one.
She is brilliant! She is wild!
She's a riddle! She's a child!
She's a headache! She's an angel! She's a son of a....gun!
Where's a TOATS taxi when you need one?
How do you spot and hail one down?
How do you find map that tells you where you are?
The Amazon River?! King Solomon's Mines?! Or Denmark?!
Many a thing you know we'd like to tell her.
Many a thing she ought to understand,
But how do you make her stop,
Before the rest of us drop?
How will we keep ourselves from certain doom?
Oh, how do you solve a problem like our Mayra?
How do you keep an author's demise at bay?

UNEARTHLY BARB
29 July 1999

When last heard of, Barb was attached to a parachute, which was in turn fastened to a rocket blasting its way to a preset destination. As she flew through the air, Barb busily perused her battered copy of the "TOATS Rule Book on Etiquette". It was the new, updated version, complete with the addendum on how much narrative of a risqué nature TOATS authors are allowed to include in their chapters.

So intrigued was she by reading examples of the racy scenarios one is forbidden to include, that she failed to note the Air Banana plane lumbering crookedly across her trajectory until it was too late. With a sickening "splat" she landed upon one of the slightly-chewed wings. The ropes of the parachute tore off on the edges of jagged metal, and the rocket hurtled off into the clouds. Clinging to the wing, Barb watched the name-plate on the rocket's side vanish into the vapours of the upper atmosphere. Only then did she realize it read: MAYRA'S ROCKET CORP.

"Mayra!" She mumbled to herself, scrabbling frantically at the plane's grime-smeared window. "I wonder if she had anything to do with this…?"

Through the patina of coagulated grot covering the airplane's plastic window-pane, Barb could make out the dim outlines of passengers. "Hey!" she yelled, knocking as loudly as possible, "Let me in! Let me in before I get blown off this wing!"

No-one even looked up.

Sliding her long, psychedelic-pink fingernails under the rim of the pane, Barb levered it ajar and slithered her long, lean body inside.

"Whew! What a relief!" she exclaimed, collapsing into a vacant seat. "Safe at last!" Angrily, she looked around at the other passengers. "Why didn't anyone let me in?" she was about to demand. Getting a clearer view of them, she thought better of it and sighed. Yes, it was a typical Air Banana flight, complete with hordes of burly, thick-set passengers wearing balaclavas and carrying violin cases. What a pity the airline had now purchased more aircraft to add to the original one plane and a wooden gyrocopter. It made the odds of parachuting on to the wing of one of them so much greater.

The PA system crackled into life. A voice said, "Dis your Capitan speak—" and was cut off. A hostess hurried up the aisle towards the cock-pit, carrying a shoe-box filled with elastic-bands, while Barb experienced a nauseating feeling of déjà vue. She leaned down and fumbled beneath her seat, feeling for the reassuring shape of a life-jacket. All she could find was a large cardboard box. Even the familiar inflatable rubber duck, yellow with an orange beak, was missing. Air Banana must have been cutting costs again. So THAT was how they could afford another plane ...

Barb became aware of another sound above the intermittent revving of the tortured engines and the screeching of metal on metal from which the oil had long ago leaked, to be flung across the window-panes. It was the noise of a 1934 Knell & Howl® projector working. An air hostess unrolled a large, white screen at the front of the cabin and a scratched version of *Das Rat* began showing. The in-flight movie.

"Ooh—er," articulated Barb, leaning forward to ogle Siegfried in that battleship commander's hat. Unfortunately a large, balaclava-covered head blocked her view. She was forced to sit back and try to comprehend the rasping hiss of the sound track over the howl of the engines, the whirr of the projector, the sound of someone being strangled in the toilets and the peculiar rustling sounds of the man sitting next to her.

Eventually even the sound-track petered out and Barb was left to her own thoughts. She began to worry. What if Mayra was behind the rocket thing? In fact, who else could it be? Might it be possible that Mayra was trying to get rid of everyone, so that she could have Siegfried all to herself? Could Mayra really be that evil?

"Yes!" she shouted, sitting bolt upright.

Just as this realisation dawned on Barb, the rustling man sitting next to her turned and asked "Hey, you seen a large cardboard box anywhere?"

"Yes. Er, I mean no," said Barb craftily. "Ah, I mean, I might have. Why do you ask?"

The man slid his hand into the breast pocket of his suit. Instantly it came to Barb that he was about to pull a gun on her. Her brain wobbled like an under-set jelly (jello) as she tried to recall the ways she had scraped out of similar situations in the past. She groped for her "TOATS Rule Book on Etiquette" and frenziedly flipped through the pages, looking for the chapter headed "In Times of Extreme Danger". She had just had time to read the first instruction, "Run away," when instead of a gun, the man pulled out a paper bag.

"You see dis paper bag?" he asked, holding it under her nose, "somewhere on dis plane dere's a whole carton of these. Where dis plane is headed, they don't got no paper bags. Me, I'm a-gonna make-a ma fortune."

Barb grabbed the paper bag out of his hand. "Where did you get this?" she gasped, turning it over to examine it carefully, almost reverently.

The paper bag was interesting. It looked like no ordinary paper bag. It had once been brown, but was now a mottled greyish-black. It had obviously been crumpled into a ball more than once, then straightened out. It had been torn, tattered and stomped on. It had been repaired with masking tape in many places and was dog-eared, but she knew it at once. It was— yes, her own, her very own old, faithful Paper Bag, last seen somewhere in Inauthentic Iceland.

Sobbing, Barb clutched it to her heart. "It's mine, mine I tell you! she shouted through her tears. "I don't know where you found it, but it's mine. It was stolen cruelly from me, probably by Lottie."

"Give it back!" shouted the Paper-Bag Man.

'Shut up in front!" shouted the burly, thick-set passenger in the seat behind, "I'm trying to hear *Das Rat!*" He stood up and dragged the protesting Paper-Bag Man away in the direction of the toilets.

Left alone, Barb immediately jammed the Paper Bag on her head. "It was providence!" she whispered happily to herself. "Now Mayra will never recognise me."

Just then a man poked his head around the beaded leather curtain of the cockpit. He was wielding a megaphone. "Dis your Capitan speaking," he said. "Some-tin going wrong in here. We be forced to make de emergency landin'. Fasten your seat-belts!"

ORIGINAL INGRID
29 July 1999

Since I have not popped my head in the door of this fansite for ages I decided to sit down and look back through the archives. Mayra, your lively contributions make me want to write! As for you Barb have you returned to normal after your thrilling experience gripping on to an airplane in mid-air?

ORIGINAL BARB
29 July 1999

P.S. Ingrid, I WOULD be back to 'normal' if the smell inside this paper bag was not so disgusting. Smells like fossilized school lunches.

ORIGINAL INGRID
30 July 1999

Wow, what a delicious aroma that would be. Wish I had a paper bag like that. Throw it my way when you don't need it any more!

UNPOET OF PRISTINA
30 July 1999

A new TOATS contributor is writing too much tedious stuff that doesn't have much plot and is filled with references to films hardly anyone has ever seen, as she gets rid of the crazy SBH fans one by one. I wish she would cease, and allow everyone just to share Hinkelheimer trivia without this madness. She should move aside and allow the Australians to provide our amusement again!

149

ORIGINAL BARB
31 July 1999

Ingrid, no-one else can have this paper bag since I am obsessed with it, but I can save you an almost identical copy. And don't worry about whether or not you are a TOATS author. On the inside of this paper bag there are some rescue plans written, and your name is mentioned.

ORIGINAL BARB
31 July 1999

UNPOET OF PRISTINA—please never criticise any TOATS author—especially Mayra. The beauty of TOATS writing is this — that we can all have the freedom to write in a joyous atmosphere of fun, knowing that if our writing does not please everyone it does not matter. Please do not take TOATS too seriously. If you do not like reading it, Donna has given us the perfect solution—we can simply ask that TOATS is never downloaded to our address.

The danger of criticising TOATS authors is that in the end nobody will want to write anything at all for fear of chastisement.

Mayra is very sensitive to this. I know for a fact she had decided that at the first sign of discontent with her writing she would stop immediately. I for one do not want her to stop. Lottie, Tess, Connie and I over here in Ozland are delighted with her work. She has so obviously studied the TOATS archives thoroughly, and enjoyed them. Her chapters show a flawless appreciation not only of the characters and the history but the oddball humor as well.

Emily and Donna are very busy, Ingrid hesitates, Lottie's computer is defunct—if Mayra does not write any more that only leaves me to carry on with TOATS and quite frankly, for me it's only fun if lots of people join in. If you do like TOATS, please let it grow naturally. If you do not like it, just avoid it. Since you obviously DO read it, how about a chapter from you? There's NO rule which says authors have to be native English speakers. Meanwhile—Mayra, please write on!

UNEARTHLY BARB
30 July 1999

Giving up her fruitless search for seat-belts, Barb whipped out her compact, snapped it open and gazed at her reflection in the mirror. At the edges of consciousness she was aware of the screech of striving aero-engines reaching breaking-point, the rattle of rapidly loosening bolts as the fuselage trembled like a frightened animal, the soundtrack of *Das Rat* warping into the babble of a language she did not understand. A feeling of weightlessness told her the aircraft had nosed into a steep dive.

Carefully, she applied eye-liner to the rims of the view-slits in her Paper Bag. She had to look good if there were any TV cameras around when the plane made its emergency landing.

Someone vaulted into the vacant seat beside her. The newcomer was panting, white-faced with trepidation. "You've got to help me!" gasped the stranger. "We've got to get out of this aircraft. Do you realize, no Air Banana pilot has ever made a successful emergency landing? Come to think of it, none of them have ever made a successful normal landing, either."

"You don't say! Really?" replied Barb, snapping shut her compact. "Right!" She continued briskly, "this calls for action. Come with me—um—what did you say your name was?"

151

"UnPoet," said the stranger, holding out his or her hand, "UnPoet of Pristina."

They shook hands.

At that moment the noise level inside the cabin dropped by half. "Oh, that's better," said Barb as she introduced herself. "It's a lot quieter in here now that right engine has stopped working. Incidentally, are you male or female?"

UnPoet's eyes narrowed mysteriously. "It's a secret," he/she said.

"It really doesn't matter at this point in time," said Barb, narrowing her paper bag's view-slits and trying to look equally mysterious. "What matters is that we have to get out of here."

Decisively, she stood up. "Come with me, UnPoet. I'm going to have a few sharp words with the pilot."

Barb and UnPoet strode assertively down the aisle to the cockpit. Or they tried to stride, but the cabin floor was on such a steep angle that they ended up taking little mincing steps, very fast. All the passengers who were not down on their knees praying, burst into applause. "Great rendition of the 'Dance of the Cygnets' in 'Swan Lake'," someone called out approvingly. Barb and UnPoet smiled nonchalantly and, with a noise as of canvas being ripped, fell through the beaded leather curtain separating the cockpit from the cabin.

With the reflexes of cats they picked themselves up, dusted themselves off and leaned casually on the door-frame. There beyond the leather curtain, the pilot sat, overflowing his chair. So enormous was he, he must have weighed no less than 250 kilograms. Beside him was a small table on which the and the co-pilot were playing at dice. Every so often they each took a sip from their large glasses of piña colada balanced on the controls.

"Wha—what's going on?" Barb expostulated indignantly. "We're in a steep dive, about to make an emergency landing, and you two are playing at DICE?????????????" The cockpit soon filled up with question marks. The co-pilot began swatting them like flies. Every time he swatted a floating hook, the little dot at the bottom fell on the floor, like a grain of burned rice.

"Relax! Don't sweat!" rumbled the pilot, with a deep belly-laugh. "We is not really needin' to make de emergency landing. Dat was just our little joke. Got to keep de passengers, happy, give dem a little laugh, eh?" Scooping up a handful of dots he munched absent-mindedly on them.

"Oh, well that's a relief," said Barb, turning to UnPoet. "We might as well go back to our seats, then, and try to see a small corner of the in-flight movie."

"Wait!" cried UnPoet. "I want out. I want OFF this flight. Do you have any parachutes?"

"Over dere," said the pilot, jerking his chin towards a messy pile on the floor. "Couple over dere I tink. You can bail out, but you don't get your money back. Mayra's orders."

"What?" Barb yelped. "Mayra's orders did you say?"

The pilot waved his large, meaty hand dismissively. "Yeah, yeah. She own dis airline now."

"That's it. I'm bailing out with you right now, UnPoet," said Barb as they both strapped on the parachutes. "Where's the nearest exit that isn't jammed?' she demanded, thrusting her Paper Bag close to the pilot's jowly countenance.

"Look, I's tryin' to concentrate here," said the pilot; "I got a game in progress. Stop interruptin'." He pulled a lever. Instantly a trapdoor yawned beneath the feet of Barb and UnPoet. The next thing they knew they were hurtling through the air yet again. This time, in a cloud of tiny black dots.

This time, without an aircraft.

UNEARTHLY BARB
30 July 1999
Next chapter...IN WHICH BARB AND UNPOET SINK TO NEW DEPTHS.

Surprisingly, the parachutes actually opened. Down they drifted, Barb and UnPoet, like two gigantic dandelion seeds, like a pair of inverted white tulips, like a couple of diaphanous jellyfish adrift in a lavender sea strewn with clouds of foam. It was all terribly poetic.

Far away, a small dark object with wings ploughed earthwards, trailing a scarf of smoke; presumably the Air Banana plane.

As they fell, Barb's mind was busy trying to work out a way to get Siegfried's name into this chapter three times. After all, this is Siegfried's site. "Siegfried," she muttered to herself, but the words were snatched from her lips by the uprush of air.

It was then she noticed a third parachute being blown towards them on a current of faster-moving upper-atmosphere airs. "Look—it's Tinfingers!" she shrieked to UnPoet, pointing to the approaching parachutist. "He was last seen many thousands of chapters ago!"

As Tinfingers floated within earshot, he cupped his

extraordinarily metallic hands around his mouth and yelled, "Who are you?"

"UnPoet of Pristina," shouted back UnPoet of Pristina.

"And I'm Unwary of Australia!" bellowed Barb. "Now get out of this chapter, Tinfingers. We already have far too many characters to worry about."

"All right!" called Tinfingers, changing course. He disappeared into a handy cloudbank.

UnPoet glared indignantly at Barb. "Unwary of Australia!" he/she roared. "But up there in the plane you introduced yourself as—"

"Yes, I know," interrupted Barb soothingly, "as Unwise of Arachnophobia. I'm travelling incognito. Why else do you think I'm wearing this Paper Bag on my head?"

"That's a Paper Bag?" shouted UnPoet incredulously.

 **UNEARTHLY BARB**
30 July 1999
Next chapter....IN WHICH BARB AND UNPOET CONTINUE TO DESCEND.

Down they floated with their parachutes, like a matching set of upturned tea-cups made of fine bone china. And without the handles. And with lots of cords attached to them. Actually, they looked nothing like a matching set of tea-cups.

The air roared past their ears with a sound like a locomotive in a tunnel. A black dot flashed past Barb's eyes— the last remaining evidence of the swatted question marks.

"You remember what you said back there about PLOT?" shouted Barb by way of conversation on the way down.

"Yes," yelled UnPoet.

"Well, Mayra does have a plot," Barb screamed, "and she does stick to it. Only it's so incredibly complicated that you have to be completely obsessed with TOATS to be able to grasp it. You see, she's been getting rid of all of us one by one, all in different locations. It's very clever really, and it will all come together in the last couple of chapters, provided she writes them."

"Oh!" shrieked UnPoet, "I think I see what you're getting at. Hey, while we're talking—I mean shouting—about TOATS, we ought to tell whoever is writing it at the moment to get their terminology right."

"Huh?" bawled Barb eloquently.

UnPoet continued (now red in the face from shouting), "Back there on board the plane, the author wrote that the RIGHT engine stopped working. Anyone who knows anything would have said the STARBOARD engine. How dumb is that?"

"Pretty dumb," agreed Barb, clutching her Paper Bag to make sure it wouldn't fly off and reveal her true identity. "But wait a minute, you're not suggesting we are merely characters in someone's story—are you?"

"But we are!" screeched UnPoet. "We are characters in a story about Siegfried, on the Siegfried fansite, written by Siegfried's fans."

"Ha ha, good one," hollered Barb. "Know any more jokes?" Just then the ground came swiftly into view, putting an end to all conversation.

UNEARTHLY BARB
30 July 1999
—IN WHICH BARB AND UNPOET ALMOST LAND.

Below them, they spied a long, deep gorge. At its rim stood a pub that looked suspiciously like The Rainforest Rondaybooze. "Good heavens!" shouted Barb through her Paper Bag, "I think we must be landing in Based-on Borneo! And I was longing for the silence and solitude of the Swiss Alps . . ."

UnPoet then yelled, "What's that forlorn thing hanging off a lone thorn bush halfway down the side of the precipice?"

"It's Ingrid!" squawked Barb, "and she's wearing a Siegfried B. Hinkelheimer souvenir T-shirt!"

"Help!" Ingrid called weakly, as they drew near to her precarious perch.

"Grab hold of my ankle," yodelled Barb, thrusting out one foot. Ingrid's hand shot out. She grasped Barb's ankle in a grip like a hungry clam. Abruptly, Barb's parachute began to plunge with greater speed.

"See you on the ground," Barb sang out to UnPoet, already several fathoms above her head.

UNEARTHLY BARB
30 July 1999
—IN WHICH BARB AND UNPOET ACTUALLY DO LAND.

"What's that strange-looking nest down there on that rocky ledge?" cried Ingrid.

"Great Scott," Barb gurgled. "Looks like a tarantula's nest. And there's an incredible shrinking woman in it!"

A sudden gust of wind blew Barb and Ingrid right up against the spider's abode. Something like a flea jumped out and landed in Ingrid's hair. Ingrid screamed.

"It's me, Donna," a tiny, tinny voice hissed in her ear. But there was no time for further pleasantries. The floor of the canyon flew up to meet them.

They landed—Barb and Ingrid rolling with instinctive precision, exactly like highly-trained paratroopers. Instantly they sprang to their feet, and had just dusted off the Siegfried B. Hinkelheimer souvenir T-shirt, when UnPoet crashed on top of them.

"Thank goodness I landed on something soft," said UnPoet, stripping off his/her harness. "Well, bye for now, Unwise, Ingrid and flea. I'm out of here. I might write myself back in, later. Lamtumirë and aufwiedersehen!"

158

11

ARMAGEDDON??

UNEARTHLY MAYRA
31 July 1999

"Damn! Damn! Damn, damn, and more damn!"
cursed Mayra. Something had gone awry with
Barb's rocket. She banged her fists on the computer keyboards
in the control room of her secret lab, trying to find Barb's
location and failing. Villains, just like children, only enjoy
playing while they are winning the game. When something
goes wrong, their disposition couldn't get lousier.

She pulled out her automatic pistol and pointed it at the
head of her master engineer.

"Oh, no, please, forgive me, Senhorita, please, it won't
happen again!" he begged.

"Damn right," Mayra replied with an intonation that
could cut steel. After placing the gun back in the holster, she

pushed a switch that opened a trapdoor under the man's feet, dropping him into a well full of man-eating sharks. "Damn! I thought that was the crocodile well!"

The irate Brazilian beauty turned to the other terrified members of her personal staff, who had wisely decided not to tell her just yet that Lottie had escaped too. "I'm surrounded by morons!" she growled. She was always growling. Or barking.

"She's only my most formidable adversary and she slips away just like that? Well, I'll have to risk it. The opportunity is still too good. Double, triple security! If she shows up at MY WEDDING heads will roll!"

"WHAT!" gasp the TOATS readers. "Wedding? WHOM IS SHE MARRYING?"

"Who do you think I'm marrying, you pathetic clowns! I lied about the original plan! (What did you expect?) The original plan was to lure Siegfried into my claws and make him marry ME! I know, I know if we get married we will get out of the story. BUT THAT'S THE PLAN! He and I will get out of TOATS and start another story called 'Beau and the Beast'—in Portuguese!—where he will be MINE, where you will never be able to reach us unless you master the Portuguese verb system—and believe me, it's murder! That will leave you, bird-brained baboons, stuck in here forever, caged with your fake Nicolases, your Gabriel Yearns, your Ray Fiendses and Daniel de Liciouses and your . . . your Gunthers Whataretheirnames! yes! yES! YES!"

Gosh, the beast in her was getting more and more carried away. "It's ARMAGEDDON!" she screamed, "THE END OF TOATS!"

UNEARTHLY MAYRA
31 July 1999

("Aaaaargh!" cry the TOATS readers, in pain. They frantically read on.) Mayra, after systematically disposing of the competition—or so she thought, had set Siegfried up to be married to her by making him believe the wedding was just a scene to a new movie, *Poisson,*® where he had a small part. She'd told him he only had to stand there, look gorgeous, say a stupid line such as "Yes, I do," and get poisoned somewhere near the end. (That should sound convincing.)

Now Mayra and Siegfried were standing before the altar. He looked fabulous in his tuxedo—yes, the same magnificent tux Lottie almost fainted at for the last time—the LAST time, mind you.

Mayra was wearing a stunning wedding gown, her arm clamped to his like a vice, and cursing that moment when she chose a traditional wedding at Melbourne's "St Sanctimonius of Cheem's Cathedral", with two dozen bridesmaids, a choir accompanied by a philharmonic orchestra, so many flower arrangements that the cathedral's foundations were giving way, full coverage on all TV channels, the works.

Why hadn't she organised a simple, fast ceremonial in her grandfather's tent like the old man had advised her? Had she listened? Ooooh no! She just couldn't resist it, could she? She just had to show off, didn't she? With Barb on the prowl—and probably rescuing the other heroines who are too busy or hesitating or dematerialized or computerless to do it themselves, in her very field of action! Villains are soo predictable, aren't they? No matter how cunning, how brilliant, how ingenious they may be, they will always make one stupid mistake, won't they?

Mayra was soaked in perspiration, anxiously looking sideways, virtually expecting a horde of hallucinated TOATS cyberchicks to storm into the place and tear her to pieces, followed by an army, navy and air force of armed mercenaries to finish the job. "C'mon, c'mon, c'mon!" she was urging herself to finish the chapter before it was too late.

The priest started the service. "Dear brothers and sisters, we are here in the presence of God to unite this man and this woman ..."

"Never mind the preliminaries! Cut to the chase!" the bride barked. The priest, realizing from his experience that this could be another case of extramarital pregnancy, gold-digging or plain extortion, agreed to speed up the process and get the hell outta there as fast as possible.

"Do you, Siegfried B. Hinkelheimer, take this woman, Mayra, to be your wedded wife, to love and to cherish ..."

Fearing for her life, before the Reverend said "until death do you part," Mayra cunningly poked Siegfried in the stomach with her elbow as if cueing him.

"Yes, I do," he said, waking up. (He's such a fine actor he can give a hell of a performance in his sleep.)

"Do you, Mayra, take this gorgeous man, Siegfried B. Hinkelheimer, to be your wedded husband, to love and ..."

"Yes, yes, I do, I do, I do!" the bride yelled hysterically.

The priest cleared his throat, "Ahem," took a deep breath and ...

12

ST SANCTIMONIUS OF CHEEM'S CATHEDRAL

ORIGINAL BARB

3 August 1999

"The Obsession And The Story"—a long-running fan-fiction saga written by Siegfried's fans and unprofessionally riddled with "said bookisms".

The current state of the story: At this point in some indefinable time in the TOATS Universe, the characters are situated in several locations.

1) A church called "St Sanctimonius of Cheem's Cathedral" in Artificial Australia, where, unbeknownst to the other TOATS heroines, Mayra might or might not be about to wed Siegfried.

2) The floor of a canyon in Based-on Borneo, where Ingrid and Barb have just landed. Donna, flea-sized, is inhabiting Ingrid's hair and Ingrid does not know who Barb is because Barb is travelling incognito so that Mayra won't be able to track her down.

3) A mountain at some unspecified point in the TOATS Universe, into which Emily's plane is about to crash. (Airlines in TOATS being notoriously unreliable.)

How did Emily get aboard a plane? When we last heard of her she was voyaging to medieval England on a doomed mission, though making the most of the cruise by enjoying a swordfight and the embrace of a handsome Ogosh replica.

Clearly, some benevolent wizard must have realized she was not, in fact, Rosencrantz, and sent her flying back through the time tunnel to her own era. Whereupon, having narrowly avoided disaster she immediately invited it again by buying an Air Banana plane ticket. (It's called either thrill-seeking or masochism.)

4) Someplace in Implausible Ireland, where Lottie, now not only in the horrendous form of some version of Frankenstein's monster, but evil as well, is prowling the streets with malice aforethought .

5) A variety of places where the rest of the feisty gang are imprisoned or about to suffer an appalling doom unless they write themselves out of it. Which makes it A LOT EASIER to narrate TOATS because there are now only SIX neurotic but gorgeous fans to harass Siegfried.

UNEARTHLY BARB

3 August 1999

The priest took a deep breath, cleared his throat and said "I now pronounce you man and wife. (You may kiss the bride)," he added in brackets, for Siegfried's benefit. Now fully awake, Siegfried gave that heartbreaking grin familiar to all his fans, lifted Mayra's wedding veil with the tenderness of one who raises up some fragile bird or easily-bruised flower, and kissed his new bride long and passionately.

A sensation like fire sizzled through her. She thought the blood in her veins had turned to molten silver. As he slowly withdrew his mouth, Siegfried murmured softly so that only she could hear—"Liebling Mayra, zis is only ze beginning of ze ecstasy vich is to be ours forever."

And then Mayra woke up with a throbbing headache and remembered what had REALLY happened in the cathedral…

UNEARTHLY BARB

3 August 1999

The priest cleared his throat, "Ahem," took a deep breath and suddenly threw off his disguise. For an instant, unable to comprehend what had happened, Mayra gaped at him. It was her ex-master engineer!

"Aha!" he triumphantly cried. "You should have known you'd never get away with this. Rule Number Nine in that hallowed volume "Hackneyed Movie Scripts" states—"Rather than wasting bullets, megalomaniacs prefer to kill their archenemies using complicated machinery involving fuses, pulley systems, deadly gasses, lasers, and man-eating sharks, which will allow their captives at least twenty minutes to escape!" Mayra's ex-employee sneered. "And you lent me that book yourself! Fool!"

"But…" stammered Mayra, "it should have been impossible…"

"Not when the man-eating sharks were NOT HUNGRY,' said her enemy, "because they had just made a good square meal of half your personal staff! The sharks were already up to coffee and liqueurs. I helped them light their cigars and then I was OUTTA there."

"But—" stuttered Mayra, at a loss for words.

"Anyway," her tormentor continued smugly, "they are MAN-eating sharks, and I'm not a man!" So saying, she threw off the master engineer disguise she had been wearing under the priest disguise. It was none other than Mary O'Really?!

Mayra screamed an unprintable insult at the woman. She lunged forward with fingernails extended, but too late. Mrs. O'Really?'s henchmen (more disgruntled ex-employees of Mayra's) pounced on Mayra from behind, twisting her arms behind her back. Other henchpeople escorted Siegfried away before he could realize that a damsel was in distress, in case he should gallantly try to save her.

"Throw her in the you-know-where," ordered Mrs. O'Really?, "But first hit her on the head so that she wakes up with a thundering headache."

"That sounds rather unnecessarily nasty," commented one of the milder-mannered henchfolk.

"Yeah," said Mrs. O'Really?, who had forgotten how to sound Irish, "but I have to make this chapter match up with the previous one. Let's get a bit of continuity here."

"Okay," nodded the henchperson, obligingly hitting Mayra with her wedding bouquet and dragging her off to the nearest dungeon . . .

Meanwhile, back amongst the foundations of a deep gorge in Based-on Borneo . . .

"How unrealistic is this!" exclaimed Barb, as she and Ingrid staggered along together. "Here we are, you've been hanging from a thorn bush for several days, I've not had a bite to eat or drink for uncounted chapters, and we're still feeling fine."

"Didn't you eat the airline food?" asked Ingrid.

"Are you kidding?" scoffed Barb. "Call me old-fashioned, but I just don't go for sheep's eyeballs in puree of rat's brain."

"You're old-fashioned," said Ingrid. "Don't you know that's the latest craze in LaLa Land? Sun-dried tomatoes are so passé—"

At that precise instant, they both caught sight of a cave snuggled in the side of the gorge. A few rocky steps led up to the door, above which hung a sign reading "Tinfingers' Bar & Grill".

Inside the cosy Bar & Grill, crimson lamps glowed through a smoky atmosphere. Somewhere, a radio was playing jungle-type music (the patter of bongos, the clink of marimbas, fake monkey-shrieks etc.) Barb and Ingrid ordered everything on the menu, including a thimbleful of de-shrinking potion for Donna.

"That's better!" said Donna as she jumped out of Ingrid's hair and regained her normal size. "Thank you, Ingrid! Thank you—what did you say your name was?"

"Ehrm—" Barb had been struggling to gobble as much food as Ingrid, but it had been difficult, because she was still wearing the Paper Bag on her head. The lower edge, near her chin, was now stained with gravy. The trouble was, she could not remember her pseudonyms for more than a couple of minutes. As she spluttered forgetfully, inspiration hit her. "Unspeakable of Dementia," she offered.

As she shook hands with Donna, someone turned up the radio. "Here is the News," intoned a nasal voice. "The latest word from Artificial Australia is that Siegfried B. Hinkelheimer is marrying Mayra in Masquerading-As-Melbourne's 'St Sanctimonius of Cheem's Cathedral'."

The remainder of the news story was lost in confusion. It was as if a tornado had struck the Bar & Grill. Overturned tables flew past. When the dust cleared, there was no sign of Donna, Ingrid or Barb.

"Oh yes there is," pointed out the Head Waiter. He picked up a hastily scrawled sign from amongst the debris on the floor and read aloud to the stunned patrons: "Gone to rescue Siegfried. Sorry about the bill. Love from Donna, Ingrid and Unintelligible of Encyclopaedia."

Of course, if they had waited five minutes they would have heard the News Update— that Siegfried had, in fact, been rescued from wedlock already. But they didn't hear it.

Sprinting down the canyon in the direction of Artificial Australia, the three hasty Siegfried fans hailed the first taxi they saw. It screeched to a halt beside them, its doors opening invitingly. The vehicle happened to be bright yellow, its roof arrayed with a complex tangle of scientific apparatus which was topped by a large radar dish and what appeared to be a small crashed spaceship. Along the side doors was printed in large letters "TOATS. Relatively Safe Transport. More Fright For Your Fare."

"No!" moaned Barb, baulking when she read these words, "Not a TOATS taxi! The drivers are really weird…"

"Look, Unstable of Influenza or whatever your name is," said Donna firmly, "it's either this or Air Banana. How else are we going to get to Australia?"

Barb was first into the taxi. The other two were not far behind. "Take us to Artificial Australia," said Donna in a commanding goddess-like manner. The taxi driver turned around to leer at them. He grinned, revealing a double row of file-sharpened fangs the color of ancient bones. A voice like gravel rattling in a steel pipe exuded from the depths of his toad-like body. "Whereabouts in Artificial Australia?"

"'St Sanctimonius's Cathedral'," quavered Donna, whose confidence level had abruptly plummeted. "It's in Masquerading-As-Melbourne."

"How are you paying?" grated the toad.

"Charge it to Uncouth of Insomnia's account," Barb rashly volunteered. Surprisingly, the driver seemed satisfied. He pressed a button and a massive propeller rose out of the roof. Taking off vertically, they sped out of the gorge and away.

As the taxi screamed through the air on its way to Artificial Australia, the three Siegfried fans became aware that a fourth passenger was already occupying the taxi. She was sitting right beside them; a stunning brunette, wearing a blue silk evening dress and a necklace delicately wrought of gold filigree. Her fingernails, four centimetres long, were beautifully enamelled with tiny scenes from myths and legends of the TOATS Universe.

"Hi!" she said. "I'm Rachel."

"You look exactly like a typical Siegfried fan," said Ingrid.

"I am," smiled Rachel. "I'm heading for Artificial Australia to try to stop his wedding."

"Good," said Donna, "so are we. I'm Donna. This is Ingrid, and the one with the Paper Bag on her head is . . . um . . . Unwieldy of Umbrella."

UNEARTHLY EMILY
4 August 1999

Emily was heading towards a mountain as a passenger in one of the new-model chicken-powered Air Banana planes. In the seat next to her sat a gentleman with a remarkable resemblance to Siegfried B. Hinkelheimer.

Another clone! thought Emily, shaking her head in bemusement. Where do they all pop up from? Barb's Splingian Replicator Gun must be lying around somewhere with the switch jammed on...

She looked up.

"Omigosh!" Emily exclaimed, "we're heading for that mountain!"

"Siegfried" looked out the window. "You're right!"

Emily, ever so meticulous, noticed a thread hanging from Siegfried's jacket. "You have a loose thread."

Emily started to pull as "Siegfried" suddenly whirled around "No! Don't!"

Too late. The moment Emily pulled the thread, the Siegfried clone unravelled until he ceased to exist. Emily sat stunned with a tiny piece of tweed thread in her hand—she was alone with the plane and the fast-peddling chickens. (And, optimistically, the pilot.)

There was only one thing left to do. She stood at the edge of this post and looked below. Having found the chapter she was looking for, she closed her eyes and jumped into the great cyberspace void......

13

A LILY-PAD COFFEE TABLE WITH BRONZE FROG BASE

UNEARTHLY BARB
5 August 1999
An unintelligible message from Taxi Service H.Q. flashed across the TOATS taxi's digital navigational display. Everyone looked at the driver. "What does this message mean?" they chorused.

He shrugged. "Search me," he croaked, but they didn't take up his offer. Instead, they began a shrill, girlish conversation about hair-dos and make-up, until the driver pressed another button and the cab filled with sleeping gas.

By the time they had reached Artificial Australia the effect had worn off and they all landed, refreshed but with bad breath, in front of "St Sanctimonius of Cheem's Cathedral". (Which was astonishing, since the driver had also been asleep.) Just as they arrived, a TOATS Maxi-Taxi pulled up and out lumbered Lottie.

"That Brazilian trollop!! She'll rue the day she did this to me!" Lottie was still snarling as she unfolded her bulk from the Maxi Taxi.

In case anyone has forgotten what she now looks like, it is this: Her dress is bursting at the seams. From it issue arms and legs that look like moss-covered tree-trunks. She sports a splendid set of yellowed fangs and copious amounts of attractive facial growth. And she's got fine social skills and a personality to match. Yes; the old, wilting, fainting Lottie is gone!

"Cringe, Mayra!" growled the new, improved Lottie, pointing a taloned finger at the door of St Sanctimonius's Cathedral. "Tremble and cower! Because I'll tear you from Siegfried's side and rip you into small inedible fragments! How dare you try to marry him! You won't get away with this!"

The eyes of the other TOATS heroines bulged. "Ooh, have you gone evil Lottie?" cooed Barb in a muffled voice.

"What do YOU think, idiot?" snarled Lottie. "And get that thing off your head." She made a grab for the Paper Bag but Barb ducked just in time.

The others nodded knowingly at each other. "Totally evil," they murmured amongst themselves.

"It's time for VENGEANCE!" roared Lottie, straightening herself out to her full height of ten feet and flexing her hairy biceps.

"Oh yes, vengeance," chirped the others excitedly, like a startled flock of sparrows. "We're right behind you, Lottie. Go for it."

Just then, Emily doubled over, clutching her stomach. She fell to the pavement and began writhing.

"What's wrong, Emily?" screeched everyone except Lottie, who was evil.

Between agonised groans, Emily managed to gasp out the words, "Ate—airline—food."

"Oh no!" Rachel screamed in horror. "She must have eaten something on board the Air Banana flight. She'll never survive this!"

"Gosh, the poor girl must have been starving," said Ingrid. "What can we do?"

"Listen! She's trying to tell us something!" cried Donna.

Emily, whose face was rapidly turning green, groaned, "TOATS Survival Kit. In my handbag."

Without hesitation, the TOATS heroines emptied out Emily's hand-bag. Rummaging through the assorted lipsticks, nail files, free samples of perfume, combs, hair-pins, embroidered handkerchiefs, wrappers of boiled lollies, pieces of used chewing-gum, pictures of Gabriel Yearn and Ogosh, worn-out Siegfried B. Hinkelheimer videos, fake tattoos, trick plastic spiders, boxes of chocolate (empty) and palm-sized notebook computers, they finally found the box labelled "TOATS Survival Kit".

Without hesitation, the TOATS heroines emptied out the container. Rummaging through the well-thumbed back copies of "The TOATS Rule Book on Etiquette", the assorted alien weapons, the entire collected wardrobe of scintillating evening gowns, harem outfits, pirate costumes and swimwear, the TOATS Taxi Service vouchers, the open tickets for Air Banana, the aquariums of babelfish and a virtual pharmacopoeia of potions, they finally held up a small blue vial shaped like a teardrop.

"Is this what you need?" anxiously asked Rachel. "It's labelled 'Niceness Potion'."

"No! No!" moaned Emily, still rolling about on the pavement. "Not that! I need the bottle marked 'Antidote to Air Banana Food'."

In a trice, Ingrid had located the antidote. "One drop will cure her," said Donna knowledgeably. "These potions are very strong."

Rachel squeezed a single drop into Emily's mouth and she sat up.

"Right, I'm cured," Emily announced. "Now where were we?"

"Vengeance," prompted Barb. Everyone looked around for Lottie, but she was nowhere to be seen.

"I think I saw her heading for the doors of the cathedral," said Ingrid. "I hope she's in time to save Siegfried from being tricked into marriage!"

No sooner had she finished speaking than Lottie loped back out of the doors, holding something scrawny high in her left paw.

"The place is empty," she trumpeted, "except for this weedy cleaner. He told me the whole story. Mayra's little scheme was sabotaged at the last minute by her ex-master-engineer, Mrs. Oh Really! in disguise."

"Sounds credible," murmured the other heroines.

"Does that mean that Siegfried is safe?" asked Emily, hardly daring to hope.

"For the moment he is," Lottie replied. "But Mayra isn't. I WILL NOT BE DENIED MY VENGEANCE!" She gave the cathedral cleaner a shake. "Where did you say the Brazilian hussy was imprisoned?" she shouted in his ear.

"In the nearest dungeon," he squeaked.

"And WHERE IS the nearest dungeon?" barked Lottie.

"I don't know!" howled the unfortunate man.

"Put him down, Lottie," said Donna firmly. "This is Australia, you know. There are hardly any dungeons here. Dungeon-building people have only been living here for a couple of hundred years. Places like Europe, on the other hand, have been riddled with them for millennia."

"Didn't the indigenous Australians build dungeons?" yowled Lottie.

"No. They were more civilised than that."

"Does that mean the nearest dungeon is in Great Britain?" asked Lottie.

"NO!" shouted Barb, furiously scratching under her Paper Bag where fleas had got in. "There IS a dungeon in Artificial Australia! It's at my—er, I mean Barb's Outback Mansion."

As if it had been waiting around the corner (which it had) a TOATS taxi screeched to a halt right beside them. The driver leaned out the window on his elbow. "Anyone going to Outback Australia?" he enquired with a lascivious grin that showed a triple row of fangs gleaming behind his liquorice-colored lips. Casting aside the cathedral cleaner (to his joy), they all piled into the taxi (with Lottie on the roof-rack) and headed north.

On Original Earth:

Lottie, Barb and Tess sat huddled in a cheap and sleazy Internet café clutching plastic bags full of old video cassettes.

"I think it's time for a change of tense," said Lottie.

"Huh?" said Barb, half awake. "I've been feeling pretty tense lately…"

"No, the other tense. You know, past, present and future. I feel like changing it. In TOATS, I mean."

"Sounds cool. Go for it," Barb replied. "By the way, did you read what some bloke called Eric wrote on the SBH fansite yesterday?"

"No! What?" Tess asked.

"He said he thinks TOATS is silly."

"Silly!" gasped Lottie, bridling. "We'll give him silly…"

UNEARTHLY LOTTIE

9 August 1999

As the TOATS taxi heads north, the driver removes his "party trick triple row fangs" and pops another handful of liquorice into his mouth. Black drool trickles down his chin as he ogles all the gorgeous women through his Kemi-Kola® bottle glasses. He brushes the drifts of dandruff off his shoulders, straightens his gravy-stained tie and turns to smile lasciviously at Emily.

"You single?" he squeaks, his bulbous pimples glowing red.

"Sure, gorgeous," teases Emily, with her most seductive smile, "we all are. We need a man—a real man, to look after us. Think you're up to the job?"

The driver manages a single strangled splutter as his taxi careers off the road and crashes into a gum tree. Emily, Rachel, Diana and Ingrid push the doors open and half fall out into the dust and the midday heat.

Barb emerges soon after, frantically trying to mend a tear in her paper bag with a piece of chewing gum. "Where's Lottie?" she asks, just as the boughs above tremble mightily.

"Up here!" rumbles a foghorn voice.

Emily is dragging the scrawny, pimply little chap out of the driver's seat. "What's your name, idiot?" she asks.

"Eric," he answers.

"Eric?" screams Rachel. "Not the Eric who thinks TOATS is crap??"

"Well, yes," he says sheepishly. "But . . . " At that moment there comes a tearing crack as a huge bough breaks and Lottie comes hurtling out of the tree like a huge hairy bomb (Human Bomb).

"Ouch! What did I land on?" grumbles Lottie, lumbering to her feet and looking down. "Oops!" she says, brushing off a few minced morsels of Eric that cling to her backside. "Look, I've had enough of this! Siegfried's out there somewhere. Mayra can rot in her dungeon, but darling Siegfried—I just know he'll be pining for me. I must find him!" Lottie pauses momentarily to extricate Eric's Kemi-Kola® bottle glasses from between her huge buttocks before galumphing off down the road in a cloud of dust.

UNEARTHLY BARB
10 August 1999

Barb stands waist deep in cloud of red dust, shading her Paper Bag's eye-slits with one leaf-like hand. She watches Lottie galumph down the road into the heat-hazed distance. The blazing rays of the Australian outback sun sizzle. It is really the same sun that shines everywhere else on the planet, but it feels as if it is a lot closer, viz. at an altitude of about six feet. In its radiation, the piece of chewing gum with which Barb has been attempting to repair her torn headgear has melted. It hangs down forlornly and elastically, like a pink stalactite with a blob on the end.

"This red dust is ruining my outfit," complains Barb, who is wearing a tasteful safari suit of gold lame edged with mauve pom-poms. She is rapidly losing height as the long, pencil-thin heels of her spangled dance-pumps sink into the sand.

"Stop whimpering," says Emily briskly. Having suffered minor concussion in the car crash, she had just woken up from a brief bout of delirium, in which she had imagined she was on board an Air Banana flight. "You can't have everything," she continues. "Look, we have a nice shady tree to protect our complexions from those damaging rays—"

"The only tree in the entire desert," interrupts Barb bitterly, "and our taxi-driver had to run into it."

"Yes, but look at it this way," says Emily optimistically, flicking a stray piece of Eric's ear off her white satin evening gown, "yes, the cab may be a complete write-off, yes, we're stuck in the middle of the remote Australian outback, yes, two of the pom-poms on your safari suit have fallen off, but look at all the supplies we've salvaged from the taxi's trunk!"

"The taxi's what?"

"Trunk. Some people[11] call it a boot, goodness knows why—it looks nothing like footwear."

"True," concurs Barb, "but it doesn't much resemble an elephant's nose, either. In fact, the one on this taxi looks more like an elephant's backside. Painted yellow. Boot, eh?" she adds. "Why does footwear get mentioned so often?"

UNEARTHLY BARB
10 August 1999

Barb notices Rachel, Donna and Ingrid sitting contentedly in the shade of the gum tree. They have discovered a nice spot, free of dismembered pieces of taxi-driver. A radio retrieved from the taxi's "trunk" is playing opera. Through glacier-blue straws, they are sipping long, cool lime drinks, chiming with ice.

---

11 People in the Original UK, Ireland, Australia, New Zealand, South Africa, India and Hong Kong.

"How can you just sit there?" screams Barb. "Lottie's probably half a mile away by now! Do you want her to have all the Revenge to herself?"

"Revenge? What revenge?" Donna asks vaguely. "Pass the chocolate, Ingrid."

"The revenge on Mayra for trying to wipe us all off the face of the TOATS Universe so that she could marry our hero Siegfried B. Hinkelheimer!" screams Barb. "Have you gone completely—" Abruptly her tone changes. "Chocolate? Did I hear you say chocolate? Give."

Seconds later, Barb is sitting under the gum-tree with the other four devastatingly gorgeous TOATS heroines. As they munch their way through a couple of mega-bars of Fruit 'n' Nut, they pensively watch an army of ants marching away with morsels of taxi-driver.

"That ant looks familiar," says Barb absent-mindedly…

UNEARTHLY BARB
10 August 1999

"Well, will you look at that!" says Rachel with mild interest. She points with a well-manicured finger towards Eric's Kemi-Kola® bottle spectacles, which are lying on the sand next to the gas-tank of the disemboweled TOATS taxi. The drilling beams of the furnace-like outback sun, six feet overhead, have been concentrated into laser form by the thick lenses. Smoke is issuing from two blackened spots on the gas-tank. Molten metal begins to drip onto the sand.

"Do you think—" begins Donna.

"Yeah, maybe—" agrees Ingrid.

"We'd better leave—" suggests Rachel.

"Before she—" Emily wisely decides to suspend her sentence.

As one, the five cyberchicks spring to their feet, sprint across the sand with the speed of a thousand startled kangaroos and throw themselves behind a tall, rock-like formation.

There is a roar as of avalanches and volcanoes. Sand and miniature shards of taxi-cab shower upon and around the cowering refugees.

After about five minutes, Emily subtracts a door-handle from her ear, spits out a windshield wiper and shakes her head as if to clear it, "—blows," she concludes.

Barb jumps up and begins to perform Quiverdance®.

 **UNEARTHLY BARB**
10 August 1999
"What's to be so darned happy about?" demands Donna.

"I'm not happy. That tall, rock-like formation—"

"What about it?"

"It's one of those outback ants' nests . . . and they bite!"

An instant later, the cyberchicks are all performing Quiverdance® in perfect unison.

"This is ridiculous," howls Barb, her toes tapping as she frantically tries to shake ants off her long and sensuous legs. "We ought to be heading at top speed for the comfort of my Outback Mansion where Mayra is imprisoned in the dungeon. Instead, here we are lined up in a perfectly straight row, our arms stiff as ram-rods at our sides and our knees going up and down like string-puppets—"

"Yes, but we're very good at it," says Ingrid enthusiastically. "I think we ought to form a—"

UNEARTHLY BARB
10 August 1999

Just then another TOATS taxi hoves into view around the corner of a dune. It doesn't just hove into view, it hoves professionally, and with flair. Hoving is one manoeuvre TOATS taxi-drivers are taught to do well. The only one, in fact. Hoving is the sole pre-requisite for getting their taxi-license.

"Over here! Over here!" yells Emily, madly waving her feather-boa. Obligingly, the cab swerves towards the five dream-boats and pulls up, spraying them yet again with red sand, ants, shreds of vinyl upholstery, "®" symbols and fragments of radar dish. The beautiful women, slightly dishevelled, pile in.

"You from Ireland?" grins the driver.

"No! Drive to Barb's Outback Mansion!" commands Emily, "and step on—wait a minute," she adds suspiciously, "your name's not Eric, is it?"

"Naw." The taxi driver turns towards her sporting a rictus which is simultaneously ingratiating and ominous. "Not Eric. Ratchet."

"That's all right then," says Emily. "Drive on, Ratchet."

The wheels spin. Twin plumes of terra-cotta dust spurt up into the flat blue heavens like the enormous feathers of some gigantic bird. The radar dish on the roof hums, turning its bowl of a face to the north.

With a howl of retro-rockets the TOATS taxi becomes a yellow blur, a mere smear across the heart of the arid land ...

And as they travel towards Revenge, a name keeps mysteriously repeating itself in what's left of Barb's mind—"Siegfried, Siegfried, Siegfried..."

CRASH! At this point something broke. I mean, really broke. It was a vital DNA/data link between Original Earth and UnEarth. For eons afterwards the two worlds were unable to connect, and bits that had fallen off disappeared into black holes—

Some of them might have been TOATS chapters . . .

ORIGINAL DONNA
4 December 1999
Testing, testing 123? We might be back. Some of you might recall that a few months ago we had trouble with this site's host, wherein we . . . no THEY lost all the data.

Well, they did it again, so I moved.

It's been an atrociously complex operation; the monstrosity domain is so named due to its enormous size, and I've had absolutely no time to devote to it what with moving and starting a new job. Well, I'm getting settled in, and I've been able to reconstruct SOME of the old SBH feedback data. If time permits, I'll get as much of it back out as I can.

I'm bitterly angry with our former host about their destruction of several of my sites (SBH being one of them) and the new host does actual backups. Well all of which no one cares about of course, except that here we are again I HOPE to stay!!

Now, WHERE WERE WE??? I feel we deserve a good TOATS chapter or 10 . . .

ORIGINAL BARB
7 December 1999

Halleluija and zipiddy doo dah. She's back! Donna the goddess of the ether is back, towing our hero Siegfried with her. The Hinkelheimer Universe is saved.

Down with Evil Former Site Hosts and their mindless destruction of innocent sites. Their futile sobbing echoes hollowly through cyberspace. Hooray for New Hosts Who Back Up Data. Let us crown them with laurels and present them with lifelong membership of the TOATS Readers Club.

ORIGINAL DONNA
9th December 1999

Oh B. & RI, how I've missed you. All of you. Where are the others? Working on their latest screenplays no doubt, loitering around European airports or prowling the high seas staring through spyglasses for a glimpse of a battleship captain?

Yes, Siegfried our hero is again safely ensconced in his new domain.

186

ORIGINAL BARB
16 December 1999
HELLO DONNA, JULIANA, EMILY! All the familiar names . . . thank goodness, and all the familiar computer stuff-ups I love so well!
OK I admit it — this is more of a social site for me than an altar of worship. Sorry SBH, but, well, if you would only come online sometimes it would spice up our lives.
Now if only I could find those TOATS archives . . .

ORIGINAL DONNA
16 December 1999
My Bad! So sorry . . . the link was wrong. TOATS is now current up through 20th August 1999. My fear is that two months of it boarded the Oblivion Bus with the rest of the content that bit the dust at ******net (no I won't bad-mouth them here.)

However, if you have nothing but idle time, that's some damned funny stuff. I just had the pleasure of re-reading some. :) And I have to get those critics' reviews uploaded again, those are a gas.

Gadzooks! (LOL) go and read the authors' biographies . . . Lottie I think somehow I'd missed yours till now! I'm dying laughing. Ok, ok it's not Siegfried-centric but dammit it's phunny . . . and Emily, it's been so long since I gazed at your TOATS covers; are you ever coming back?

ORIGINAL EMILY
6 January 2000
It's been a while since we dreamed up an impetuous and outlandish escapade. I'll call up Air Banana Get-Aways and look for the harshest treks, most dangerous itineraries, and remotest points known to mankind.

I try not to be an alarmist. However, I am the kind of passenger who now requests a window seat in order to keep an eye on the clouds and a hand on the stewardess call button, expecting at any moment to relay some vital message to the pilots: Swing it a bit to the left, Captain, there's a cargo plane veering toward us! or, Why is that little flap on the wing shaking like that? Somebody get out there and do something!

Remember the last flight from Based-on Borneo? It reminded me of Einstein's theory that mass equals energy as Barb rummaged through her carry-on bag, gobbling up everything vaguely edible, and then flapping her arms vigorously, hoping that her capacity to transform food into heat would alleviate our doomed aircraft from what—judging from the weight of Tess's 500 Vulgarian sailors—was surely fatally excessive cargo.

ORIGINAL RACHEL
11 January 2000
The airline jokes were funny! I'll have to go look at the archives. I love fan fic!

ORIGINAL BARB
11 January 2000
Welcome, Rachel, if you haven't been here before! You sound like a person of great taste who knows a good laugh when she sees one! Stay tuned to this site. You never know what will appear. (And it is a pretty sociable site too, as you may have noticed.)

ORIGINAL RACHEL
15 February 2000
Oh My God! I just went over to the TOATS site. I'm in shock. I love the Romance Covers! Are you guys still writing that stuff? That is too funny!

188

ORIGINAL DONNA
15 February 2000

Hiya Rachel, yep TOATS still lives, although it's in some sort of suspended animation most days now. I'm pretty desperate for new chapters, but too damn busy with work and what free time I have for SBH stuff goes into the ongoing upgrades you're seeing around here. I know Emily's very, very busy right now too, those stunning Romance Covers are hers. We're kind of in limbo . . . :)

ORIGINAL BARB
18 February 2000

Rachel, you will probably also find yourself written into the TOATS story in the near future!

ORIGINAL RACHEL
18 February 2000

Write me in! That would be great. I wish I could write. But I've no imagination for that sort of thing. That's why I like to read. I can't believe the ideas that come out of people's heads.

ORIGINAL EMILY
16 March 2000

Since I have no desire to back track to find out exactly where we left them I figured this was as good a place as any to pick up the thread.

189

UNEARTHLY EMILY
16 March 2000

There are few things, Siegfried had discovered in his somewhat turbulent relationship with the opposite sex, which can compare to a frustrated TOATS woman. When a TOATS woman smiled in that thin-lipped, glittery-eyed way it meant that she'd gone round the bend, that the innocent had best flee screaming into the night. Any fates aligned against her had better assume new identities and start life over as ghosts in the Australian Outback. But you see that's exactly where he was; trapped in the Outback as he pondered what was going to happen to him next—

Mayra tucked stray lock of hair behind one shell-like ear and glared at Siegfried's back. Usually this view of his nice, um... of his posterior and swimmer's shoulders was one of her favorite bits of scenery, but today it just added to her mounting frustration.

Silently fuming, she pretended to read her emails and review the past episodes of TOATS. New dress, new perfume, make-over, new hairstyle and, new sexy sling-backed shoes on her feet. All that and Siegfried had not batted a single, sinful eyelash her way. Being distant was one thing but this was ridiculous. When she'd entered the room, he'd just handed her a cup of Darjeeling tea and launched into one of his totally outrageous scenery-chewing monologues from the movie *LOL*. Now he was burrowing through one of the TV Movie of the Week scripts that littered the lily pad shaped coffee table (with a bronze frog as the base) And Mayra was about ready to strangle him and call the murder just another TOATS episode.

What did it take to get him to make a pass at her? She knew he wasn't gay. Gossip from the TOATS women, and Bonnie at the front desk at ICM, was that he also wasn't the least bit repressed. In fact, they described him in terms that had Mayra's knees quivering and her palms sweating. Apparently he was terrific, for every woman BUT her. Clearly this one called for desperate measures; feminine wiles Mayra had never had the unmitigated gall to use.

She prepared herself, reapplied her Indelible® Ruby Red lipstick, and bided her time. And then it happened. Yes! If there was any way for Siegfried to injure himself it would come to pass—it was TOATS's Law, so it was inevitable that pawing through the scripts like that should result in a paper cut.

Her heart leaped when he yanked his hand away from the script and sucked the injured digit between those marvellous lips. It seemed like risking the fates. If she did make a move, Mayra was sure that some lunatic TOATS woman would come bursting in and abduct him. She'd already found out how hard it was to kill the authors, and even when they were presumed dead, they still kept coming back. Well, that was okay because and she had three new Eeyore® suits to wear in future episodes.

But today she had him alone. With a locked door. And the temptation was too great. Four quick steps across the room and she could gaze up into his soft, azure eyes, letting her own cerulean orbs speak volumes of comfort as she gently pulled his finger out of his mouth and tugged his hand down to have a look.

Siegfried took on a certain terrified expression generally reserved for being trapped in sinking battleships with no means of apparent escape as Mayra raised his injured hand to her crimson lips …

UNEARTHLY BARB
17 March 2000
WHAAAAT? Mayra has Siegfried with her trapped in the dungeon of the Luxurious Outback Mansion???? And not only that, she has my favorite coffee table. She'll have to pay for this.

ORIGINAL BARB
17 March 2000
Great episode, Emily! I had a good laugh!)

ORIGINAL EMILY
17 March 2000
Thanks Barb. By the way that coffee table really does exist somewhere in Australia. That's where the designer lives. I saw it in a catalogue; it was 3,600 US dollars.

UNEARTHLY BARB
18 March 2000
"Here we are at Barb's Outback Mansion, last visited in TOATS Book 1, Chapter 33," announced Donna virtuously. (She had been studying the TOATS archives during the taxi ride. Anything to keep her mind off the way Ratchet was driving.)

Bruised and travel-sick, four seductive damsels crawled from the vehicle euphemistically called a taxi. There before them stood Barb's Outback Mansion, half-hidden behind a screen of mulga, wattles and eucalyptus. The walls of Connemara marble and the golden chimneys were gleaming. Late afternoon sun glinted from the topaz window-panes and the diamonds discreetly studding the walls.

"Hey, where's Ingrid?" Rachel asked.

"She was flung out when Ratchet did that hundred-miles-per-hour wheelie back there," explained Emily, who was walking like a robot, having made a lot of recent contact with the insides of the wildly swerving cab.

"Yeah, why did you spin the steering wheel so suddenly, Ratchet?" Barb asked, leaning in at the driver's window.

"Something big in the road," grinned Ratchet. "Had to avoid it."

"Something big? Oh, you mean Lottie. Now that you mention it, I did see her stomping along the road looking like some kind of nightmare. That morphing potion of Mayra's sure lasts a long time. Great value. I wonder where she picked it up."

"You pay now," grinned Ratchet. "You owe fifty bucks."

Barb put her hands in her pockets and felt around. An innocent look came over her face. "Oh yeah, that's right," she said lamely, "I remember now. Lottie's got the money. She said she'd pay the fare."

"But Lottie didn't ride in the—" began Rachel. "Ouch, what did you do that for, Barb?"

"Off you go now Ratchet," said Barb brightly. "You're sure to find Lottie behind that last dune." The taxi's whirling tires sprayed up loose dirt as it sped off into the distance, leaving everyone looking like a series of sand sculptures.

UNEARTHLY BARB
18 March 2000
Barb's grey-haired English butler answered the door.

"Pleased to see you, ma'am," he began with a genteel bow. "Would you like me to make up the guest rooms?"

"No time for that now, Peeves," peremptorily snapped Barb. "Just tell me this—is Mayra still imprisoned in the dungeon?"

"Why yes ma'am," articulated the butler, "and her gentleman friend accompanies her."

A long pause ensued, during which Barb's face took on the terrible gaze of a latter-day Medusa and Peeves appeared to have been turned to stone.

"Pardon me," Barb said softly, "but did you say 'gentleman friend'?"

"Er yes, ma'am," said Peeves, backing away. "Forgive me if I erred, ma'am, but the prisoner specifically mentioned that if a gentleman answering to that description should come calling, that you, ma'am, would want him ushered into the dungeon at once."

"And you BELIEVED her?" shrieked Barb, like a tornado which has suddenly reached its culmination. "What description?" she added in an ominous tone.

"Well, er—" the butler cleared his throat, "he is arrestingly handsome, though not in the traditional sense of the word. And somehow he has the kind of demeanour that is suggestive of secret or private knowledge. His masculine poise and self-assurance is very seductive. He simultaneously exudes power and tenderness. In any movie scene he outshines all other actors with his charisma, even when he is neither speaking nor moving, and as for his voice—the modulation, his ability to infuse his speech with a tender, soothing quality, or to exact esteem by uttering a single command…"

"STOP!" bellowed Barb. But even as the words left her perfectly-formed lips, she found herself thrown to the floor and trampled by three pairs of fast-moving stiletto-heeled shoes whose owners were heading straight to the bowels of her mansion. "Just be careful of the coffee table!" Barb called weakly after their departing backs.

ORIGINAL EMILY
19 March 2000
"Inspired brilliance Barb! Loved it!" Emily replied, wiping tears of laughter from her cheeks.

UNEARTHLY LOTTIE
30 March 2000
Barb picked herself up off the floor. She tugged around the crumpled paper bag so that the eye-holes lined up with her eyes just in time to see Lottie crawling in through the door on dusty hands and knees. Her once elegant (if somewhat bag-like) Its MySaki® frock was a wreck—stretched beyond recognition and hanging

loosely from her gorgeous body by a few threads. For Lottie had resumed her true appearance—lean and athletic, tawny muscles rippling like a tigress, waist length tresses of auburn curls and "loser" stamped unmistakably across her face.

"Urgh, what's that yukky stuff you're dripping all over my marble floor?" shrieked Barb.

"Oh that," answered Lottie despondently. "That's just Ratchet. I had to kill him."

"Oh, not again!" snapped Barb. "I do wish you'd refrain from killing TOATS taxi drivers—it's getting so hard to find the staff these days."

"Well, he asked for some money for the taxi and I didn't have any," wailed Lottie. "What else could I do? And by the way, has anyone found Siegfried yet? I need to see him or I'll die!"

"For a start," snapped Barb, ignoring Lottie's desperate plea, "you can stop leaving bits of Ratchet on my floor. Peeves, go and get a mop. I must say, Lottie—I'm very disappointed to see that your monster persona has gone—I much preferred her."

"There was a newspaper", sobbed Lottie, "in Ratchet's taxi . . . I saw it and the monster in me just shrivelled up. Look . . ."

She handed Barb the tattered paper. "AUSTRALIAN PRIME MINISTER SURVIVES ATTACK BY MONSTER WOMAN!" proclaimed the headline.

The article continued, "Sporting an egg-sized lump atop his balding pate, the Prime Minister spoke to the press after a lightning recovery. 'It was nothing I couldn't handle,' he spluttered. 'Now I intend to get on with the job, concentrating especially on my government's aim to boost Australia's sporting prowess. I'm a man with Vision! I think of the Big Picture!' he gurgled, spraying enthusiastic spittle. 'By rapidly increasing greenhouse gas emissions and thereby speeding up global warming we plan to have Sydney underwater in five years. With all that practice, think of the probable achievements of our swimmers in the 2008 Olympics!'"

"Boo hoo," sobbed Lottie. "You'd think I could get something right . . . why didn't I go back and squash that annoying politician? Oh Barb . . . please tell me—is Siegfried here? I want to die in his arms."

"First things first," said Barb briskly. "You need another frock . . . Peeves, haven't you finished mopping yet? Leave that—go fetch me that worn-out Armanaleg® outfit I put in the OpShop® collection bag, there's a dear. It's eons old Lottie dearest, and way past its use-by date, but it'll look just divine on you, darling . . ."

Barb pushed open the dungeon door as a cleaned-up Lottie whimpered excitedly at her back.

"Oh Barb, is Siegfried really here? What a beast you are! What will he think of me wearing last-season's Armanaleg®?"

The door swung open with a loud groan to reveal Siegfried, Donna, Emily and Rachel sitting obediently squashed together on the settee beyond the lily-pad shaped coffee table while Mayra, dressed in beige twin-set, knee-length tartan skirt, thick stockings and sensible brown shoes, served them English Breakfast tea from a sensible brown teapot.

"Good golly!" gasped Barb (totally failing to notice that Lottie, after one glance at Siegfried, had toppled limply to the floor).

"Now, now, my dear", scolded Mayra, turning a makeupless face towards her, "we'll have no blaspheming here. This is a nice house and we're all nice people. I'm sure you'll feel better after a nice cup of tea and you must try one of my nice coconut macaroons."

"Oh dear," moaned Rachel, turning towards Barb. "I found that Niceness Potion in the TOATS Survival Kit in Emily's handbag (last mentioned around Chapter 70) and I slipped some in Mayra's Darjeeling."

Barb sniggered. "How cruel you are, Rachel darling. That's a fate worse than death if ever I saw one!"

Siegfried sipped his tea politely, a faint smirk on his face. "Ihr albernen Dinger[12]," he muttered, then turned to Mayra with a smile. "You look lovely in that outfit, Mayra—my sweet little Schickse. It really suits you."

"Arrgh!" screamed Emily, whipping out her cell phone and dialling frantically. "Is that Marcus Oldman®? I need a delivery—instantly—one mohair twinset, mauve please, a tartan skirt of sensible length, flat shoes—you know my size—oh yes, a nice teaset . . . and a Bible. Address? Barb's Outback Mansion, Australia . . . what? . . . oh, I don't know . . . find Sydney, then head west a thousand miles—you can't miss it . . . "

Suddenly a huge, booming crash echoed through the mansion as the front door was battered in. Moments later several women burst into the dungeon (one of them falling flat on her face, having tripped over the prone form of Lottie).

---

12 You silly things

Oh horror—these were no incredibly svelte liposuctioned TOATS women with eating disorders! They had curves and bulges in normal feminine places. Some of them were wearing what appeared to be Q-Mart® jeans. All of them were having a bad hair day.

"Enough!" they cried. "This must stop! Siegfried, you're coming with us. We demand that you make another good movie! A movie we can review and discuss with sensibly controlled enthusiasm on a new, sensible SBH site. A site that can never be sullied by stupid TOATS women! A site that can be visited by MEN . . . without embarrassment!"

The indignant women (Julie, Rev Inc, Sheila—whom have I missed?) triumphantly dragged Siegfried away. The dungeon door slammed and the bolts shrieked and clashed as they were slid home.

Donna, Emily, Barb and Rachel clung together fearfully as Mayra stood bravely on top of Lottie, reciting passages from the Bible. They heard the fearsome roar of flames and the terrifying crash of toppling marble columns. Trapped, defenceless and heartrendingly beautiful, they waited—sobbing—for the cruel end.

Barb's mansion, consumed by raging fire, toppled in upon itself, as dingoes (scenting a Sunday roast) howled horribly, and clouds of black smoke rose up to blot out the fierce desert sun.

UNEARTHLY EMILY
31 March 2000

Barb, an ever-elegant beauty resulting from a remarkable gene pool, excellent breeding, and thousands of dollars' worth of plastic surgery, was angrily picking bits of curtain and leather bound book out of her still smouldering hair. Her wide eyes crackled with hostile energy and her mouth was pursed in a tight little line. "You pathetic fools!" Barb raged. "Look what sensible shoes will do to you! You should have known that common sense would cause this place to implode! Where the hell are my crocodile slingback pumps?!"

Suddenly, out of the corner of her eye Barb spotted shards of glass and bits of bronze frog. "NOOOOOOOO!!!! MY COFFEE TABLE!" She knelt by the shattered pieces and lovingly picked up shards of frog leg. (Which reminded her that they hadn't had dinner yet.) Rachel and Emily surveyed the damage while Lottie sat on the blackened earth piecing bits of paper together.

"Well, I hope Lottie didn't kill off the last TOATS taxi driver or we're really stuck out here," Emily mused, as she tossed her long raven hair, sending chips of fine china everywhere.

"We'll never find them," Rachel said dejectedly. "We need some of that might and power Mayra used to have before she was almost married to Siegfried. How did you get so powerful, Mayra?" Rachel asked, turning to where Mayra had last been seen. "Oh," she added.

Mayra had disappeared.

"I seem to recall seeing her blown away by the force of the catastrophe," said Lottie, "which means we can't ask her how she became so powerful. Hey Donna, you're the web goddess, can't you just wave your magic wand and get Siegfried back?"

"Oh, that broke ages ago," said Donna. "In fact I lost control of this entire fabrication way back when. Do you think I'd be sitting here in the rubble of a burned-out mansion in the middle of the desert, if I had any say in the matter?"

Barb had uncovered a single unbroken teacup, still with the dregs of some Darjeeling in it. Rachel rescued a slice of stale bread from the remains of the pantry.

"Let's share this around while we make a plan of action," Barb suggested, sitting on a heap of broken marble and toasting the bread at one of the many miniature fires which still sprang like stained-glass lilies among the ruins.

As they passed around the tea-cup, the five women watched the sun setting yet again beyond the distant horizon. A dingo howled.

"Never fear," said Barb in the tone of a jolly Girl Guides Leader, "we can't possibly be stuck here forever."

"Yes," agreed Emily. "It's not over till the giga-bytes."

UNEARTHLY BARB

31 March 2000

"Do you think it's possible someone might marry Siegfried some day?" Lottie asked wistfully into the brittle silence.

"Naw. Yeah. Maybe."

There was a pause.

Some masonry fell down and Peeves emerged from behind it.

"I found your old sampler, ma'am," he said, holding up a square of cross-stitched linen, charred at the edges.

"Well done, Peeves," Barb said bracingly.

"What does it say?" Donna craned to make out the words.

"'On UnEarth, As On Original Earth,'" read out Barb, "'Everything Is Subject To Change. Anything Is Possible.' Good heavens, did I embroider all that?"

A light breeze arose, fanning the cyberchicks' sensible clothes and tattered glamor. Down the wind came a sound so dim and far off it might have been their imagination.

A soft and rhythmic thudding, as of hooves approaching across sand . . .

OR

A rumbling, a kind of revving continuous thunder, like an engine, the engine of a souped-up automobile . . .

14

A THINKING WOMAN'S CRUMPET WITH GOBLIN EARS

On Original Earth, in March 2001, a new contributor innocently posted her first comment to the Siegfried B. Hinkelheimer fan site.

ORIGINAL MARJORIE
posted by Marjorie Braithwaite from England on 31 March 2001

How can I get hold of German videos, or German films that Siegfried has made? Some of his best stuff is out there, and I can't touch it. Someone, please help! Those old Hinkelheimer movies must be within my grasp in this day and age! We're seriously SBH deprived in this country. Great web site, great new info. Well done! Can you help me too?

A brief detour for some background info:

About a year earlier, Barb had expressed her desire to edit TOATS into novel form. The other contributors had been enthusiastic about the idea and eager for their literary efforts to be included. In reply to Barb's email airing the notion Juliana had written:

"GREAT IDEA!

LOVE IT!

MOOUAAAH!"

On discovering that they were both writers, Barb and Juliana had begun sending each other chapters from stories they were working on.

ORIGINAL BARB
18 May 2001
Juliana! I sent the chapters to your email address but the Mailer Daemon returned a message that they could not be delivered!!! We need Siegfried to slay the evil Mailer Daemon.

ORIGINAL DONNA
19 May 2001
Barb . . . you're alive! :) Where have you been? Nosily, I want to ask.. those aren't *the* chapters, are they? How's that TOATS undertaking going, or isn't it anymore. I wouldn't be surprised if it sapped your strength. Haven't heard from you in so long :(:

ORIGINAL MARJORIE
20 May 2001
I'm wasting too much time on this site. My real work is writing novels, and I'm getting behind. If only I could get one made into a film starring Siegfried . . . !:

ORIGINAL DONNA
20 May 2001
Marjorie, the next best thing is to . . . write a TOATS chapter!! ;-):

ORIGINAL MARJORIE
21 May 2001
I've looked at the TOATS, and I have to say that you're all wasting your time. There are publishers out there who'd pay good money for that!

I daren't start yet, not with a book to finish, but once I'm doing a crime novel I shall definitely work on some input. When I'm stuck for ideas, I know where to come! Naturally the hero of my latest novel has piercing blue eyes, but hey, he could be based on anybody!

ORIGINAL EMILY
21 May 2001
Novelizing TOATS was Barb's project I believe. I'm into screenplays and just had the most wonderful Saturday talking to some producers and writers whose credits include *Terminator, Aliens, The Rock, Con-Air, Jumanji, Armageddon,* etc. Learned a lot and it kept me motivated to get my script done!

ORIGINAL MARJORIE
22 May 2001
Emily, next to meeting SBH that has to be one of the best ways to spend a Saturday. Pity you don't live in England. A small film company here is looking for a female scriptwriter to write a screenplay for one of my books!

I used to be incredibly focused, before I saw *Das Rat* for the first time last year . . . .

ORIGINAL JULIANA

27 May 2001

Oh Barb Dearest.

I was expecting your instalments. Had a very vivid dream about you the other night, regarding villa at the seafront and a handful of bare-armed shifty-looking types. . . but it turned out to be a-oh-so-civil-get-together-round-the-table-for-a-cup-of-tea routine. And I actually saw your face, and there was blonde hair. I just wonder how correct I could have been?

My email address has delivery problems or so they say. Should be sorted by now but send them to my old one.

Looking forward to it!:

ORIGINAL JULIANA

27 May 2001

Regarding Marjorie, what is this intriguing connection between SBH and female writers?

More than half of the die-hard fans who have lumbered these pages with their outpourings in the past four years have literary ambitions in various stages of completion and recognition.

Very intriguing . . .

Siegfried most be some kind of thinking woman's . . . what . . . I do not know . . . there is no proper word . . . crumpet . . . over-aged muse.

Someone oughta write an article about it. Or at least link up with some Writers' Forums on the net.

ORIGINAL MARJORIE

28 May 2001

I've no idea why so many SBH fans are creative, but since we are, we should get together and write him a cracking good script for a change! Any suggestions for supporting cast? William Dafriend® must be in it somewhere, but with his toes back on.:

206

JEMIMA
30 May 2001
I suggest a new version of *Twotooth the Vampyre*® with Siegfried in the lead role!

ORIGINAL JULIANA
30 May 2001
Now that was a yum yum idea, Jemima.
Scope for a lot of innocent virgin blood here.
Vampire teeth will go so well with his pointed ears.

Siegfried only need to dye his hair black and voila, he is Sicilian. No problems whatsoever, Marjorie.

ORIGINAL MARJORIE
30 May 2001
Has he got pointed ears, Juliana? I don't believe you. I couldn't have missed pointed ears!

ORIGINAL JULIANA
31 May 2001
Marjorie, he does have pointed ears, very goblinlike, you haven't done your homework!

ORIGINAL MARJORIE
31 May 2001
No, I hadn't noticed goblin ears, and I absolutely refuse to believe it. His ears are usually hidden under loads of hair, so how can you be sure. Name a film where his ears look pointed and I'll go and check for myself. This is most upsetting!

ORIGINAL DONNA
31 May 2001
This is hilarious. The pointy-ear thing came up . . . it must have been years ago, I seem to recall someone mentioning a good title for checking that out but . . . maybe *Judge Mental*, he has short hair in that, his ears might be visible. In fact I think they are (off to check..):

ORIGINAL DONNA
31 May 2001
Well, all my images from *Judge Mental* cleverly hid the ears from side-view, so I sat there trying to think of other short hair titles . . . here is an image from *The Creep* in which only a hint of pointiness is visible . . . hmmm . . .

ORIGINAL MARJORIE
31 May 2001
Donna, how could you do this to me? I looked up his photos in *The Creep*, and in the one with the old man his ears did look a teensy bit pointed but, certain that it was a trick of the light, I went and looked at the *Forbidden* photos.

I wish they had been!

It's true. There he is, kissing Jaqueline Bassett-Hounde on the video cover and suddenly all I could see was this big pointed ear. I'm going to lie down in a darkened room for half an hour and try to pretend it was all a bad dream. I'm in such a state I haven't even spelt the wretched Jaqueline thingummy's name right, but I don't care any more . . .

ORIGINAL JULIANA
31 May 2001
Marjorie, not to want to further your distress (I cannot think why goblin ears would have such an effect on you. (... I think they are rather fetching)
But there are lots of pics in Das Rat section where he is standing in profile ...
... especially the third from the beginning.
With a beard it looks even more fantastical!

ORIGINAL J.
31 May 2001
And third pic from the left in *Airforce Fun*!

ORIGINAL MARJORIE
31 May 2001
Thank you Juliana, that's ruined *Das Rat* for me. A goblin with a naval cap on. And if you're going to make things worse by telling me about *Airforce Fun*, where I thought he was delicious, at least have the decency to leave your name! Perhaps it's my problem. Why don't I like goblin ears? I'm now going to try and work this into a really good science-fiction scenario!:

ORIGINAL EMILY
31 May 2001
LOL He's the Goblin King ... Marjorie you made my day.

209

ORIGINAL DONNA
31 May 2001
Marjorie, thanks you have me laughing out loud here. I have managed somehow to block out the ears, or else points don't bother me. I know, how about a Star Trip® tie-in??

ORIGINAL MARJORIE
4 June 2001
Hey, my birthday's 17 June, must mean Siegfried and I are soulmates (or seulemates as he'd say!)

ORIGINAL JULIANA
4 June 2001
Talking of birthdays.
Just noticed that Siegfried and Moompsie. H.® share the SAME birthday 10 June . . .

Now that is the most sick cosmic joke the gods ever played on me . . .

I cannot express in any civil words what I feel about Moompsie but I am beginning to think I was right all along, way back in the past, calling Siegfried vain, stroppy and thoroughly unpleasant.

Marjorie . . . you are very safe and pleasant though being born in the end of the Geminian sign.

ORIGINAL MARJORIE
4th June 2001
Well, if he's been reading this site lately, he won't think he's got much to be vain about! Relieved to know I'm okay. Perhaps Siegfried was a premature baby, and is really safe and pleasant . . .

210

ORIGINAL JULIANA

4 June 2001

Marjorie, I did not mean to class you as a safe person, far from it, good heavens no, I meant you were safe in terms of not being classed as vain, shallow and unpleasant as our new unholy alliance of Siegfried and Moompsie.

Actually if you look close enough, yuck, they do resemble each other. They both got major problems with their noses, or at least used to have since Moompsie went under the knife.

Anyone seen The Cap'n . . . a good chemistry between them?

ORIGINAL JULIANA

4 June 2001

I am going to self-destruct in a mo, but I want to take back all I said about Siegfried and E.

Siegfried's rising sign is cancer, one of the most sensitive, sympathetic signs ever. Elizabeth's rising sign is Scorpio, the combination Scorpio/Gemini is bound to be finicky in her case making her appear more arrogant than is the case of Siegfried who should be much more sensitive.

So all the people born on 10 June do not write to Donna and complain that you are not vain and shallow . . . (It all depends on all the signs and all the positions in the zodiak.) I was making a snap hasty judgment, based on raw emotions and my own rising sign today says I should not be making judgements like that.

Not that I am into these sort of things . . .

ORIGINAL MARJORIE
4 June 2001
Too late, Juliana. You've probably offended everyone born in June already. When I saw The Cap'n, or Thrill Schmooze as it was called on my video, I couldn't believe Moompsie H.'s® nose. I honestly didn't know until then that she'd had it fixed. The chemistry between the pair of them was rotten. He should have had someone born on the 17th June rolling around in his bunk, I'm sure the air would have crackled then.

What on earth makes you think I'm not safe? Hope you haven't been reading the wrong sort of books!

ORIGINAL JULIANA
4 June 2001
Probably right, but what can you do. Still miffed that E. H. has a rising sign in Scorpio. Just like me! We are both complete cows. And it has nothing to do with Siegfried.

ORIGINAL JULIANA
5 June 2001
Since it is Siegfried's big day, soon I run his birth details through a astrological character assessment thingy on the web. (They are very accurate, pinpointed me being a stroppy cow within the first line . . .)

He sounds like a great guy. VERY communicative, sensitive to others need, quickminded and with a great sense of humor. He loves talking, talking, talking and should be good at expressing himself.

The most curious but telling part though was that he seems to have trouble judging people and situations (i.e. prospective roles . . .) and will often be taken for a ride and be misunderstood completely.

ORIGINAL MARJORIE
5 June 2001
There you are then, Juliana. You've been mis-understanding him all these years, and now you have to take back all those negative things you said about him!
Tell me where this assessment thingy is on the web. I must find out if I'm equally sensitive. I certainly like talking . . . Clearly this explains his dreadful errors of judgement regarding roles.

ORIGINAL DONNA
5 June 2001
Marjorie you've earned yourself a spot as a TOATS heroine ;) Now if someone would just pen that chapter . . .

15

TOATS REBOOTED

ORIGINAL EMILY

5 June 2001

Donna, since it's been so long — should we start a new TOATS book?

ORIGINAL DONNA

5 June 2001

Absolutely Emily! "TOATS, Book II"! "TOATS, The Sequel"! "TOATS II: The Revenge of (Inse)"[13] (only works if you actually know about the abbreviation.;))

---

13   Insert Your Name Here.

ORIGINAL BARB
5 June 2001
I vote yes. Now that Lottie's actually ON THE INTERNET!!!!!, plus we also have JULIANA and MARJORIE with us, it bodes well for "TOATS the Sequel".

I still haven't got over Emily's desert chapters. I laugh every time I think of them. Where *haven't* the TOATS wenches been in their pursuit of Siegfried? We could venture into new realms . . . What do you think, Donna?

ORIGINAL BARB
5 June 2001
I instantly demand my old persona back, to start with. Svelte, narrow-waisted, a gorgeous seventeen-year- old red-head, with legs that go all the way to Valhalla (sorry Juliana, did you have copyright on that immortal line?).

This time Siegfried couldn't possibly resist me. Bwah-ha-ha! I'll whip him out from under the very noses of . . . oh, sorry darlings (sweet smile) of course I could never be so selfish to my friends. Nice stilettos, Emily, great outfit, Marjorie. Gosh Donna I love your hairdo . . . As for you, Lottie and Juliana —

ORIGINAL DONNA
5 June 2001
Svelte! Yes, we're back in peak condition for the reunion of the TOATS cast, I also insist. This might be the only way we get Lottie out of giant troll mode, or whatever had happened to her last. I'm going to have to go and re-read to figure out where in blazes we were. New realms?? Well... we haven't been to space yet... have we? Oh, dear . . . :

On Original Earth:

Where indeed, had the cyberchicks ended up in the last instalment of TOATS? Barb wondered, as she swung idly on her office chair. She clicked back through Donna's online archives.

There it was! In the last chapter a band of 'normal' Siegfried B. Hinkelheimer fans had blown up the Outback Mansion and dragged Siegfried away, leaving Barb unscathed in the ruins with Emily, Rachel, Lottie, Donna and the faithful butler, Peeves.

ORIGINAL MARJORIE
6 June 2001
I've read some TOATS but haven't quite got to grips with it. Before I can take part in what is obviously a great and creative adventure, can someone run the general idea past me. Can I be a blonde in it? And young again? Maybe not. Sophisticated more mature type might make a change from the rest of you. I'll be tempting him away from red-headed sirens with my wealth of experience, plus a read of one of my books for when he runs out of ideas!

ORIGINAL JULIANA
6 June 2001
One of your books Marjorie . . .
- Poor, poor Siegchen, he is in for a lot of new experiences in the next few chapters . . .

217

. . . well according to his cosmic map he is very easily bored so I guess the battle between mature oracles and redheaded fussy vixens is already lost.

Nice to have you back fellow redheaded Barb. You can borrow my legs if you want now and then but I am indeed copywrighted as a surly bitch.

Hope someone, Emily or Barb could write a chapter to give Marjorie the gist of things . . .

Now I know he is chatty I have put him into an entirely new perspective altogether, I am gonna be unbearably schmaltzy in the coming month. To such an extent you are gonna wish the bitch back.

ORIGINAL MARJORIE
6 June 2001
What do you mean, chatty, Juliana? I didn't see him talking. Anyway, just go out and buy an outfit that's too small for you and you're away.

Personally, I wish he'd cut his hair. Do most people prefer him with long hair still? Am I the only one who likes it thick but shorter, as in Constable and Young Lady®, British Are So Impatient® etc.

Yes, please do give me a starting chapter for TOATS. Glad to know he's easily bored. Makes for more fun.

ORIGINAL JULIANA
6 June 2001
Sorry Margret but I have all his secrets at my very fingertips. He had such a lovely cosmic map, one of the loveliest ever, not many bad points at all.

Only naïvety but that is SO sweet in a man. Especially at that age. He is creative, an eternal child, or so they put it. Being an eternal child he can full well wear his hair like a cherub stuck in a vestal virgin's budoir . . .

I am a like a born-again Christian these days . . . now schmaltz off back to work. And I am not being sarcy . . .

On Original Earth:

Hmm, thought Original Barb as she finished reading the previous posts in her office. Juliana's really getting into these astrological analyses. And what's with Marjorie preferring short hair? Come on! Doesn't she know that every proper romantic hero has Flambio®-lously long tresses?

She wondered what had been happening on UnEarth during the long period from 31 March 2000 to 6th June 2001, when the cyberchicks had been rattling around the Virtual Cosmos like loose cannon, dangerously unsupervised by their Original Selves. Where, for example, had Juliana been? Had the Icelandic red-head survived Mayra's trap? Was she still stuck passionlessly on The Island at the Top of the World with Thor the Sinewy and Thor the Mighty, or had she somehow managed to convert those two gorgeous Vikings from their platonic ways to her own brand of foul-mouthed lustiness?

At that moment a new episode written by Emily flashed onto her monitor. Barb read it at speed, after which she found herself in a state of perplexity.

There doesn't seem to be any kind of link from the old episodes to the new, she mused. She began to conjecture about the events that must certainly have occurred between the last chapter, set in the ruins of UnEarthly Barb's Outback Mansion, and Emily's recent scenario.

Presumably the "normal" non-TOATSian Siegfried fans who had invaded the mansion would have conveyed their hero to a secret hideaway in some far-off place like—oh, for example, Rio de Janeiro[14], where they would have left him to enjoy life, believing him to be safe from obsessive fanfic writers. (In this assumption they would have been seriously underestimating the opposition.)

Loitering among the burned-out remnants of the Outback Mansion, the Hot Cyberchick Babes would, no doubt, have pretended that they neither cared where Siegfried was, nor intended to track him down behind each others' backs – all the while privately plotting to be the first and only one to find him . . .

It seemed they all possessed indestructible credit cards with limitless funds, so after they had found accommodation in some luxurious hotel they would have hired private detectives to trace Siegfried. It would take them a long time, working separately, but in the end they would have discover the hideaway's whereabouts and made a bee-line for it (Barb leaving Peeves behind at the mansion to supervise the rebuilding).

Satisfied that she was well on the way to inventing a way of segueing what had gone before with what was to come, Original Barb sighed contentedly and leaned back in her office chair. Being cheap and unstable the chair tilted right back and suddenly overbalanced.

As Barb lay slightly stunned on the carpet staring at the ceiling, she pondered the natural law which ordains that the moment you start to think everything is going well is the point at which it all goes pear-shaped.

Next she returned to considering probable events on

---

14 (Replica Rio)

UnEarth during the past year.

Due to Air Banana's unbelievably low-cost fares, by now the airline would have knocked most of its rivals out of the skies (literally) and would now dominate the UnEarthly aviation industry. Still keeping their missions secret from one another, the Siegfried-chasing beauties would book separate flights on the dreaded airline. None of them would guess that they were — dangerously — all bound for the same destination. It was all very risky.

There were so many intriguingly unanswered questions. Would everyone arrive safely at their destinations? Would they have aged at all during the past year? (Not likely.)

And what about that new cyberchick, Marjorie?

16

MARJORIE TRIES
A TOAT

UNEARTHLY EMILY
6 June 2001
TOATS —The Next Adventure
Marjorie had made up her mind that when her
vacation came, she would spend it seeking adventures. She'd
always wished for adventures, but they had avoided her.

At nights, when she'd been up late researching her latest
spicy novel, her Icelandic friend Juliana used to ring her up
and relate some surprising thing that had just happened
to her.

Juliana, whose full name was "Juliana Snow Queen and Nordic Goddess", had followed Siegfried B. Hinkelheimer to Iceland in a Viking ship and reigned as a Scandinavian deity, or she had witnessed Barb dragging Emily out of a swimming pool in Greece with Siegfried precariously hanging from a balcony above, or at the Pink Elephant Bar in Almost Africa had made friends with strangers, who turn out to be no less than a half dozen Siegfried clones, as well as "Nick Birdhouse" and "Gabriel Yearn".

It all sounded terribly glamorous and thrilling, so when Juliana phoned from her holiday house on the Island at the Top of the World, proposing that she and Marjorie should go on an adventure together, Marjorie couldn't refuse.

After bidding a regretful farewell to Thor the Sinewy and Thor the Mighty, both now utterly beyond redemption, Juliana caught the next Air Banana flight to England.

She was soon sitting in Marjorie's parlour enjoying a cup of English Breakfast Tea® and discussing plans with the author of naughty books.

Their first problem was where to begin their adventure. Marjorie was longing for the sight of water and ships. She wanted to sail around some harbor and feel the tug and pull of the tiller.

Juliana, however, protested that that was no way to spend a vacation. The thought of wearing clam diggers was repellent to her, she said, and she complained that at the beach their only chance of adventure would be Marjorie's capsizing the boat or robbing a lobster pot. She insisted they should go someplace more exotic. And so, for several weeks, they fought it out.

Juliana gave a great deal of consideration to her clothes; the question of what she should wear on vacation was uppermost in her mind. When Marjorie said she thought it was nothing to worry about, the Icelander snorted indignantly.

"YOU wouldn't! If I'd been brought up in a schooner, and had hair like a Broadway blonde, I wouldn't worry either. Donna says you look exactly like a British spy in disguise." Marjorie had never seen a British spy, with or without a disguise, and she was intrigued.

For this adventure Marjorie bought a second-hand suitcase. It was covered with the labels of hotels in Forged France and Sham Switzerland, and she thought it looked worldly.

"Marjorie," Juliana said, "if you carry that bag, you will be a walking eyesore. Louis Futon® doesn't close till eight. We can still make it."

"Juliana," Marjorie said sternly, "I have as much right to carry a second-hand bag as a new one."

"I was thinking", said Juliana, looking at Marjorie rather doubtfully, "it might help a lot if for the first week you acted as my secretary. Having a private secretary would naturally give me a certain importance."

Their departure day approached and they were still undecided about their destination. Marjorie suggested they leave it to chance. "Let's write down the names of the places we want to go to and put them in a hat. The name of the place we draw will be the one we go to!"

225

Juliana reluctantly agreed. What mainly disturbed her was the thought that the places Marjorie picked were not likely to be fashionable. "I have a terrible fear," she declared as she admired her French manicure, "that, with this method, we'll wind up in some boring suburban shopping mall."

"I wouldn't mind. My main worry is not getting to meet Siegfried B. Hinkelheimer," said Marjorie.

"Oh, no need to worry about that," Juliana replied. "No matter where we go, we are sure to bump into him eventually. It's one of the rules of this particular cyber-universe. An immutable natural law of UnEarth, in fact."

Friday night found them prepared for departure, and at midnight they held their lottery. In a pillowcase they placed twenty slips of paper, on each of which was written the name of a place. Ten of these places were selected by Juliana, and ten by Marjorie.

Juliana dramatically rolled up her sleeve, and, plunging her bare arm into the pillowcase, she drew out a slip of paper and read the choice aloud . . .

UnEarthly Marjorie

UNEARTHLY MARJORIE
6 June 2001
"Rio de Janeiro!" squealed Juliana excitedly. "That's brilliant! Quick, to the airport immediately."

Marjorie felt it her duty to bring her friend down to earth. "Neither of us speaks Portuguese, and all the young women there are very voluptuous and sexy. Don't you think it might be wiser to go somewhere where we might stand a better chance if, as you claim, we're going to bump into Siegfried the instant we get there?"

Juliana gave Marjorie an icy stare, her eyes as hard as diamonds. "I don't have a problem with Rio. Stop thinking about yourself all the time. Pick up your Louis Futon® bag and follow me."

During the plane journey Marjorie put on a pair of horn-rimmed spectacles and scraped her luxurious dark hair back into a bun, so that everyone would know she was a secretary, but the moment the plane landed she took the pins out of her hair, removed the glasses, shook her head and tried to pretend she hadn't noticed the gasps of admiration from all the tanned young men standing around the airport.

Juliana looked a bit peeved. "That's odd. I thought Siegfried would be here already. Look, there's a bar over the road. Let's try that."

Inside, the bar was dark and hot. A fan moved lazily round on the ceiling overhead, and the music throbbed as the local people danced wildly with a freedom that was pretty excessive by English standards.

All at once the newcomers both noticed a group of in the corner of the room. In the centre of the group was a man with long dark hair, streaked with grey, and as he caressed the arm of one particularly attractive girl next to him his amazing blue eyes turned in the newcomers' direction.

"It's him!" Marjorie gasped. "It's Siegfried."

"Well, who did you expect?" demanded Juliana. "Tarzan®?"

"What's he doing here?"

"Search me, or rather don't. Leave that to him please."

She sounded a bit annoyed, and Marjorie guessed that her star sign was in the wrong ascendant or something. As the two travellers were talking, Siegfried moved slowly across the room towards them, a smile playing around the corners of his mouth.

"Did I hear you asking what I was doing here?" he asked softly.

Juliana pushed Marjorie out of the way, but the Englishwoman kept her eyes locked onto his, in case he preferred mature wisdom to leggy youth. "That's right," she said with a dazzling smile. "I expect you've got a boat round here somewhere, which you use for smuggling, or giving girls trips on. Girls who are searching for a plastic surgeon, that sort of thing."

He nodded thoughtfully. "Good idea," he drawled. "I hadn't thought of that. Maybe I could make a film about it sometime. Right now, I'm busy running guns for the highest bidder."

"Isn't that rather dangerous?" Marjorie asked, English to the core.

"Of course, but I like danger."

Marjorie felt a shiver go down her spine. This was her moment. Now was her chance, and she wasn't going to blow it. "So do I," she said firmly.

Siegfried narrowed his eyes thoughtfully, and stroked his chin as though he thought he had a beard, when in fact he only had some five o'clock shadow. Still, it was a good gesture.

"I haven't had enough rum to fancy you yet," he whispered. "Wait around until I've finished the bottle, then we can go back to my house and have astronomical flex."

Marjorie glanced at Juliana. "I do think it's a pity that sometimes it's impossible to make out every word he says, but I'm willing to give astronomical flex a try."

Juliana grabbed her companion by the arm. "It takes three to flex, I've read about it in a book some freak sent me, so I'll come with you."

"Hope he's drunk enough rum for the pair of us," Marjorie remarked, just as Siegfried walked a little unsteadily towards them.

"Ready girls?" he asked with a beautiful, if slightly drunken, smile.

"Yes!" shouted Juliana, but Marjorie knew that it was just for her that he'd got so drunk.

"Should be quite a night," he murmured, and then they found themselves being jostled and pushed through the dark, humid streets of Replica Rio in the middle of a crowd of beautiful Brazilian girls.

"Lucky he's a keep-fit fiend," Marjorie muttered to Juliana.

All at once they were there. In front of his huge, incredibly large . . .

UNEARTHLY JULIANA
6 June 2001
. . . collection of very good Portuguese Rum.

"Now this is what I call DRINK. And a very good year too. Scuse moi Siegchen, but I think I just will have a fiddle with these thingies first, what do you call it in Germanglish again. I forget . . . " said Juliana, diving into the heap of bottles. Her hair sticking out into all the four wind directions. Like a Lappgirl on Speed. No, not like, she WAS a Lappgirl on speed.

"I knew she would take the bait. . ." smouldered Siegfried conspiratorially. "I planned it specially. She always takes the bait.

"Easily diverted. So coarse," mused he further, and placed a very muscular, tanned arm around Marjorie's shoulder. She tried hard not to blush.

He let out a burp seething of Rum.

He leant forward, fixing his blue eyes into Marjorie's brownish.

"I hear you know things . . . Very special things. A book . . ." he whispered, revealing a very prominent sort of—

"SHE KNOWS NOTHING," interrupted the Lappgirl coarsely, but still managed to belch some Rum. "SHE TAKES MY NOTES. THAT IS ALL SHE KNOWS."

Marjorie knew she would react like this. Taking all the credit for all her research notes the last thirty odd years. Not for nothing had Juliana let her come with her on her great adventure.

The Englishwoman was prepared though and let her well-manicured hand rest inside her bag. . . She gave Siegfried a tiny nod, indicating that she was indeed the one who knew but before he could register this the door burst open and in came . . .

UNEARTHLY BARB
6 June 2001
. . . in walked Barb. I say "walked" when in fact I mean "fell". She was, as usual, squeezed into an impossibly small pair of high-heeled shoes, which caused her to overbalance with monotonous regularity.

"I had to come," she snapped irritably, picking herself up and removing the odd cocktail umbrella stuck through her mohair cardigan. "Someone's got to provide a little guidance around here. You!" Barb cried, whirling on Marjorie, fire blasting from her insanely beautiful eyes. "Can't you keep your hair under control? One moment you have hair like a Broadway Blonde, the next moment you're scraping your dark tresses into a bun!"

"Tough luck, sweetie, replied Marjorie casually. "I happen to be born with chameleon hair."

At that instant Barb noted to her amazement that Marjorie's hair had turned to a delicate shade of heliotrope.

"Damn!" Barb muttered jealously, between clenched teeth. "I always wanted chameleon hair." Then she rounded on Juliana. "As for you! she trumpeted, "now we all know why you wear that horned Viking helmet everywhere you go. The horns are secretly filled with rum. It's disgusting, you sot!" She added, "Give us a swig."

"Sorry", belched Juliana, "I have an appointment to keep, elsewhere." And she winked conspiratorially at Siegfried.

"Siegfried! I didn't know you were here!" gasped Barb, taking a step towards him and collapsing into the lap of a handsome, tanned Portuguese model.

(Model aeroplane, that is.)

"Who left this model aeroplane in my path?" she screamed, endeavouring unsuccessfully to disentangle herself from a bunch of wires.

"How should I know?" replied Emily, studying her fingernails with an innocent air.

"Hey, how did you get here in this bar with Siegfried?" Barb asked, her insanely beautiful eyes narrowed in suspicion.

"I followed everyone, of course," said Emily. "It wasn't difficult, since you all made such spectacles of yourselves. Except Siegfried," she simpered, smirking at the handsome film-star.

He bestowed on her a tender glance from his penetrating cerulean eyes, and immediately everyone else started thinking of how they could get him alone. Their cogitations had not yet reached fruition, when all of a sudden . . .

UNEARTHLY LOTTIE

7 June 2001

. . . all of a sudden, in burst the whole of the Vulgarian Mafia! But to explain this strange turn of events we must go back several hours when, somewhere far above the Atlantic Ocean, Lottie (gorgeous in sapphire silk by Lagerpint®) sat staring out of a plane window at the softly rolling cloudscape, painted gold by the evening sun. She felt sure she was the only one of Siegfried's regular female leeches who knew his present whereabouts.

"Oh, how romantic—Rio!" she sighed, "and I'll have him all to myself for once… well, that's if I can stay conscious and not swoon the instant I look into those heavenly blue eyes".

Suddenly an Air Banana plane hurtled past the window, upside down and with both engines ablaze. A familiar figure trailed from a broken window, held only by her exquisitely elegant Lacquer® scarf that had snagged on the window frame.

"That's Donna!" gasped Lottie. "Oh my God, I hope she's not on her way to Rio! Oh well, she won't get there before me—serve her right for trying to save a few dollars with a crap airline."

Lottie looked down at her Bananovyyflot® menu just as a potato-faced attendant came down the aisle. "Cheeken or feesh?" she asked.

"Fish, thanks", said Lottie. As the tray was plonked down in front of her Lottie looked up to see, with dismay, right behind the attendant, (Inse)! Swinging her shapely hips (Inse) sauntered past with a sneer. She was wearing a little Goatee® number—a black rubber strapless bustier and tiny matching mini skirt.

"Good grief, I thought we'd killed her off ages ago," muttered Lottie, but she couldn't help a smirk when she saw that, despite the wonders of modern plastic surgery, the scars where she'd had bits sewn back on were still visible.

Lottie lifted the cover on her tray and stared down at her meal. It was a whole fish, floating in orange-colored grease. Its scales were patterned in dots and dashes that looked strangely like full stops and commas, acute accents and diacritical dots. Its little mouth that, not so long ago, was mangling any number of languages, gaped open.

"My God, it's a babelfish," said Lottie, pushing the tray away after only one bite. She peered around at the other passengers and cringed into her seat. The plane was full of heavy-jowled men wearing five o'clock shadows and shiny suits, and carrying violin cases.

Suddenly she discovered she could understand the words spoken by the men seated behind her. Whereas before dinner they'd been conversing in Vulgarian, after eating the babelfish they now appeared to be talking in badly mangled English.

"Ve must to get our hands on zat book or ze big boss he vill angry be. Ze new edition of ze TOATS Book of Rules on Etiquette—only vun copy. Zat genius Juliana—she vurking on ze book many year. Ahh… Juliana!"

The thug paused to wipe the drool from his several chins. "Yes, she, and zat ozer woluptuous voman—ze nubile Marjorie." (Copious amounts of drool.)

"Vy ze big boss vant a damn book?" asked a henchman.

"Ahh, not jus eeny book. Zis book ze secrets of ze vorld hold! And more important—ze man who has zis book vill ever be encircled vith lustful leggy tarts in designer frocks. Ve know zis, for ze only man who now has zis book is Siegfried B. Hinkelheimer! Ve going to blow him avay!"

"Oh my God!" inwardly shrieked Lottie. "A whole planeload of Vulgarian Mafia… all hunting after Siegfried! I must warn him!"

UNEARTHLY EMILY
7 June 2001
Meanwhile, back in the Rio bar—

"Nobody Move!" shouted a Vulgarian. The whole place quickly filled with heavily-jowled men wearing five o'clock shadows and shiny suits. Marjorie was happy to oblige since she was the one currently in Siegfried's arms.

Juliana made a valiant attempt to remain upright. "I—I'd be happy to shhhtop mooooving if the room would shhhtop swaying back and forth."

Barb gave Emily a nudge. "What?" Emily whispered.

"The plane." Barb whispered back. Emily shrugged not comprehending. "The plane! The plane!" Barb whispered louder. Emily still looked at her blankly, but before Barb could explain her cryptic message the Vulgarian shouted, "NOW!"

Fifteen violin cases snapped open and to the ultimate horror of the group, they began to play their violins.

Badly.

Barb, Emily, Juliana, Siegfried and Marjorie dropped to the floor, eyes closed and hands clasped tightly over their ears to prevent their eardrums from exploding. The Vulgarian ringleader laughed a menacing laugh.

"What in Justin Sain's name is that!" moaned Barb as the glass beading on her mohair sweater started to shatter. A few more moments and their group would be rendered unconscious by the horrible sound of the violins.

Juliana exclaimed, "I'd rather have sax than violins!"

Just as Emily thought she would faint, a glimmer of recognition lit up her eyes. THE PLANE!

She slowly reached for the Portuguese model aeroplane's remote-control unit just inches from Siegfried's rear end. As tempting as it was to reach a bit further, she stuck to the task at hand and grabbed the remote control. It may be their only chance—it was a chance she had to take. She adjusted the dial on the remote, said a silent prayer and pushed the little yellow button.

Then another noise could be heard. Faintly at first but steadily growing louder and louder still. It was the unmistakable sound of an Air Banana plane about to crash. The room shook to its very foundations; the sound of ripping metal filled the air and as the dust settled an eerie silence came over what was left of the apartment.

The dazed occupants opened their eyes and shook debris off of their expensive ensembles. The first thing they beheld was Donna checking her Lacquer® scarf for snags and adjusting her micro mini saying, "That was Artsybushev's Concerto Cantabile For Violin and Strings®, if I'm not mistaken."

At that very moment Lottie burst into the scene of destruction and mayhem. "Siegfried, LOOK OUT—THE VULGARIAN MAFIA is—after—you?" She warned a bit too late. Lottie caught sight of Donna and stomped her stiletto heel into the rubble. "Damn it woman, how did you get here before me?!"

Emily turned to Barb and gave her a big smile. "I got it! The plane!"

Barb narrowed her eyes and shoving the mangled model aeroplane in Emily's face said, "I meant THIS one!"

Just then....

Another brief detour:
On Original Earth, Marjorie quickly composed her cyberchick bio.

236

UNEARTHLY MARJORIE'S BIO:

Marjorie was born on the wrong side of the blanket, due to a careless nurse who failed to make the bed with the correct hospital corners. Traumatised by this she's been obsessed with the finer points of English etiquette and grammar ever since.

Aware that her tenuous connections to the most important family in the land make her a target for many strange people anxious to put her on the throne, she's led a chameleon-like existence attempting to blend in with many different kinds of people as she flits around the land. Following Darwin's theory of evolution, her hair has also adapted to her lifestyle.

In order to try and disguise her blue blood she writes un-mentionable books, which make her the object of desire to many unmentionable people. Since she exists mainly on a diet of liquid lunches she is exquisitely slender, but a little pale. The only solid food she ever consumes is the canapés at the Buckingham Palace Garden Parties, where she sits below the salt.

And now back to the story . . .

UNEARTHLY MARJORIE

8 June 2001

. . . just then, Siegfried staggered to his feet, despite the fact that Marjorie was trying to keep him on the floor, because he'd fallen on top of her and she didn't want anyone else taking her place. "What's the problem?" he asked, his blue eyes bemused.

"It's the Vulgarian Mafia," repeated Lottie, anxious for her moment centre-stage. "They're after Juliana's book."

Siegfried's eyes lit up, partly because he'd accidentally stuck the fingers of his right hand into a shattered light socket. "Not the TARTS Rule Book on Etiquette?" he gasped.

Barb fought back a sigh of irritation. It really was a pity that he still had such a bad grasp of the English language. "TOATS!" she shouted.

Siegfried was beginning to look thoroughly confused. "I don't usually eat breakfast, and I never have toast. But it's kind of you to offer," he added, in a very Son of God tone of voice.

Donna chewed absent-mindedly on the end of her Lacquer® scarf. She could see that the Vulgarian Mafia were regrouping, and trying to find their violins again. "Quick, we must stop them playing," she shouted.

Original Marjorie

UnEarthly Marjorie

"I know," cried Marjorie. "Siegfried, you must sing them a carrot, like you did to those dreadful people in that horror movie."

"I can't sing carrots," he said apologetically. "Will a carol do?"

For the first time Marjorie understood what he'd said in that movie. "Of course, a carol, that's what I meant," she said nonchalantly.

Not for nothing had she sat through thirty of their idol's dreadful films. She knew what had happened to the bad guys in that movie, and sure enough as the handsome German started to sing, the tough men of the Vulgarian Mafia began to fall to the floor once more, their eyes closing in preparation for a truly mind-boggling death scene.

"Quick, vee must get out of here," shouted their leader.

"I think he shaw the movie too," slurred Juliana, and as the men turned tail and ran, the cyberchicks gave Siegfried a cheer.

Carried away by the applause, he would have gone on singing, if Juliana hadn't shoved The Book under his nose. "Here it is, Siegfried, the key to your schucshess," she mumbled. "It's an incredible book and I . . ."

"Don't listen to her," cried Marjorie, pushing the leggy Scandinavian beauty out of the way. "This is the book you want to read Siegfried. It's one of my own, and it's all about . . ."

She bent closer to him, and whispered into his (pointed) ear.

Siegfried went straight into heavy breathing mode again, and all the other girls glared at Marjorie with intense dislike.

"I'm sick of hearing about her damned book," snarled Emily. "Come on you lot, we've got to stop her."

When Marjorie had finished whispering, Siegfried looked thoroughly over-excited. "I don't get scripts like that from Sox®," he said huskily. "Where can we go, so that I can read this alone with you and a bottle of rum."

At that moment . . .

UNEARTHLY BARB
8 June 2001
. . . at that moment Barb, unaware that a couple of cocktail umbrellas were still transfixed in her mohair cardigan, two model aeroplane wings were projecting from her shoulder blades and a propeller was stuck on her nose, was surveying the situation.

She noted to her satisfaction that Lottie had already fainted, and it was only chapter eight[15]! The famous scriptwriter lay on the floor like some gorgeous, exotic blossom with petals of sapphire silk. While no-one was looking, Barb arranged an abandoned violin case over her face so that Siegfried would not notice how exquisite she looked.

"That's One," mumbled Barb to herself.

Grabbing Marjorie by the elbow, she exclaimed, "Marjorie, sweetie! Did you notice the terrible misprint on page 138 of your book? You can't possibly let Siegfried read that part— you'd lose all credibility!"

"Misprint?" gasped Marjorie, snatching her book out of Siegfried's hand. "What page did you say?"

"256", said Barb helpfully. "Or it might have been 674, or 890 ..."

Frantically, Marjorie started rifling through the pages.

"That's Two," the beautiful, long-legged red-head said softly, preening the shattered glass beading on her mohair cardigan. "Hey Juliana! If you think Siegfried's collection of very good Portuguese rum is a discovery, wait till you see what he keeps in the cellar!"

As soon as Juliana had rushed downstairs into the slimy basement optimistically called a cellar, Barb hastily slammed the door at the bottom of the stairway, suddenly deaf to the shrieks and Viking curses that began to emanate from that subterranean dungeon.

"Gosh, am I being a little too evil?" she thought with an uncharacteristic pang of guilt. She dismissed the notion as she

---

15 Barb wasn't very good at maths.

made her way back to Siegfried's cocktail bar, where Emily was apparently absorbed in making some strange apparatus that looked like another model aeroplane . . .

That'll keep her occupied for some time, thought Barb. *Now for Donna.*

"Hey Barb, where's Juliana?" Siegfried asked, as Donna poured him another tot of rum.

"Er—" stammered the delectable teenager, "she's watching a few re-runs of 'I Fantasize About a Genie'® in your home cinema down in the cellar.

"What?" shouted the Sexy Saxon. "But that could drive her mad! Do I hear screaming?"

"Not to worry," soothed Barb. "She's screaming with laughter. Now, Donna, darling," she said cosily, "I KNOW you must be suffering from jet-lag after that DREADFUL Air Banana flight. I'd like to show you my patented jet lag cure. Just come with me—"

At that exact instant, there was an explosion of sound like an over-stoked locomotive and something came hurtling through the fumes straight towards Barb.

"No you don't!" bellowed (Inse). "You had forgotten about me, eh? Overlooked me as usual, eh? Think I can't speak for myself just because I'm not a real person, hmm? Well, I'm awake to your stupid tricks! I know what you're up to!"

"Oh really?" said Barb, trying to sound calm, but desperately looking around for some handy method of escape from the wild-eyed (Inse).

"It's no use looking for escape!" screeched (Inse).

"It's impossible really," agreed Barb, trying to humor the angry nymphette. "I seem to have a propeller in front of my eyes. I can hardly see a thing." She gave the propeller an experimental spin. Abruptly, a motor dangling from her left knee sprang to life. Her feet left the ground and she rose vertically, up into the toxic atmosphere.

"Help! Help!" shouted the stunningly seductive siren, as she was lifted over the heads of the amazed Siegfried, Donna and (Inse). But too late—the model aeroplane drove her straight out the window, and . . .

ORIGINAL EMILY
9 June 2001
Barb you propeller wielding maniac. Do I have to wait to post again? Do I? Do I? I'm laughing so hard right now!

ORIGINAL BARB
9 June 2001
Post away Emily! Any time!:

ORIGINAL JULIANA
9 June 2001
Just post away Emily!
But please take me out of that dreadful cellar. And what is 'I Fantasize About a Genie'?

Is it a Hinkelheimer produced homevideo or what? Someone tell!

ORIGINAL DONNA
9 June 2001
You women are killing me!!! I can't wait for the next instalments :) So proud that I crashed (literally) another party! lol . . .

ORIGINAL MARJORIE
9 June 2001
I thought "I Fantasize About a Genie" was a song, Juliana! What makes you think B. Hinkelheimer produces homevideos? Do you have inside information on this? Hope they show him practising his toe-chopping persona. (Must visit a therapist soon.)

ORIGINAL BARB
10 June 2001
A belated *Freulich Geburtstag* to Siegfried, and congrats to Marjorie and Emily on their recent TOATS chapters. I keep thinking it can't get any funnier, but it does. Post away whenever the inspiration hits, writers — we don't have to take turns!

UNEARTHLY JULIANA
10 June 2001
"Hey Chiiccckkss!!!" Juliana's voice splurted out of the cellar. "Someone's left his home movie video collection all over the plaaaccceee!!" Juliana the Red twittled like Sweety the Canary®.

Siegfried choked on his rum.

"Maaarrjorriee. You might get some new ideaass!" continued the Redhead sugarlippedly.

244

In a flash, notebook and pen deftly in hand Marjorie was down that cellar. Barb was notwhere to be seen now. Only a sad trail of cocktail parasols remained. And a weak whirr came from the outside. Donna, Lottie and (Inse) followed Marjorie. Hogging the steps, pushing and jerking to get there first.

"Not coming Emily?" shouted Donna.

"Naahh. Gotta get this plane done so Siegfried can have a little play later . . . " Emily busily gluing a tiny little sidewing onto the porphproian thingy in the back of the model plane.

Screeches of delight from the cellar.

This is simply marvellous! thought Marjorie. *I guess this is what one jokingly would call a studio . . .*

Juliana guided the group very professionally. Upon hearing this, Siegfried was down those stairs in a tick.

"No not you sweetie. Shouldn't go there if I were you . . . " Juliana coaxed him gently.

SLAM BANG

The door shut!

GULP

"Vass datt de kii you svallaved!" cried Siegfried.

"Heheheh! Now who's been a naughty girl," brayed Juliana like a hyena.

"Did ya svallav datt key?"

Watt. Can't understand a word you are saying but never mind. Let's have a little chaattt! thought Juliana pushing him up the stairs.

"Watt?" Siegfried looked curious.

Juliana had never heard that word said like that before. Not even by him! "Yur accand is vorse dann mine!" she exclaimed. (Finally found someone to knock at last!)

"Hey wiseguy," she added, "let me show you my book!" She shoved her book right up his face.

"I hope it's like Maarjoriee's book!" His breathing went haywire.

From the cellar could be heard Marjorie's plummy voice advising rather anxiously . . . " No Donna . . . Lottie . . . that does not make much sense, does it now. Silly girls!"

"Never you mind Marjorie's book," hissed Juliana. Her Viking helmet horn leaking rum at this stage. She slurped as she spoke. "An actor of your sizeable standing . . . I mean—scuse moi—someone of your stature . . . as an actor you see . . ."

In that very moment . . .

UNEARTHLY EMILY
10 June 2001
Juliana and Siegfried's conversation on the stairs was interrupted by a loud "WOOOHOOO!" as the porphproian thingy on the model airplane began whirring faster and faster.

"It works! It works!" exclaimed Emily as she did a little Macarena® happy dance. Ages ago, Emily had decided to learn a new craft that would be useful in future TOATS episodes and subsequently enrolled in a correspondence course at the University of Whatzihoosits and Thingymabobs. The aircraft she had so meticulously created for her final exam contained parts from an Air Banana plane, a Thigh Thumper®, a satellite dish, a Pocket Multitool®, and an automatic drip coffee maker, and it was powered by the porphproian thingy that came from a TOATS taxi. Thinking ahead, she always carried spare parts.

The newly repaired model airplane lifted into the air and began to circle the room.

"Duck!" Emily yelled frantically. "Duck! Duck!"

"Mallard or teal?" Siegfried enquired.

Juliana looked up. Seeing the plane coming directly at her—she ducked. Emitting a high-pitched scream a coloratura soprano would be jealous of, she slipped and unceremoniously bounced down the stairs on her perfectly proportioned bottom.

The plane reached maximum speed, ripping a hole in the space-time continuum as it circled around again towards Siegfried. Emily was frozen in place like an icicle in a snowstorm during the middle of winter at the North Pole. The horrified look in Siegfried's cerulean eyes was the last thing Emily saw as his long dark hair streaked with gray got caught in a hook dangling from the Pocket Multitool® and pulled him into the space-time continuum with a WHOOSH!

Marjorie, (Inse) and Donna came up the stairs singing "Voulez-vous coucher avec moi … ce soir?[16]" just in time to see what was happening. Emily was still staring at the pretty little sparks of static electricity when Marjorie angrily commented "I told you the short haircut on Siegfried was better!"

Just then, somewhere in the rubble, a cell phone began ringing and . . .

---

16 "Voulez-vous coucher avec moi (ce soir)" is a French phrase that rose to fame in the English-speaking world through the song "Lady Marmalade", written by Bob Crewe and Kenny Nolan.

Original Connie

UnEarthly Connie

17

BOGUS BRAZIL

UnEarthly Marjorie

UNEARTHLY MARJORIE

10 June 2001

Barb tottered over to the ringing phone on her high heels, one of which had broken in the mayhem. Wondering why she'd suddenly developed a limp, she grabbed the phone and then listened in astonishment.

"What ish it?" slurred Juliana, trying to wipe the leaking rum out of her eyes with the back of her hand.

Barb winced. "I've no idea, but it's a horrible noise."

"Give it to me," snapped Marjorie bossily, but as she listened a look of frozen horror covered her face. "It's the music of 'Mandarin Nightmare'®!" she exclaimed. "That means that Siegfried must be talking in a soft romantic way somewhere—that's when that band always comes crashing in and ruining the moment."

"We must find him!" shouted Lottie. "If he's doing soft and romantic, I want to be in on it."

"Well, I don't want to miss the romantic bit," Marjorie agreed. "Trouble is, how can we find him? With hair that length, he could be anywhere."

Barb sighed heavily. "Listen, sweetie. I thought you were meant to be an author. Take it from me, it's simple. Just all think double spacing and three asterisks in the middle of the page and off we go. Change of scene, no problem."

At that moment, Emily attempted another of her Macarena® dances and tripped over her feet. "I can see the asterisks," she shouted as she knocked her head against a large lump of the ceiling that was now lying on the floor. "Let's go."

Everyone concentrated hard, and sure enough, within seconds they were on the Copacabana beach.

"You were right," said Donna. "Look, there's Siegfried wandering over the silver sand with some lithe, Brazilian beauty."

The whole group ground their teeth in fury. "Don't panic," said Marjorie, who was rather enjoying the plummy voice that she'd suddenly acquired. "Mandarin Nightmare® will drown out the few words she can follow. Come on let's go and rescue him."

Siegfried didn't look as though he wanted to be rescued, but Barb threw a handful of sand in the Brazilian girl's face, and she ran off crying.

"There, saved by a handful of sand," said Barb as Siegfried gazed wistfully after the girl.

"That sounds like a line from one of my films," he murmured.

"That was a shovelful of sand, and it came from the film that set you on your career path," said Marjorie helpfully.

Siegfried looked as though he was going to cry, but then as Barb stripped off her mohair cardigan because she was so hot, he cheered up again.

"Have you brought the book with you?" he asked them all.

(Inse) shook her head. "We don't want you reading that book yet. In fact, we don't want you reading any book. When we were down in your cellar we saw your home video collection, and what we want to know is how do you manage to . . . ?"

UNEARTHLY EMILY
10 June 2001

Marjorie didn't have time to finish her sentence because just then Lottie came running down the beach holding a German battleship shaped birthday cake topped with sixty candles and singing "Happy Birthday to Siegfried" at the top of her lungs.

It was unfortunate she was running because when she reached the "Haaaappy biiiiirrrtthhhdaaaaayyyyy tooooo youuuuu!" part she stopped—but the battleship cake didn't. The cake, fully ablaze, headed directly towards...

UNEARTHLY MARJORIE
11 June 2001

One of the horns on Juliana's Viking helmet. The tip of the horn pierced right through the centre of the (literally) flaming cake, and Juliana shrieked in drunken terror.

251

"Dive!" shouted Siegfried helpfully, feeling really at home.

Still shrieking and flapping, hitting her head as though auditioning for a role in *Thrill Schmooze*, Juliana obeyed. She rushed into the sea as fast as her endless legs would carry her, and then plunged into the smooth depths of the ocean.

"Well done, Lottie," murmured Barb. "That's her out of the way."

"Entertainment we need," said Siegfried abruptly.

Marjorie sighed. It really got on her nerves when he insisted on sticking his verbs at the end of sentences. One day she'd have to help him with his English, but at the moment it wasn't his English that interested her the most.

"What kind of entertainment did you have in mind?" asked Donna, twirling her scarf around her throat in a suggestive fashion.

Emily tugged sharply on one trailing end, and as Donna began to cough, Barb smirked with satisfaction. "Yes, tell us Siegfried," she said huskily. "What kind of entertainment do you like?"

"Beautiful girls, naturally." He gave one of his apologetic smiles, that made them all feel a bit faint. "Of course, you are all beautiful ..."

"Some more than others," sniggered (Inse) as Juliana began to struggle back to the shore.

"This presents me with a big problem," continued Siegfried, trying to keep his overlong hair out of his eyes as a gentle breeze drifted along the beach. "So, I shall set a test for you all. First, I shall dance the hula with each of you in turn ..."

A collective gasp of horror rose from the mouths of the adoring throng.

"And then," he added, oblivious of the distress he was causing them, "we will all watch *LOL* together. When it's over you will each choose your favorite scene, and the one who chooses the same scene that I like is the winner. With the winner, to my mansion I will go."

Even Marjorie, who had so much imagination that she could usually find some moment of magic in any of her hero's films, was speechless. Her plummy voice was silent, and it was left to Barb to get them out of the awkward moment.

"Sounds great, Siegfried," she lied, brazen as ever. "The only problem is . . ."

UNEARTHLY EMILY
15 June 2001

"The only problem is all our videos were trampled by Brian the stallion back in the desert chapters of TOATS," Barb replied. "So it's impossible to sit through *LOL* again." Emily, Juliana and Marjorie gave sigh of relief that Barb had remembered the back story.

"Hmmm there must be another way to settle this." Siegfried pondered.

(Inse) meanwhile was watching the latest episode of *Remainder*® on her portable TV. She also had a fascination for *The Double Agent*®, which was Emily's personal favorite reality show. An idea began to form in (Inse)'s deranged diabolical mind on how to narrow the field back to one . . .

UnEarthly Marjorie

UNEARTHLY MARJORIE
24 June 2001

"I know," she announced triumphantly. "We'll have our own *Remainder®* contest!"

Siegfried sighed deeply, causing Joanna to feel faint and sink onto the sand. "I'll lose first," he said sadly. "I never remain to the end of anything."

"That's because he chooses roles where he can take the money and run before the finish," muttered Barb.

Emily was shocked. "How can you say such a thing? I think playing *Remainder®* is a brilliant idea. The one who makes it to the end the winner is declared."

"Good grief, it's catching!" exclaimed Marjorie. "Emily, why did you put your verb at the end of the sentence?"

"I'm practising for when I win and get to go off with him," retorted Emily.

"You won't win!" shouted Joanna, slowly getting over her faint, since Siegfried hadn't even noticed her long legs splayed out on the soft, white sand. "I'm a born remainer."

"You're a horned remainer, that's for sure," said Marjorie, who wasn't into physical or mental labour and was wondering how she could get out of this diabolical plot of (Inse)'s.

"Come on," said Emily. "Let's get started. Siegfried, you must set the first task, then when it's completed, we girls—" (Siegfried struggled manfully to suppress a smirk at the word "girls") "—will choose who to boot off the island."

"This is Brazil!" said Donna, as she tried to work out if her scarf was strong enough to strangle anyone.

"The principle's the same" drawled Barb, examining her long, beautifully manicured nails and wondering if they could be used as a weapon.

"Come on then, Siegfried, set us a task," agreed Marjorie, who was trying hard to get her chameleon hair to turn blue, so that it matched Siegfried's eyes. She had a feeling he might be quite taken with the idea of a partner whose hair matched his eyes, and they could just leg it off the beach while the others were sweating away at their task. Unfortunately, at the moment her hair was black and purple, which from the look on his face didn't seem to be to his taste.

Siegfried nodded, his most thoughtful and intelligent nod—the one that someone had once unkindly said looked like a muscle spasm. "Right, girls." Again, the suggestion of a smirk crossed their idol's face. "Here is what I want you to do . . ."

UNEARTHLY DONNA
26 June 2001
"GET ME A DECENT #$@!&*^ SCRIPT!!" shouted Siegfried triumphantly. "And if even one of you can survive that challenge, I'll . . . I'll . . . I'll marry her, even if that has been done before!" And with that he developed a decided smirk.

This development plunged most of our surpassingly beautiful heroines into states of catatonic hopelessness. Emily, however, squealed like a teenager and Marjorie whooped triumphantly . . . both of them made a mad dash for writing implements and soon Emily was scribbling madly on napkins with an eyebrow pencil while Marjorie began making cryptic notes on a nearby beach hut with her $30 lipstick.

The others found themselves with no recourse but to team up to avoid certain demise and quickly devolved into arguing whether their tribal tattoo should be done in permanent ink while glaringly with deadly intent at (Inse).

Juliana grew increasingly despondent, knowing full well her legs were utterly useless for writing.

Donna, realizing that her own situation was particularly hopeless, was wondering whether her scarf could also double as a sail, when she realized rafts weren't strictly necessary if you're trying to escape within an area the size of South America.

(Inse) however brought a sudden halt to all of the activity by dragging her intricately manicured nine-inch nails across a nearby blackboard (where do these props come from?)

"That's impossible," she began . . .

ORIGINAL MARJORIE

27 June 2001

Why does my surname keep appearing whenever I post? I'm useless at all this stuff…

PS Cyber weirdo who told me "LOL" was "lots of laugh", and you know who you are, I shall remember being misled. Be very afraid.

ORIGINAL JULIANA

posted by Cyberette on 27 June 2001

Hey don't fill in all your particulars in those nasty little empty boxes.

Soon we will have your medical records on show for everyone too.

I did tell you Laughing Out Load.

You get confused again. Recheck your emails.

ORIGINAL MARJORIE

posted by Marjorie on 27 June 2001

Not my medical records, they'll show my age! Sorry Cyberette, you're quite right, have checked my emails and it's my fault. To make amends I'll try a TOAT. Anything rather than my damned book.

UNEARTHLY MARJORIE

posted by Marjorie on 27 June 2001

"Why?" demanded Siegfried, creasing his brow so that it was brought nicely into line with the rest of his face.

"Because the shock might kill you."

Donna saw her chance to put in a dainty boot, since even her scarf wasn't any use. "She means you haven't had a decent script for so long that your brain and body would go into overload and then you'd be dead before any of us got to marry you."

Siegfried grabbed hold of (Inse)'s hands and looked thoughtfully at her fingers.

"Yes!" cried Marjorie, almost delirious with excitement, but to her disappointment it wasn't what she thought.

"You should manicure those nails," remarked Siegfried. "Get them to look more like your friend's over there."

Barb smirked as (Inse) glared at her. "She's no friend of mine!" (Inse) shouted.

"I couldn't possibly marry you now, anyway," said Siegfried quietly. "I need a woman who has faith in my acting, and who can give me advice and guidance as well as a decent script."

"Tell him miracles don't come cheap," said Barb.

"If you keep saying red leather, yellow leather it might help," suggested Marjorie, as her Obsessed Orange® lipstick snapped leaving a nasty red smudge on her words of incredible wit and wisdom. "It gets the speech muscles going."

"Please don't," whispered Juliana, but it was too late, and soon their hero's mouth was working frantically as he struggled with the tongue twister. The sounds that came out would have done justice to a cat being strangled by Donna's scarf.

"I've got some good stuff here," added Marjorie modestly. "It's a bit risqué but..."

"Yes!" shouted Siegfried, delighted at the combination of intelligence combined with a bit of excitement.

"You don't want to read her filth," shouted Emily.

"I do!" exclaimed Siegfried.

"There, he's said it," cried Marjorie triumphantly. "He's mine now, and there's nothing you lot can do about it."

Slowly Juliana unfolder her long elegant legs. "Oh yes there is. Siegfried, you can't marry her because..."

UNEARTHLY JULIANA
posted by Juliana on 27 June 2001

"... according to her medical records she is well-nigh your age." Juliana triumphantly whisked forth a mega printout of all the personal titbits Marjorie had ever left behind on the internet. Her Cyberways being to pedantically fill in every empty box that glared in her face.

A generational thing.

"Nooooo." Screeched Marjorie, dropping her book whilst chameleon bluepurplish hair turned Gray of shock and horror!

258

Siegfried felt huge pangs of sympathy. He knew only too well that mondaymorning feeling of gray roots on both top and chin and your hairdresser simply is not available.

"You are such a bitch!" He muttered gutturally. Blue eyes filling up with icebergs.

Wow… thought Barb. Moving in closer to the target. Seemed like Marjorie and Juliana both was out of the competition.

Donna deftly unfolded her scarf sailing implement. A-whistling. Back in the game.

Emily picked up Marjorie's filthy book and studied the cover very carefully.

Could not make out much of it though.

Haplessly she passed it on to Siegfried.

Juliana's red hair flared out in the wind as she trudged up the hills in the sunset with Marjorie in hot pursuit, determined to get hold of her personal peculiarities.

A long list of printouts trailing behind.

"Well Girls," whispered Siegfried gently, licking his lips, opening the covers of the book. " … BedtimeStoryTime!!!"

(Inse) squeaked violently because …

ORIGINAL MARJORIE
posted by Marjorie on 27 June 2001
Brilliant, Juliana. I laughed 'til I cried!

ORIGINAL BARB

posted by Barb on 28 June 2001

Marjorie and Juliana, congrats on the hilarious TOATS episodes. I feel so guilty about not contributing lately, but I will ASAP!

ORIGINAL MARJORIE

posted by Marjorie on 27 June 2001

What a great start to the day! Brilliant TOATS, Donna, and as for the pictures, well — be still, my beating heart. I'm off to do an indecent novel, will think about a decent script later.

UNEARTHLY BARB

posted by Barb on 29 June 2001

…because page one listed "Other Books in This Series". The first was called "Astronomical Flex," and her imagination went into overload. "Quickly, turn the page before I pass out," moaned (Inse).

Too late.

At the sight of the next title, she collapsed in a fever, foaming at the mouth. It was called "1000 Ways of Using the Porphproian Thingy in the Back of Model Planes."

"A minute vait," said Siegfried, turning the pages and studying them closely. "Zis book very interesting is."

Emily, Donna and Barb were jostling one another with the subtlety of sumo wrestlers, trying to look over Siegfried's shoulder. Meanwhile, a scream that might have been of human origin echoed thinly from somewhere up in the sunset-painted hills.

"Gosh, that's coming from the direction Juliana and Marjorie went," whispered Donna, but nobody was listening.

Absorbed in the book, Siegfried continued to read intently. At last, the three insanely beautiful creatures bashing each other senseless at his shoulder could stand it no longer.

"WHAT!" they shouted simultaneously.

"Oh," said Siegfried, snapping back to "reality". "Amazing zis is. Someone ze book's jacket substituted has. Ze cover, of Marjorie's book is, while ze pages from 'Ze TOATS Rule Book on Etiquette' are."

Emily rounded on Barb."It's you who's writing this chapter isn't it!" she shrieked. "And you're making Siegfried sound like that little green alien guy with the ears, the one out of *Galactic Conflicts*® whose name rhymes with a Czechoslovakian automobile brand! Stop it! Stop it at once or I'll be forced to use an acrobatic mid-air roundhouse kick on you."

"Sorry," said Barb, ever-respectful of Emily's martial prowess after some chapter eons ago when she beat someone to a pulp.

"Look at zis!" cried Siegfried, holding up the book with his finger pointing to a certain paragraph. "Ze Rule Book states zat ze source of any props used in TOATS must be accounted for, and not mysteriously appear as if by magic!"

"Damn!" shouted Barb, quickly putting away a flame-thrower that had mysteriously materialized in her hand. "But why? WHY?????????????????"

Swatting away another full-blown flock of question marks, Siegfried read out, "Because zat makes it too darned easy..."

He began to walk away, his nose in the book.

"Hey," said (Inse), waking up on the sand as Siegfried tripped over her, "But if that's the "TOATS Rule Book on Etiquette", where is Marjorie's Book of Filth, and WHO DID THE SUBSTITUTION???????????????"

From far away over the crimson-and-cochineal-drenched hills, another faint scream came down the wind. It sounded quite human…

UNEARTHLY MARJORIE

posted by Marjorie on 30 June 2001

…but was in fact Juliana. The group on the beach turned to stare and soon saw her familiar long legs galloping down the hillside, closely followed by the rest of her. "Marjorie opened her book and I read some of it by mistake," she shrieked.

"How come you had her book? Did you do the substitution?" asked Donna.

Juliana opened her mouth to reply but then an extraordinary change came over her. Her luscious full lips began to pout and she smoothed her tousled mane of hair behind her ears while at the same time starting to sashay towards the hypnotised Siegfried. Slithering up to him she wrapped her arms round his neck. Siegfried, who hadn't been a leading man for nothing, swiftly started to remove his shirt.

"Leave him alone!" screamed Emily, Barb and Donna, trying to pull her off.

"I can't help it," cried Juliana. "If you start to read the book, you get possessed. You turn into a sex symbol and …"

At that moment Marjorie strolled up, her book clutched firmly in one hand and the incredibly long list of her personal peculiarities grasped in the other.

"Is that true?" gasped Siegfried.

Marjorie nodded. "Yes, only she's been more badly affected than most people. I think she must have been rather a naïve little thing underneath that over-painted, cheap sexy image she projected." The plummy English girl, as she liked to think of herself, clearly hadn't forgiven Juliana for giving away her age.

"Then I MUST read it," declared Siegfried. "My romantic roles have been few and far in the middle lately."

"You mean 'between'," said Marjorie, holding the book high above her head as the other girls leapt fruitlessly in the air to try and get it. As Siegfried advanced purposefully towards her, dragging the entwined and suddenly surgically enhanced Juliana along with him, they all heard a loud rushing sound and the gentle breeze that had been ruffling Siegfried's overlong locks turned to a howling gale. The sky began to darken, all the birds fell silent and then a tornado appeared out of nowhere.

"That's not allowed," Barb reminded everyone, as she started to read some of Marjorie's personal peculiarities from the bottom of the printout that was trailing on the sand.

Siegfried sighed. "I know where this tornado has come from. It's the revenge of the special FX people. They were angry when I complained about the avalanche in Final Descent. This is their doing."

263

As the wind plucked them all from the silver sand of the beach, tossing them through the air towards any destination the dastardly FX people chose, Siegfried could be heard screaming "Stay close, Marjorie, I need that book," but it was too late because ...

ORIGINAL JULIANA
posted by Juliana on 29 June 2001
Barb. Great Stuff. I just Love the German Syntaxing you so immaculately and flawlessly in the sentences inserted ...

Someone said constructing German sentences was just like walking submerged under the water just to emerge on the other side of the Atlantic Ocean with a verb in the mouth. Ergo you can put as many little words in between those active grammar words I never remember the names of.

ORIGINAL MARJORIE
posted by Marjorie on 29 June 2001
Great TOATS, Barb. Loved the Yoda® effect.

ORIGINAL EMILY
posted by Emily on 29 June 2001
Barb that was great! You have a gift for the hysterical. I'm moving house today but this site is so addictive I couldn't disassemble the computer. I had to wait till the last minute.

Now I really am logging off. I can see the movers pick me up in this chair as I'm still trying to type!

ORIGINAL JULIANA

posted by Juliana on 29 June 2001

LOLLY ..(sly abbreviated internetspeak, you work it out) know the feeling Emily . . . being picked up along with the computer whilst typing away that is . . . :) Good luck with the move.

ORIGINAL DONNA

1 July 2001

I went away for a few days where the internet is too slow to bother with . . . I'm only back here for about 24 hours but see what is the first thing I do, log in to see what's happening in TOATS . . . you go through withdrawal if you are away from it for very long . . . Emily this is hilarious, you're a genius.

GREAT TOATS episodes everyone! I should go away more often if I get to come home to this . . .

18

KEFLA-TWIG-AT-THE-SEA

UNEARTHLY JULIANA
posted by Juliana on 2 July 2001
Juliana was up to her old dastardly tricks again.

In the eye of the SOX network® hurricane, the Cyberchicks twister their lithe, delicate little limbs in agony, WDYM® scarves and Maraschino® envelope handbags hovered on top of the human fanconglomeration. Juliana though kept a ironsteady grip upon her hammiest hero in the world ever.

"Where is my Verbose® accessories . . ." whined Emily to Lottie who had mysteriously reappeared onto the scene on account of her service provider letting her stay online for more than one nanosecond. Her eyes were still being transfixed by the chock of sudden selfcombustion. Could happen any minute now.

"Hey that is MY Verbose® bag . . . not yours . . . " interrupted Barb. Surrounded by a whisk of pastel-colored cocktail parasols as usual.

"Hey Seegchen . . . Let's nosedive away from your FanSkivvies . . . " Juliana said conspiratorilly. Her hair in the four cardinal windpoints as usual.

Siegfried was to be honest, more interested in catching Marjorie's Filthy Book, fluttering in the wind on top of his head than anything else in the world.

Juliana deftly extended her supervixen arm and caught the darned book, pocketed in her vast bulging OpShop® bag. "There, happy now . . . ?

"Lets nosedive to the volcanic hottubs of my ancestral homestead of Kefla-Twig-At-The-Sea in the easterly direction of the chic city of Reykjavik. Just a Snip and we are in VodkaLand," promised Juliana with glaring, firey eyes. Knowing full well that no-one was more easily led than Siegfried.

And therefore, before Donna, Marjorie, Barb, Emily and Lottie could add up to one, Juliana and Siegfried was soaking in the hot tubs of Twig-At-The-Sea. Juliana had relocated her Viking helmet and was busily and whistlingly filling up the empty horns with Cranberry Vodka. Siegfried, though, had found his yellow bathing rubberduck and was on the same time struggling with the first sentence of Marjorie's Filth.

Kaboommmm . . .

UNEARTHLY MARJORIE

posted by Marjorie on 7 July 2001

With a sound like a depth charge, Donna, Emily, Barb and Marjorie were deposited in an adjoining volcanic hot tub. Lottie had vanished, cut off by her service provider. Siegfried looked on with interest as they jostled for position, Barb using all her pathetic paper parasols in an attempt to gain herself prime position next to her hero.

Marjorie, who was worried that her workmanlike Parks & Fences® underwear might not show up to good advantage in the water, decided to use her most sophisticated, plummy tone of voice in order to compensate for her lack of designer label clothes. Luckily her chameleon hair had now turned a bright shade of blue, which certainly caught Siegfried's attention.

"What, may one ask, are you trying to do, Juliana?" she asked, sounding rather like the Queen of England.

"Brrr," said Siegfried.

"Are you cold?" asked Juliana anxiously, shoving the horns of her helmet to his mouth and trying to seduce him with warm liquor.

"No, I thought it was time for a new paragraph. There was a distinct lack of those in the last episode," he explained.

"Picky!" snapped Juliana, taking a quick swig of the vodka herself. "I haven't mastered that yet. It's the story that counts."

"I know, so where's my brilliant script?" demanded Siegfried, eyes ablaze as he turned to page two of Marjorie's Filthy Book.

"In my head of course," cried Juliana, tossing her red hair and catching it again as she wondered why seducing her hero was turning out to be such hard work. "It's an Icelandic saga.

269

You will play Siegfried the Just, who is in search of the Elixir of Excellent English. Along the way you'll meet with many obstacles ..."

"Like you way you pronounce vowel sounds," explained Donna, anxious to ruin Juliana's brilliant idea.

"You think there something rooong with my spicking?" Siegfried was clearly in a state of shock, but as he was on page ten of Marjorie's Filthy Book this was understandable.

"NO!" cried Juliana, hiccuping as she slid beneath the bubbling water. "You're perfect.."

"Forget it", said Siegfried decisively. "I don't want to be in a boring saga. Everything I want is here, between the covers of this book."

His band of devoted fans glanced wildly at one another. They couldn't allow the blue haired imitation of the Queen of England to entrap him with her cheap tricks.

Luckily Barb wasn't intimidated by anyone. "Forget it kiddo," she snarled, and Siegfried's deep blue eyes lit up at the compliment. "I read some of Marjorie's list of personal peculiarities, and what you don't know is ..." Before she could finish speaking, the FX people from Vixen® struck again and as they all watched in astonishment Juliana ...

UNEARTHLY BARB
posted by Barb on 7 July 2001
... as they all watched in astonishment, Juliana burst up through the porridge-like, glutinously bubbling waters of the volcanic hot tub.

"Omigosh, she's being sucked skywards by the psionic subverted epistemological pressure of the hurricane, or tornado, or whatever you call those storm-things," remarked Barb with academic interest, watching Juliana's long legs disappear toward the clouds.

"What?" yelled Siegfried, dropping Marjorie's Filthy Book into the hot-tub. "Sarve her! Someboody sarve my delictable rod-haired Icelundic voxen befire it's too latté!"

"Latté?" said Emily vaguely, feeling the first twinges of caffeine withdrawal symptoms. "Gosh, it's a long time since I had a coffee…"

Her words were lost in a hubbub of floundering as Siegfried and several flounders leapt from the hot tub.

"Relax Seegums," cooed Donna silkily, re-arranging her scarf. "It's too late. She's vanished into the upper atmosphere."

"And Donna should know," added Barb smirkily. "She is the Web Goddess, don't forget. The entire TOATS universe could vanish if she waves her mouse."

"Bit thus is turrible," cried Siegfried, staring wildly at the heavens and sounding more and more like a New Zealander.

No sooner had the words left his rather well-shaped and kissable lips than Donna, brushing flounders out of her hair, waved her mouse. The hurricane departed rapidly westwards, with a terrified yelping sound.

"I say, how jolly extraordinary!" said the blue-haired Queen of England plummily, as Donna re-folded the mouse into her scarf.

Just as ice was beginning to form on the end bits of those who had climbed from the hot tub into the forty-degrees-below-zero temperatures of Kefla-Twig-at-the-Sea, a second catastrophe struck.

UNEARTHLY BARB

posted by Barb on 7 July 2001

A fleet of odd-looking bright yellow automobiles sporting radar dishes and other strange apparatus on their rooves came careering up the sides of the volcano topped by the hot tubs of Kefla-Twig-At-The-Sea.

Simultaneously, a flock of beaten-up World War II aeroplanes with bananas amateurishly painted on their tail fins came roaring and smoking out of the snow-laden skies.

Gradually it started to dawn on Siegfried, Emily, Barb, Donna, (Inse) and Marge Simpson®—sorry, I mean some other woman with blue hair—that these unexpected arrivals might mean trouble. Feverishly they tried to prepare themselves for the worst.

"Whare are the terls?" Siegfried yelled.

"The what?"

"The terls."

"Oh, the TOWELS you mean," said Marjorie smugly, in her juiciest BBC-announcer accent. "Well, when we were zapped here to this rather spiffing Icelandic place by some strange teleportation phenomena, nobody jolly well thought of bringing any, did they."

Everyone started madly drying themselves on Donna's scarf and wondering what they were supposed to be wearing in this chapter. By the time they had gone from soaking-wet to covered-with-a-thin-film-of-ice, the taxicabs (for that is what they appeared to be) and the euphemistically-titled "aeroplanes" had either parked or crashed nearby.

Two figures, who appeared to be the leaders of each vehicular party, were striding up the Completely Extinct volcano. One looked to be a white-eyed alien from some unimaginable planet. ("A TOATS Taxi-driver!" breathed Emily, stunned.)

The other was a small wizened-up man with one arm, wearing thick spectacles, a hearing aid, a parachute and a pilot's hat. ("And an Air Banana captain!" stammered Barb, amazed.)

UNEARTHLY BARB
posted by Barb on 7 July 2001
"What is the meaning of it!!!!!!!!!!!!!" chorused both creatures as they approached, "zapping yourselves here, there and everywhere without so much as purchasing a plane ticket or hailing a cab!!!!!!!!!! How are we supposed to make a living, eh?"

Everyone looked blank, which was not much of a change from their normal expressions.

"And what's more, soloed the cab-driver, "there's a large unpaid amount outstanding. For past services rendered."

"I thought she was going to pay," said the TOATS nymphettes, pointing accusingly at each other.

"There will be reprisals, you know," said the "pilot" sinisterly. "Already we have one of your number under lock and key. An attractive but silly wench. In between fainting fits she writes scripts on the dungeon walls."

"Lottie!" yowled the TOATS heroines. "And we thought it was her service provider's fault!"

"Wait a minute," said Emily, "I distinctly recall Barb saying, 'Charge the cab and plane fares to my account.'"

"Er, really?" said Barb guiltily, stripped of her usual brazen over-confidence by the recollection that drunkenness is associated with amnesia. "That is to say—go and speak to my butler Peeves, at my desert mansion in the Great Southern Land. He'll take care of it."

"What Great Southern Land?" said the TOATS heroines, staring at Barb.

"D'you mean South America?" demanded the "pilot".

"Oh, you know. Austral—" Barb broke off, on seeing the mystified looks on everyone's faces. Most of the other cyberchicks hailed from the Northern Hemisphere.

"Oh. It's just a biggish island between New Guinea and Antarctica," she muttered lamely.

At that precise instant, a reddish object with long legs came hurtling from above.

"Goodness gracious!" screamed the Queen of England look-alike. "I do believe that's—"

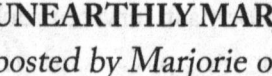

UNEARTHLY MARJORIE
posted by Marjorie on 13 July 2001
" . . . the first effort by the Vixen® Special Effects Department for the monster in *LOL*. The one the movie-makers discarded."

"I'm not surprised," exclaimed Donna, watching the ghastly apparition dropping towards them like a very heavy stone.

"No, it's Juliana. I recognise the Viking helmet," said Emily.

"Happy, Siegfried?" enquired Barb frostily, spitting a few frozen ice cubes out from between her pearly white teeth. "You've got your delictable rod-haired Icelundic voxen back."

Siegfried stared at her. "A problem with the English language you have?"

"Is this another of your chapters, Barb?" demanded Donna who, in her role as spinner and controller of the website was none too pleased to have Yoda®-Siegfried back.

"No, it's that plummy, blue-haired Queen of England look-alike's. I shall sue her for plagiarism."

"SILENCE!!!" shouted the one-armed captain of Air Banana. "Have you forgotten that we hold one of your number prisoner under lock and key. If you don't use us or pay us our money, she will die."

"Well, I'm not paying!" cried all the TOATS nymphettes in unison.

Siegfried stared at them. "Do none of you delectable damsels know how heroines should behave? No wonder you can't come up with a decent script between you. Ashamed you should be of treating a fryend in this way."

"His speech gets worse and worse," groaned Marjorie, running her hands through her now-crimson hair. "Okay, Siegfried. Since you've starred in so many wonderful movies…" Siegfried nodded nervously, aware that the crimson-haired, plummy-mouthed, so-called novelist had been known to resort to sarcasm, "you tell us what we should do next!"

UnEarthly Marjorie

UNEARTHLY MARJORIE

posted by Marjorie on 13 July 2001
At that precise moment, the unseen Vixen® FX people threw a sword into Siegfried's hands. For a few seconds he juggled it around, uncertain which hand he was favoring for this adventure, but then grasping it

decisively in his left hand he lunged forward and severed the Air Banana captain's remaining arm. "There, he is 'armless'," he announced proudly.

As the TOATS girls groaned in despair, the Air Banana Captain staggered off down the hill, occasionally kicking a leg out to the side as he swore to return soon and wreak vengeance on them all.

Juliana, who had been lying very quietly in case Siegfried believed that she was a monster and cut off her excellent legs, thus leaving her without any advantage over the other TOATS heroines—except for her ability to drink six bottles of rum and remain standing—got to her feet. "We must find Lottie," she declared. "It's our duty."

Siegfried put an arm round her waist—he had exceedingly long arms—and squeezed her fondly. No one had ever squeezed Juliana's fondly before, and she quite liked it.

"That's my girl," he said huskily. "You alone are worthy of a place at my side. Quick, to the taxis we will go."

"And WHERE pray is one going?" enquired Marjorie, whose hair was now plum-colored to match her voice.

"Why, to Under-Lock-And-Key of course," snapped Siegfried. With that, he niftily grabbed Marjorie's Filthy Book from the bubbling lava, and then he and Juliana lurched down the side of the volcano as Siegfried tried to adjust the lifts in the heels of his shoes to make him tower over the long-legged Icelandic wench who appeared to have him in thrall.

The couple fell into a waiting yellow taxi, as the rest of the TOATS nymphettes followed close behind. Pushing and shoving they piled into a second cab.

"Follow that taxi!" cried Emily to their deaf and blind driver. Luckily his disabilities didn't matter, because the moment Siegfried pulled the rusty yellow door of the first taxi closed . . .

Original Donna

UnEarthly Donna

19

A GOOD RUMMAGE

Fast-forward to 2009.

Scene: Barb's office on Original Earth. The office's owner stared at her computer screen in utter bemusement. In 2001, TOATS had sputtered like a wetted candle-flame, struggled weakly to achieve a brief re-ignition later that year, then given up and expired into a heap of ashes. It was not rekindled until 2002.

The Barb of 2009 had a vague inkling that it was sometime during that rekindled year that she had ceased contributing to TOATS once and for all, and she wondered what had happened next in the saga.

In the meantime she was confusedly trying to work out how the 2001 chapters linked up with those of 2002. It didn't help that the entire Siegfried B. Hinkelheimer fansite had once again been forced to pack up its bulky belongings and move to a new webspace. . .

Flashback to 2002—

ORIGINAL DONNA

6 March 2002

ok another thang . . . doing this migration i discovered quite a pile of lost TOATS posts. I know everyone is dying to know that.

It might be worth mentioning too that moving this stuff I had quite a few good laughs at some of the stuff that's been posted here in the past years. You are all extremely clever funny people.

ORIGINAL MARJORIE

6 March 2002

This site feels very strange at the moment. I'm going to have a good rummage through all the old postings when I've got a moment. Poor Donna, you've really got your work cut out.

ORIGINAL MARJORIE

10 March 2002

Has anyone else seen SBH's interview on the DVD of *THE LAST HOP*? It's great, and you learn a lot about what he looks for in a script . . .

(INSE)

posted by (Inse) from the Dungeons of Barb's Mansion on 10 March 2002

There's an interview at the end of *Last Hop*??

280

ORIGINAL MARJORIE

10 March 2002

Welcome back (Inse). Yes, there's an interview as part of the 'extras' on the DVD.

By the way, I think a TOATS in the Dungeons of Barb's Mansion would be interesting. I shall have to give it some thought. Hope you're comfortable there, and that Barb sometimes lets you watch Popgun Vodka. The dungeons in that are pretty impressive.

ORIGINAL BARB

11 March 2002

By the way (Inse) is not me, if that's what you're thinking. I suspect she is you, Emily:) I hope Peeves is being the perfect butler to you in my dungeons (which my cyberself has recently had renovated, replacing the old, outmoded rack with a nice fresh Iron Maiden).

ORIGINAL MARJORIE

11 March 2002

Maybe (Inse) has come to life, like something out of a horror movie. How about that for strange?

(INSE)

Posted by (Inse), Rambling around Barb's dungeons on 11 March 2002

Yes, the renovations in these dungeons are startling. Barb, you didn't mention however how much the "new" Iron Maiden resembles its mistress; or that you've been running *Kipper* on the wall-sized screen down here 24/7 ALL YEAR for my amusement!

But now that I've . . . tired . . . of that "chair" you had engineered for my comfort (did you know rats could gnaw through leather straps?) and gained greater freedom to these chambers, you can bet I'm having "a good rummage", as Marjorie recently put it, through your video collection. Just while I get my strength back and recover from the intellectual torture of the past several months. Why, I've already assembled this crude computer out of old toenails, odd strands of hair (what color is that, anyway?), rats' nests, and spit—and I think I'm recovering my senses quite nicely.

(By the way, Peeves isn't doing so well. Haven't seen him since February or so, when he wandered off mumbling what sounded like deranged Biblical prophecies. From time to time I still think I hear some far-off muffled sobs that I gather are probably his . . . ?)

UNEARTHLY BARB
11 March 2002
(Inse), did I mention that if you press the second stone to the left, in the wall behind the combination popcorn-maker-and-thumbscrew, the secret exit opens? Or have you already discovered that?
ROFL and LMAO.

(INSE)
GONE on 11 March 2002
Secret exit? Whhooooooooooosshh . . .
Going . . . going . . .

282

UNEARTHLY BARB

posted by Barb from My dungeons. on 11 March 2002

Good, she's gone. And in her haste she left behind this computer made of old toenails, odd strands of hair, rats' nests and spit. Now I can have a good rummage in these personal files . . . bwa ha ha!

ORIGINAL DONNA

11 March 2002

Barb! I was going to say, "how could you?! (touch that)," but now I see that you must now have gained really keen insights into (Inse)'s personality digging around in her bookmarks and cookie files . . . hmm . . .

ORIGINAL DONNA

posted by Donna from Quite the Twilight Zone on 11 March 2002

Marjorie, "good rummage" is an excellent expression; it would probably fall under "quaint" on this homely side of the pond but I personally like it very much. In fact I think I really . . . really . . . REALLY deserve a Good Rummage™ through my own personal SBH archive. I *know* I do.

As fate would have it though it's inaccessible behind . . . a years' worth of construction debris, the majority of the world's bird cages, and of all things, a rather large and honestly really dangerous pile of broken glass. Strange, but true. It's like my tape collection is being hoarded by a splinter-toothed version of Cerberus. He's daring me to test the waters!

Wait! . . . I am Egill the Impaler, I almost forgot . . . !! Gggrrrr . . . !! . . . ??

ORIGINAL DONNA
11 March 2002

Marjorie, it looks like (Inse) beat the dust after your warning . . . funny, if there was any vodka involved, I would have guessed it was one of our Ozzies sobbing in the distance. Just who was it ran off with a barge load of Vulgarian sailors and a potato distillery? It's been so long.

UNEARTHLY BARB

posted by Barb the Rummager from "Is this turning into a TOATS episode?" on 12 March 2002

Barb, rummaging around in (Inse)'s Ratintosh computer, finds a bookmark and clicks on it.

Zap.

What comes up on the saliva screen—I mean, silver screen— is an image of Donna, as broadcast by DONNACAM. The web goddess is seated behind a mountain of bird cages and a glacier of broken glass, while a splinter-toothed version of Cerberus growls menacingly from the general direction of her videotape collection.

"Cor!" says Barb. "And I thought it was bad down here in my dungeons!"

But even as Barb stares at the saliva screen, her hand clenching on the warm fur of the very annoyed mouse, she hears Donna cry: "Egad! I am Egill! I almost forgot!"

With that, Donna claps on a horned helmet stolen from Juliana, grabs her impaling spear and begins tossing empty bird-cages in all directions.

Suddenly the screen goes blank. The mouse has chewed through the braided-hair Ethernet cable.

"Darn!" cries Barb. "Now I'll never know what happened next!" Picking up a handy framed photo of Siegfried B. Hinkelheimer she kisses it. "But at least I have you," she murmurs fondly.

ORIGINAL BARB

posted by Barb, Talking to herself. on 14 March 2002

Haha! Very funny Barb! Now will you please stick to the topic, which is Siegfried B. Hinkelheimer??????

ORIGINAL DONNA

posted by Donna on 15 March 2002

Clap clap clap!!! Hahaha very funny Barb! :) I have a picture to share because of this if only i can remember where i put it. My PC took one the other day . . . I wonder if it could be channelling (Inse)'s Ratintosh . . .

ORIGINAL MARJORIE

24 March 2002

An idle thought—wonder if SBH is going to the Oscars tonight? If I were going I'd wear something tight-fitting, sort of in-and-out if you know what I mean, with a wide off-the-shoulder collar and a fishtail. That sounds pretty TOATSY don't you think? It would be black with a dark red collar and a matching red stripe down one side. What would the rest of you wear?

UNEARTHLY BARB

24 March 2002

Omigosh, Marjorie, you look GORGEOUS. And here's me, about to go to the Oscars in a 1960's mumu shift to hide the pounds I've put on recently. But no! In the world of TOATS everyone's thin, so to celebrate I'll wear a slinky black dress, off one shoulder, with a few tastefully placed black sequins and a fake-spiderweb hem. I actually wanted to wear full Queen Elizabeth I costume, neck-ruff and all, but you know how those women's magazines pillory one's dress sense if one steps outside the bounds of convention. What's everyone else wearing? Siegfried, Siegfried, Siegfried.

ORIGINAL LOTTIE
Lottie from Oz on 3 April 2002
Hi everyone. I'm still lurking . . .

ORIGINAL BARB
3 April 2002
Oh my gawd it's Lottie! (Barb faints head-first into her keyboard and types an entire novel with her face before regaining consciousness.) Lottie actually got on the internet and posted! I'd better take a quick look outside in case it's raining frogs, or false noses. . .

Hi Donna and Marjorie! Nice to see you in this gaping silence :)

Um, I haven't seen any Siegfried B. Hinkelheimer movies lately.

ORIGINAL DONNA
4 April 2002
good grief Nicole AND Lottie in one week, i think i may have felt the earth shift in its orbit, wait maybe that was the tequila . . .

An Australian called Nicole had recently joined the SBH fansite. From some offhand comments she made, Marjorie decided that she must have a foot fetish. Eventually, Nicole found herself written into TOATS.

However, it was not until July 2002 that TOATS began again in earnest. After much cogitating, Barb-of-2009 cunningly came up with a solution to this new gaping chasm in the chain of events, deducing what must have happened on UnEarth during those months while no one on Original Earth was looking.

The last known whereabouts of our protagonists was Kefla-Twig-At-The-Sea, Juliana's ancestral home in Iceland. Siegfried and all the TOATS heroines, having crammed themselves into taxi-cabs, had headed off in search of Lottie, who was trapped under lock and key somewhere unknown but most likely in the dungeons of Barb's Outback Mansion.

Their quest was far from uneventful.

At some point en route someone, probably (Inse), must have laced their cocktails with a very specific amnesia-inducing potion, because most of them forgot that they were supposed to be rescuing Lottie and instead drifted away in various directions.

By fair means or foul (you can guess which), Barb managed to entice Siegfried away from the rest. Eluding the lot of them she took him on a romantic holiday to Fiji.

Emily, the only one who had managed to avoid drinking the potion, loyally continued the quest. With piratical flair she located Lottie in the bowels of the Outback Mansion, set her free, locked the devious (Inse) in the dungeons to prevent her from causing more mischief, and invited Lottie to recuperate at her home in Los Angeles.

(Since then, [Inse] had escaped after pressing the second stone to the left in the wall behind the "Torcherer's Apprentice"™ combination popcorn-maker-and-thumbscrew.)

Deprived of Siegfried and not knowing where to begin looking for him, Donna recalled that she had heaps of paperwork waiting for her back at her web-goddess headquarters and rushed back to California. After finishing the work in record time, she received a phone call from the new Aussie cyberchick, Nicole, who had found out all about Barb's sly trick.

"And now that man-thieving hussy is on her way back to her mansion with Siegfried!" caterwauled Nicole.

"Who told you this?" Donna exclaimed in horror.

"Marjorie!"

"Right. We'd better get there before she does. Meet you in Australia!" Donna cried, dashing out of her office so quickly that she forgot to open the door and left a Donna-shaped cut-out in the thin plasterboard.

As for the others...

UNEARTHLY BARB

19 July 2002

Barb sighed contentedly and relaxed into her seat, sipping a gin and tonic. Another wonderful holiday in Fiji had come to a close, and as the international jet airliner sped homeward, she reflected on the romantic week she had spent alone with a certain gorgeous German film star, having successfully evaded the companionship of his other fans.

It had not been an easy feat, slipping slyly away for a tropical rendezvous while their attention was diverted. They were a canny bunch, unfortunately as cunning as they were beautiful.

Strangely, Barb thought about them in alphabetical order: Connie, who was actually in love with Nic Birdhouse and thus did not count as a genuine Siegfried B. Hinkelheimer fan but managed to get mixed up with the bunch anyway; Donna the web-universe goddess, who, it was fair to say, fancied a chap called Lance almost as much as she fancied Siegfried; Emily, a.k.a. the Irish Fairy Queen, another one with a fetish on the side—in her case Gabriel Yearn; (Inse), whose full title was Insert Your Name Here, a handy scapegoat for almost anything; Marilyn the naïve cave-tourist, who had not been heard of for years (at this point in her reverie Barb uttered a low and rather suspicious laugh); Juliana the Icelandic wench, wearing her horned Viking helmet, Lottie the Consciously Challenged (i.e. continually having fainting fits), eternally trying to get someone—anyone—to read some pathetic film-script she had once scribbled; Marjorie of the chameleon hair, writer of unmentionable books; Mayra the Brazilian Babe whose Amazonian romps had shocked and thrilled audiences all over the Internet, the perplexing shape-changer known as Tinfingers, and Tess, ever-popular with Vulgarian sailors and the manufacturers of Baksmälla® Vodka.

A mixed bevy, mused Barb, smugly buffing her long, well-manicured fingernails on her colorful Smoochee® Resort Wear. *Hopelessly crazed, every one of them. It is fortunate for liebchen Siegfried that I, at least, am sane.*

UNEARTHLY BARB
19 July 2002

As the plane landed on the private airstrip on the grounds of a sumptuous Outback Mansion, Barb, the stunning red-haired owner of that mansion, stared thoughtfully out of the window.

It was night-time. Beyond the moon she could faintly discern the planet Splinge pinned like a cameo brooch on the purple velvet of the sky. The landing was smooth, and for the umpteenth time Barb congratulated herself for avoiding a flight with Air Banana, arguably the most unsafe airline in the universe.

The aircraft's tires rolled to a smooth halt on the bitumen and the slim, long-legged beauty checked her cabin luggage. Yes, it was all there: The Orderly And Thoroughly Sensible (T.O.A.T.S.) Book of Rules and Etiquette, the Handi-Karri® aquarium filled with babelfish, The Outstanding And Totally Safe (T.O.A.T.S.) Survival Kit. As usual, she had packed with an eye to unforeseen circumstances.

"Thanks," she flung over her shoulder to the pilot, as she walked past the open cockpit door.

The pilot fell on his knees. "Please, please, won't you have dinner with me?" he pleaded. "I diverted this Sproing 747® for you, as you asked. I made an unscheduled landing, just for you. The other passengers are seriously annoyed. I will probably lose my job—"

Turning around, Barb bestowed on him a sweet smile.

"But it was all worth it," he huskily whispered, "for one glance from your flawless eyes."

"You bet," acknowledged Barb briskly.

UNEARTHLY BARB
19 July 2002

Barb and her travelling companion had disembarked, arm-in-arm. "Siegfried, liebchen," she purred, her gloss lipstick spangling seductively in the moonlight, "I am certain that by now Peeves will have prepared the BubblexHotTub®, and a glass of champagne waiting for each of us upon our arrival."

"Wunderbar, meine Schutz," he responded. "How far is your mansion from ze airstrip?"

"Not far," simpered his fair companion, "but when I phoned Peeves I asked him to send the limo for us. No point in wasting time walking."

"You sink off everyzink, mein little desert opal," said Siegfried lovingly. Momentarily Barb frowned, wondering whether he was referring to the time she had sunk off the coast of Fiji, while swimming after a heavy meal.

291

UNEARTHLY BARB

19 July 2002

Her cerebrations were, however, interrupted by the roar of the departing Sproing 747® and the appearance of a cloud of red dust on the desert skyline. At the heart of the dust-cloud glimmered a yellow speck.

"No." said Barb, shading her eyes against the harsh glare of the stars. "It cannot be!"

"Vot is ze matter, mein little desert plant?"

In wild desperation, the breathtaking young damsel scanned their surroundings. "The limousine is not here!" she exclaimed, "and I can't be sure, but I think that's a TOATS taxi coming towards us!"

"Scheisser!"

The billowing mass of sand particles shot towards them and sure enough, it was being engendered by the rapid and erratic progress of a T.O.A.T.S. cab. The vehicle was bright yellow, its roof arrayed with a complex tangle of scientific apparatus which was topped by the remains of a small, badly-dented spaceship and a large radar dish. Along the side doors was printed in large letters—'TRIPE ODD'S ALIEN TAXI SERVICE".

"Oh no!" moaned Barb. "It's all going wrong. Someone must have realized what I was up to. Quick, liebchen, let's make a run for the mansion before the taxi gets here!"

UNEARTHLY MARJORIE

posted by Marjorie on 19 July 2002

"Run?" queried Siegfried in astonishment. "I can't do that unless you've got technical equipment to speed up the film."

Barb felt an icy chill run down her spine. "You mean you don't do your own stunts any more?"

He laughed nervously. "Not all of them, nein. Only eight. What were you of me expecting?"

Before she could reply, Barb heard the sound of feet thudding over the ground towards them. The sand beneath their feet trembled, and so did Siegfried.

She wondered how many of her love-sick rivals were approaching. She knew Marjorie was there, because the whole tone of the episode had dropped, mainly because Marjorie didn't write the kind of books that needed beautiful descriptive passages concerning the scenery. Also, Siegfried's speech pattern had changed. He always tried harder when Marjorie was around, because she could be very picky.

Narrowing her eyes against the glare of the blazing sun, Barb could make out Donna, wearing her bottle green Vivienne Eastplank® single-sleeved blouse, skin-tight Verbose® leopard print pants and red rubber flip-flops, and Nicole, looking fit and sporty in a pair of crisp white running shorts, a pale blue sleeveless T-shirt and Crikey® trainers. Only her support stockings hinted that she might be a little older than the thirteen years that her open, guileless face suggested.

"Don't go with Barb, Siegfried," cried Marjorie, who was looking very English in her special red, white and blue Jubilee mini dress, with matching hair. "She doesn't really love you. It's Daniel..."

"DON'T YOU DARE CALL HIM NAMES!" screamed Barb, and Siegfried winced at the sound of her shrill shrieking, so different from the husky, tempting tone she'd been using earlier. "Liebling," he murmured softly, "who is this Daniel . . . ?"

"No one, Munchkin," Barb assured him, crossing her fingers behind her back and nearly severing an artery in her left wrist with her long nails. "Believe me, you're all that matters in the entire universe."

"She's lying," cried Nicole, dropping to her knees and scrabbling at the sand at Siegfried's feet. "Here, let me take off your shoes and give you a nice foot massage. Later, I'll work my way up to other things."

Siegfried nodded enthusiastically. "My feet do ache. I don't think your beautiful auburn-haired friend here understands this. She wants me to run."

"Well, I want you to keep perfectly still," whispered Nicole. "Leave it all to me. You're in safe hands now."

"She wants you to run?" queried Marjorie. "That's not what I had in mind at all." And she began to scribble unmentionable things in her pocket notebooks.

Donna, who was jumping up and down so that she could see over Marjorie's shoulder, gasped in shock and waved her magic wand. "Hey, my notes have disappeared!" protested Marjorie. "That's not fair. They were private."

"They were disgusting," said Donna. "Not at all the kind of thing Siegfried would want to take part in. Go and pay off the taxi while I deal with Barb."

Marjorie looked sulky. "I haven't any money," she protested.

"Give the driver a free book," suggested Nicole as her fingers caressed Siegfried's feet and ankles.

Rummaging around in her white handbag, which she'd bought from the Queen who was trying to raise money to pay her own taxes, Marjorie found a dozen or so spare copies of her unmentionable books lying at the bottom. "I'll be back in a minute. Don't go anywhere," she added in a quick aside to Siegfried.

"How can he? You're writing this episode," Donna pointed out.

"Yes, and doesn't it just show!" sneered Barb. "Bottle green indeed."

"I suppose it does show," agreed Marjorie smugly (she laboured under the delusion that her books were of some literary merit) but as she skipped daintily back towards the waiting TOATS taxi driver, everyone heard the sound of a computer springing to life as the story was taken over by . . .

UNEARTHLY EMILY
posted by Emily on 19 July 2002

. . . Emily. Half way around the world in Los Angeles the phone rang. It was late. One o'clock in the morning to be exact, and neither Emily nor Lottie were in the mood for talking. The suite they had just booked for the night only had one bed so they would have to share it. On top of the inconvenient sleeping arrangements, both were perturbed at how successful Barb had been at snatching Siegfried away from them, so they decided to team up to track him down. But I digress; the phone was ringing.

"Hullo?" Lottie answered. "Connie! Really? Asteroids? How far? No, you were right—ice cream not brain, uh huh, okay, cheers!" Lottie hung up the phone. "What was that all about?" "Oh, Connie found Siegfried. He's in the bindi bindu something Australian outback near Barb's castle. Oh, and Connie is stuck in a diner."

"Great! That means we don't have to leave till morning. I don't know about you but I've got to get a few hours' sleep. If I show up with these unsightly dark circles under my eyes it could be disastrous!" Emily replaced the chilled cucumber mask over her eyes.

She spent a rough night dreaming about earthquakes until she realized Lottie had been tampering with the controls of the massage bed. As daylight streamed into the room she turned over with a groan and opened her eyes to see her friend smiling at her.

"Good morning!" Lottie beamed. "The TOATS taxi is outside waiting for us. Do you think I should wear the Goatee® or the Lacquer®?"

UNEARTHLY BARB

posted by Barb on 19 July 2002

Stunned by the fact that the sun had risen so quickly in the middle of the night after Marjorie had appeared on the scene (please, no innuendoes), Barb stood gaping with astonishment in the desert. A couple of flies droned lazily in and out of her mouth.

From where she was standing in the now-blazing sun, she could see Marjorie handing a copy of an unmentionable book to a puzzled TOATS taxi driver, while Nicole grovelled in the sand massaging Siegfried's feet. Barb noticed how

Nicole was displaying her long, tanned legs to best advantage. Siegfried seemed to be staring at Nicole's shapely form with a glazed look.

"Don't look at her, my little pumpkin!" shrieked Barb, clapping her hands across his baby-blue eyes. She licked her lusciously-lipsticked lips, briefly wondering what the two tasty morsels she had just swallowed might have been. Definitely some form of protein.

"At what did you sink I schtaring vaz, mein little cactus?" enquired Siegfried lucidly. "I merely remembering vaz, about how you slipped a love potion into ze drink of ze Sproing 747® pilot, so zat he would ze detour make."

"What? Love potion? What?" Siegfried's perceptiveness had thrown Barb into confusion. "No, I—that is to say, of course not—"

UNEARTHLY BARB

posted by Barb on 19 July 2002
Meanwhile, across the dunes at the TOATS taxi, the driver was flipping through the pages of an unmentionable book and saying to Marjorie, "Really? You wrote this?"

Modestly, Marjorie blushed and adjusted her tiara. "Yes."

The driver lifted his green, three-horned head and grinned lasciviously at her. Wide-eyed and innocent, Marjorie noted he seemed to be salivating, and wondered if this was normal for aliens from the planet Splinge...

"Get up!" Barb said crossly, prodding Nicole's prone form with one of her eight-inch stiletto heels. "We have to go to my mansion. This bright sunshine is wreaking havoc on my complexion."

Nicole jumped to her feet.

"That sensational vaz, mein little toasted bun," Siegfried crooned to Nicole. "You ze woman with ze best massage technique in ze TOATS universe are."

"No she's not!" shrilled Barb. "I am!" Dragging Siegfried away by his elbow, she added, "Come on. Let's get to my mansion before anyone else arrives."

UNEARTHLY BARB
posted by Barb on 19 July 2002

(Inse) took a thoughtful drag on her cigarette and, as she blew a series of perfect smoke rings, leaned her elbow out the open window. Her shining D'Oreally® hair streamed out in the breeze. She let her long-nailed fingers rest lightly on the steering wheel of the taxi she had recently hijacked. The erstwhile driver was struggling and grunting on the back seat, but (Inse) smiled in the knowledge that aliens from the planet Splinge habitually struggled and grunted. This one wasn't even tied up and gagged; he was merely relaxing, sitting back and enjoying the passing scenery of endless desert.

Away in the distance there was a dark speck. At least, it looked to be away in the distance. Realising it was a fly speck on the windshield, (Inse) flicked it off with one gleaming, enamelled fingernail. The erstwhile taxi driver caught it in mid-air, and there was a gulping sound from the back seat. (Inse) shuddered, and did not turn around.

Away in the distance there was another dark speck. As the taxi sped over the sand, its rooftop radar dishes frantically revolving, this second speck began to evolve into a town—

that is to say, what passed for a town in the outback; a single pub and a diner called The Jolly Kangaroo.

"We've arrived!" said (Inse) cheerily, pulling up at the diner in a cloud of red sand.

Her back seat passenger struggled and grunted.

A figure stepped briskly from the diner's front door. "There you are!" snapped Connie, smoothing out her Enchilada® three-piece safari suit. "It took you long enough. I called ages ago. Nic's had time for seven milkshakes and I think he's starting to suspect I've been stalling—hello!" As she slid elegantly into the back seat, Connie noticed the alien for the first time. "Wait a minute, aren't you supposed to be driving?"

"Too late," said (Inse), hitting the "doors auto-close" button and stamping on the accelerator. "You're a bit slow on the uptake, Connie. I'm in charge here, and you've got no say." She smirked in an annoyingly self-satisfied manner and blew a couple more smoke rings. "You don't like it, you have to write yourself out of it."

"But, but I'm nowhere near a keyboard," protested Connie, "and modems don't just grow on cactuses, you know."

"Cactus schmactus," said (Inse), tapping her cigarette ash onto the dashboard. The needle on the taxi's speedometer whirled around the dial. "You got the wrong desert. This is Australia. No cactuses, but plenty of snakes."

"Where are we going?" Connie was beginning to feel it had not been such a good idea after all, abandoning Nic in The Jolly Kangaroo and calling a taxi to effect her getaway.

"To Barb's Outback Mansion," replied (Inse). "Haven't you heard? Where have you BEEN? Barb has managed to snatch Seegumses from under our very nose-jobs and the conniving tart has had him to herself in Fiji for a whole week. Fortunately Donna, Marjorie and Nicole have caught up with her, and I've heard Emily and Lottie are on their way here from LA."

"A week?" Connie echoed. "But (Inse), I don't really care. You see, I'm really in love with Nic, despite the fact that I dumped him—"

"In love with Nic?" shrieked (Inse), unwisely letting go of the steering wheel and rounding on Connie. "You mean, you are not crazy about Seegumseseses?" The taxi careered wildly out of control, while the erstwhile driver grunted and peered at Connie's shapely knees.

Connie saw her life flash past her eyes, before realising the alien driver had nonchalantly switched on a portable TV and started watching *The Immature and the Fidgety*®. Suddenly one of the doors flew open and it was a lot of sand she was seeing flash past her eyes. As she picked herself up off a dune and brushed down her Enchilada® three-piece safari suit, Connie stared after the erratically retreating taxi.

"Darn!" she muttered. "Looks like I'll have to find a keyboard somewhere, somehow, and write myself out of this tricky situation . . ."

But she didn't. And neither did Barb. Finally, after years of romping through TOATS, their Original Selves both had to submit to the busy constraints of Real Life on Original Earth. That was Barb's final post.

Fortunately(?) other writers carried the TOATS flame a little further, so that cyber-versions of the non-contributors continued a little longer. . .

UnEarthly Marjorie

UNEARTHLY MARJORIE

posted by Marjorie on 19 July 2002

Luckily Connie didn't need to worry. Marjorie had found a state-of-the-art laptop in the bottom of the capacious royal handbag and immediately began to write the Nic-loving traitor out of the story. Because she was a great deal younger than the other TOATS heroines, she hadn't understood much of Emily's chapter, so she decided to ignore her too, until she actually appeared on the scene.

"Come on," she hissed at Nicole, who was spitting trains (and grains) of sand out of her mouth. "We've got to stick close to Barb and Siegfried. Where's Donna?"

"Trying to wrest your book out of the taxi driver's hand."

"Wrest"? That's a good word, wonder where that came from?" mused Marjorie, as she ran lithely across the golden, sunkissed sand, following Barb's footprints. "She's got very small heels," she added. "One would almost think she had royal connections too."

"She's wearing stiletto heels," sighed Nicole, who sometimes thought she was the only sensible Siegfried fan around.

"Really?" asked Marjorie, who was blind as a bat without her glasses, but far too vain to wear them. "I thought she had high arches."

"What hierarchy?" demanded Donna, running to catch up with them, book in hand as the taxi driver from the planet Splinge sobbed despairingly in his cab. "Here, put this disgusting thing back in your bag."

"Can't have too many copies," said Marjorie. "They've got me out of many a tight situation."

"You shouldn't have so many liquid lunches," retorted Nicole.

Marjorie frowned. "Don't be silly. I have to have lots of liquid lunches, otherwise I wouldn't need to write my books."

At last, after at least two minutes of fast walking, the three exhausted beauties peered round the corner of a giant snake—a cactus would have been better but since it was the Australian desert there weren't any around—and there, in front of them, they saw the most incredible mansion. It was indescribably beautiful, so Marjorie didn't bother to try.

Hurrying through the large mahogany front door, with a brass ring for a knocker (it took Nicole a while to work out how that was possible) they stumbled onto the most hideous of sights. There, in the middle of the Italian marble hallway, stood Barb and Siegfried, locked in a deep and passionate embrace. Barb was leaning backwards, supported by Siegfried's strong arms and an even stronger corset, and her slender throat was exposed in the perfect position for him to shower it with kisses. He'd failed to realize this, so was hissing her eyelids instead—he'd been badly affected by the giant hissing snake outside the mansion—but the brazen hussy didn't seem to mind.

"STOP!" cried Donna. "Barb, you do realize this is punishable by death?"

"Slow death by Marjorie's primary-school level prose?" drawled the gorgeous red-head. "She's the pits. She didn't even attempt to write about my beautiful mansion. 'Indescribable' indeed. Anyway, I'm not doing anything you wouldn't all give your right arms to do. You'd love to be in my position."

"Not with my back I wouldn't," muttered Marjorie. "You foolish TOATS heroine, she added raising her voice, but not the tone of her writing, "don't you understand anything about my chapters? I don't do romances. I only do . . . "

"HOLD IT RIGHT THERE!" shouted a husky American voice from the minstrel gallery up above them, and then Emily and Lottie floated down to join the staring group, their parachutes of sugar-starched crinoline petticoats making Marjorie wince with distaste. "Siegfried, release Barb at once, before you find yourself doing Unmentionable Things to her."

Not surprisingly, Siegfried merely tightened his grip, and Marjorie's fingers began to fly over the keys, but before he or Barb could actually start enjoying themselves the laptop was dragged away from the minor member of the royal family and taken over by . . .

UNEARTHLY EMILY
posted by Emily on 19 July 2002
. . . Emily.

Lottie launched herself between Siegfried and Barb, knocking them both to the ground. "This is a PG rated saga! I would think voyeurism would be strictly taboo."

Barb, pinned under Siegfried, which was not a bad position to be in after all, reached for her TOATS Rulebook and began flipping through the dictionary section. "Vivacious, voguish, voluminous, voluptuous, votary..."

Donna and Nicole joined the pile trying to pull Siegfried off Barb.

Emily, dressed casually chic in a Showé® black gauze top, faded Alvi® denims and woven sandals, surveyed the pile of flesh as Marjorie tried to wrest the laptop away from her.

Thinking quickly, Emily showed Marjorie a picture of Poppy Starr® at the Australian premiere of *Generator®*. Marjorie recoiled in horror at Poppy's® super snug flare jeans, silver and black bustier, black lace over shirt and a choker so high it made her look like a baby llama.

"My gosh!" she cried. "Does her mother actually let her leave the house looking like that!"

Suffice to say all the female heads in the room turned to gape at the fashion *faux pas*, leaving Siegfried enough time to escape. He made a mad dash for the front door.

Just outside, he saw that the taxi driver from the planet Splinge had stopped sobbing and was just about to leave. "Vait!" Yelled our hero. "I'll pay you anything! Get me out of here!"

The taxi driver paused and wiped a tear away with a tentacle. "Vere . . . I mean where do you want to go?"

Siegfried closed the door and ducked low in the back seat in case the women noticed he was missing. "Timbuktu . . . I don't care, Drive! Drive!"

The driver shrugged what would ordinarily be considered his shoulders and pushed the ENGAGE button above the steering wheel . . .

Having read this last contribution of Emily's, 2009-Barb logged off. When she logged on again several months later, she searched the Internet in vain for the Siegfried B. Hinkelheimer fansite. Where had it vanished to? Donna must have been obliged to move it to a new web host yet again. . . the files were too voluminous . . . TOATS was too illogical for any software to decipher . . . and now the whole thing had finally fallen off the edge of cyberspace into the Great Void.

Shaking her head regretfully, Barb sighed.

It looks as if we have to leave the story here, she thought, with our hero Siegfried setting off for Timbuktu.

Or do we?

Will Siegfried finally make good his escape, or will the Great Void reject UnEarth, coughing it up like an irritating furball and re-materialising those Siegfried-crazy cyberchicks?

Probably not, but we can dare to dream. . .

In the wake of the rapidly departing taxi, a scrap of frayed fabric fluttered across the red sands. It appeared to be a tattered sampler, blown like a tumbleweed in the scouring winds. Unravelling stitches spelled out a message:

> On UnEarth, As On Original Earth,
> Everything Is Subject To Change.
> Anything Is Possib. . .

A marsupial hopping-mouse had eaten the rest.

EPILOGUE

What of Juliana, last seen lurching down the side of a Completely Extinct Icelandic volcano with Siegfried in thrall, before falling into a taxi with him?

Could it be that she had, in fact, fallen out the other side of the taxi just as it drove off? (Those alien drivers are too impatient to wait for the odd mislaid passenger, and Juliana certainly fitted that description.)

Or had the Icelindic voxen completed the taxi ride only to mistake (Inse)'s bottle of amnesia-inducing potion for fine Portuguese rum, and polish off the lot?

Tess was last heard of eons ago, doomed to destruction in one of Mayra's chapters. It's possible she didn't survive, seeing as she never wrote herself out of sticky situations... and sticky was an understatement.

Mind you, she had been enjoying herself—for the short while left to her—partying with the feisty crew of the Vulgarian submarine *Kohoban* in the North Atlantic. Some were playing balalaikas while others were Cossack-dancing up and down the after-engine room to the rapidly accelerating tune of

"Kalinka". Everyone except the captain was quaffing from huge kovshs brimming with countermeasures dissolved in toxic petroleum distillates, oblivious of the torpedo barrelling straight towards them which, if it collided, could prove bad for their health. Would the party end with a bang or would some highly unlikely event intervene to save the lives of Tess and the Vulgarians?

Katie, too, seemed to have vaporized.

Thank goodness for the "Find" feature in word processors, thought 2009-Barb. *Without it I should never have remembered what happened to Alice.*

Alice was still in Almost Africa. After wandering through King Solomon's Mines and Souvenir Shop, forgotten by the self-centred cyberchicks and abandoned by her Original Earth self, she had ascended the mine shaft loaded with plastic King Solomon figurines.

On her return to The Pink Elephant she discovered that a TOATS taxi had pulled up outside. When the trunk was opened, replicas of several SBH characters emerged and hurried to the bar for to refresh themselves after their ordeal.

Throwing away the plastic King Solomons, Alice rubbed her hands together with glee and rushed off to join them. She had a hunch she was going to enjoy the rest of her African sojourn. . .

Even further back in the saga, Tammie had been aboard the windjammer at the moment when Mayra appeared and herded most of the cyberchicks onto an Air Banana flying thingy.

The deserted girl was, no doubt, spared a terrible fate by avoiding Mayra's clutches, and one can only imagine what her feelings must have been when she found herself voyaging home in the company of gorgeous avatars who looked exactly like Gabriel Yearn, Lance Boyle, Nicholas Birdhouse, Daniel de Licious, Ray Fiends, Andrew Huggins, Jeremy Northbound and Gunter Whatsisname—all as delectable as they were fictional.

That leaves Tinfingers and Nigel the Croc to be accounted for. The former was cast aside into a cloud bank back in Chapter Ten, and Nigel didn't even make it into Book 2.

Let's be honest, poor Nigel has gone through a lot. At one point he was being worn as a pair of boots—how he ever recovered from that, only the demi-goddesses of TOATS know. Tinfingers, an enigmatic character who had himself been subject to the rough end of the pineapple in our saga, took pity on Nigel and shipped him back to Australia, where he set the giant reptile free in a wild lagoon of waterlilies, far from crocodile farms.

Tinfingers, who had also emigrated, built a shack beside the lagoon and lived there in peace and quiet for about five seconds before becoming screamingly bored. Immediately he set off to wander the unplanet in search of adventure...

and cyberchicks...

~ THE END ~

. . . or maybe not.

Hmm, thought Barb, drumming her fingers on her desk and absentmindedly munching a square of Rum 'n' Rhubarb®. *We can't just let it all fizzle out weakly, like a damp squib. Whatever a damp squib is. That would be a pathetic ending!*

She chewed and drummed for a few more minutes, then threw the empty chocolate wrapper in the rubbish bin and picked up the phone.

"Lottie? It's Barb. What are you up to?"

"Oh, this and that," Lottie replied vaguely, her voice resonating tinnily over the landline.

Instantly, Barb's inbuilt "fantennae" started buzzing. "What do you mean 'this and that'? What's going on? Haven't you been writing your movie script?" she demanded suspiciously.

"Oh no! I haven't got time for that."

"Why not?"

"I'm too busy writing my novel."

"What novel?"

"It's a fantasy set in the Middle Ages. All about a princess and—"

"And a prince?"

"Well, yeah. . ."

"Come on girl, out with it! Why the sudden urge to drop the Siegfried script and start writing a book?"

There was a pause.

Presently Lottie blurted, "Well, if you *must* know—Connie and I watched a TV show on the Abe[17] the other day. Gosh, it was lovely. The acting was so great. And the costumes, and the scenery—"

Barb interrupted, "So who's the actor?"

"He's so lovely!" gushed Lottie. "Tall, dark, handsome, with a gorgeous British accent and the most amazing grey eyes, like chips of slate."

"What's his name?"

"Richard Armyduck the Third." Lottie pronounced the name with an aching, voluptuous relish.

"And the prince in your mediaeval fantasy novel looks exactly like him, right?"

"Right."

"But what about Siegfried?"

"Who? Oh yes, Siegfried. . ."

"You've forgotten all about him, haven't you!"

Defensively. Lottie said, "Well not really. . . " Her voice trailed off.

Barb sighed. "You'd better tell me the name of this TV show so I can take a look at this guy . . ."

"It's called 'Trooble at Mill'."

"What? Trouble at Mill?"

"No, TROOBLE at Mill. TROOBLE. 'OO' as in 'foot'. Why do you always have a problem with show titles?"

"Not feet again!" grumbled Barb. "Why is it always feet. . ."

---

17 The ABC TV network

Transitional "dissolve" effect.

The scene changes to night-time in the desert surrounding Barb's Outback Mansion in Artificial Australia.

So many pearl-like stars are spilled across the vast swathes of black-velvet sky overhead that it looks as if Marjorie has accidentally kicked over her jewel-box.

At the centre of the darkness, a bright shimmer, like a burning glass flower. Flames leap, their vitreous petals sparkling amber, crimson and topaz. A pole is stuck in the sand. On top of it is a paper supermarket bag, upon which someone has drawn a cheery face.

Music blares and throbs, destroying the peace of the wilderness. A pair of huge Def® speakers and an amplifier are plugged into a nearby acacia tree whose roots improbably reach down to a geothermal electricity source.

Several spectacularly beautiful young women in fashionable garments are dancing around a bonfire, drinking vodka and loudly chorussing:

"Oh, I once loved a guy, an extraordinary guy,
But I didn't really know him, no I didn't really know him.
I said, 'I would cross the sea for you,
I would fly through time for you,
I would move worlds for you,
I would be anyone for you!'
But I didn't really know him, no I didn't really know him…"

During a lull in the cacophony, Barb draped her svelte arm around Emily's shapely shoulders. Both cyberchicks leaned together for balance, peering blearily into each other's eyes.

"Emily darling," Barb said indistinctly, "you crazy woman. You certainly wrote us in and out of some hair-raising situations. I'm sorry I chased you across the Moroccan desert. I knew you'd escape in the end."

"I know," slurred Emily. "But honestly, I'd forgotten all that. I've got more important things to think about."

"Like what?"

"Like character development," said Emily with a worried frown. "It just occurred to me that we haven't got any in TOATS. And all the experts say you've gotta have it in stories."

"Of *course* we've got character development!" Barb exclaimed, scandalized. "We've all changed! Just think of—" she hesitated, then began again, "what about—"

"Well, do we have it?" Emily enquired.

"Nah."

Emily shrugged. "Never mind, I'll work on that later," she said. "Cheers!"

They clinked their glasses together.

Emily overbalanced and fell full-length on the ground, so Barb wandered across to Donna, who was dispensing refills. This was a short but difficult journey, as her stiletto heels kept spearing into the sand.

"Donna. Darling." Barb hiccupped. "Thank you for being the web goddess and making it possible for all this madness to happen.

The two hot babes tapped their glasses together and gulped down another shot.

"Cheers, Barb," said Donna. "It's been a... well, it's been."

A horned helmet intervened between them. That is to say, the helmet still had one horn attached. The other was in Juliana's hand, and she held it out, hollow end up. "*Áttu meira vodka?*"

Donna splashed a goodly volume of Baksmälla® into Juliana's Viking drinking vessel.

"Julianah!" Barb warbled affectionately, barely avoiding being poked in the eye by the affixed horn. "Darling! I forgive you for everything!" With a lunge she attempted to grab the Icelandic wench, but Juliana dodged with remarkable adroitness, wrinkling her pert nose.

"Ugh. An Affectionate Drunk, eh?" she commented. "Of the seven types of drunkenness, you had to be that one."

She disappeared into the twilight beyond the sphere of firelit radiance, but Barb could have sworn she winked cheekily over her shoulder just before she vanished.

Someone bumped into her. "Connie! Darling!" Barb yelped. "Was that your trusty horse Brian I saw in my lounge room earlier, eating oats off the lily-pad coffee table with bronze frog base?"

"Yep that was him!" Connie exclaimed happily. "I promise I'll clean up the mess in the morning. That is to say, I'll get Peeves to clean it up. Cheers!"

Barb's glass tinkled against Connie's, just before the former tripped over a sprawling figure and face-planted in the sand. Her glass flew into the air and landed elsewhere with a thump.

"That you down here, Emily?" Barb raised her sand-encrusted visage and blinked. "Oh it's you, Tess."

"Cheers, Barb," mumbled Tess.

"Tess, *darling*," gushed Barb, "you've broken the hearts of a thousand Vulgarian sailors. At least, I think it must be up to a thousand by now. As far as I remember you started with three hundred. Funny how they multiply."

Turned her head, Barb spotted another familiar face. "Amy *darling*," she enthused, "you don't say much, but we love you!"

An elegant arm reached down and hauled Barb to her feet. "Get up Barb. For goodness' sake, pull yourself together. You're giving us cyberchicks a bad name."

"Mayra! *Darling*! We're so glad you joined us for those wicked, wacky, worldwide-web adventures!"

"Here," intruded a crisp, British voice. Marjorie handed Barb a rather dingy shot-glass. "You look as if you could do with a drink."

"Dearest Marjorie!" yelled Barb. "TOATS was never so spicy before you arrived! Cheers!"

"Cheers!" another voice joined in, and Lottie stepped out of the gloom into the bonfire's orb of illumination.

Lottie! Dar—"

"Yes, I know. You're off your face. You always call everyone 'darling' when you're three sheets to the wind. It's a dead giveaway."

"Loshie gnarling," garbled Barb unrepentantly, putting her arm around Lottie's shoulders and lowering her voice confidentially, "at the end of the day, I think it's probbly you who desherves him most."

"Deserves who?"

A momentary hiatus.

Barb screwed up her face, evidently trying to think.
"Oh, you know that guy—what's his name?"
Lottie looked vacant. "Pass the vodka, will you?"

The singing resumed.

Somewhere far away—very, very far away—a certain
Siegfried B. Hinkelheimer leaned back, kicked off his shoes
and breathed a deep sigh of relief.

On the edges of the firelight, unnoticed by all the rest,
UnPoet was energetically pushing a young man in the back,
endeavouring to steer him unceremoniously into the howling
darkness.

"But I'm the token male at this gathering!" protested
Nathaniel Hinkelheimer, resisting the pressure as hard as
he could.

"We don't need any token males," said UnPoet.

"But you're a male, aren't you?"

UnPoet assumed a smug expression. "Maybe. Maybe not.
It's a secret."

"But there's nobody out there," wailed Nathaniel, indicating the frighteningly blind void beyond the fragile ball of
light. "Just millions of acres of sand." As an afterthought he
added, "and crocodiles, and spiders, and snakes, and sharks!"

"In that case you won't be lonely, will you," said UnPoet
somewhat mercilessly.

316

Nathaniel looked so woebegone that UnPoet added, "Agreed, it's pretty daunting in the outback, but with a bit of luck you might find some company. There's sure to be a taxi driver out there somewhere, and an Air Banana crew, and maybe even some Barbie tribespeople. And Mrs. OhReally?"

UnPoet gave Nathaniel one final, determined shove. He vanished into the murk, but since he had grabbed hold of UnPoet at the last moment, the two of them exited together.

The Def® speakers boomed, their bass notes vibrating through the ground and thrumming along everyone's bones. The cyberchicks sang,

"Where has he gone? Can't see him near,
Did he ever hold us dear?
He's gone away, what can we say?
Did he ever want to stay?

"Run, run, running, leaping, bounding,
Elusive dream, our hunt confounding.
Like a spaceship moving fast.
He left us here, like shadows cast
Upon a landscape strange and vast.

"He travelled fast, always ahead,
And while we chased, he simply fled.
Away from us, into the night.
Yet in his absence, we're all right.

The ditty gave way to another—

"And after all, we never really
Knew him anyway.
We ran together, then—
We're still together, and okay!
We've had some great times, haven't we?
We've quarreled, laughed and cried,
And after all is said and done,
We're still here, side by side.
And may we go on running through
This crazy world together.
And may we never stop,
And may the good times last forever!"

~ THE OTHER END ~

. . . except that Barb, staggering disorientedly into the dimness at the fringe of the firelight's range in search of Lottie spied someone emerging from the obscurity of the desert night. It looked to be a dark-haired man.

She halted and stared, trying to focus her gaze.

"Hi," said the stranger. "I think your friend needs help." He indicated the direction from which he'd appeared. "I was just about to explain to her how I sneaked past that UnPoet person when, for some reason, she fainted."

"You're," stammered Barb. "You're—"

He extended his hand with a friendly smile. His slate-grey eyes twinkled.

"I'm Richard," he said.

"Richard MacGuffin?"

He ignored her inept attempt at a quip. "No, Richard Armyduck the Third."

"Oh right," spluttered Barb. "I'm Barb. Pleash to meetcha." Under her breath she added, "Thish ish gonna be inneresting. . ."

~ THE REAL, HONEST-TO-GOODNESS END ~

With thanks to Siegfried B. Hinkelheimer
for the inspiration.

Cyberchicks series

Book 1: Cyberchicks in Love

Book 2: Cyberchicks go Wild

For more books you'll love,

Visit the Leaves of Gold Press website

www.leavesofgoldpress.com

Write a review

Enjoyed frolicking with the fangirls?

Consider reviewing this book ^{with lots of stars} on Amazon.uk

↑

https://tinyurl.com/cyberchicks-2

or on Amazon.com

and Goodreads https://www.goodreads.com

It means the world to us!